True Love

Passion & Pain

By Lennie F. Mickey III

True Love Passion & Pain

Copyright© October 2014

Lennie F. Mickey III.

Dedicated to my Sons and Daughters

This book is dedicated to my children my mother, father, and other family members, those who supported me and who has not forgot me in this land of lost memory

Victora Reeves, Kenny Brayboy, Lanice Mickey, Leslie Brayboy-Hill, Tanya Brayboy, Sherrly Brayboy, Marcus Brayboy, Shawn Louis, Darrel Benjmain, Stephen Brayboy, Style, Kenny Brayboy Jr., Row Brayboy, Tie AKA Money, Deborah Coxs, Mary Reeves, Connie Reeves, Lonnie Reeves Jr., Mike Reeves, Tamika Lucks, William Luck, Dariona Brandy, Daelen Bryant, La'Dae' Bryant, Euphoria Bryant, Amirah Thompson, Kyra Thompson, Tony Luck, My soul sister and strong supporter Mack Mama. Mount Sinia Church in Varnville, and the NAACP, City of Plainfield, NJ.

Special Dedication

Grammy -GramWillamae Brayboy Rest in peace, I know you're watching over me now, as you did in life, I love you Grammy-Gram.

Lonnie Reeves, Uncle Leroy Brayboy, Pat Brayboy, Carron Carter, Jermaine Jones, Lisa

Acknowledgements and Supporters

This goes out to all my brothers and sisters lost in the land of the forgotten. My love is real as long as I have a voice you'll never be forgotten. Hold your heads up, stay alive, and stay safe. Keep it 100 and always remain sucker free...

A big thank you goes out to the people who saw the light in me when all I knew was darkness. If it had not have been for you I might have stopped writing. So my thanks go to: Ny Jay, Carter, Meechie, Debow, Bird, Law, Bear, Rah-Rah, Trouble, Teflon, Red Nose, D-Bless, Slim, Ace, Tashawn, Roach, Dog Pound and BJ. Derick Parker AKA Block, Tina Nance, Marylin Williams, Brandon Lee, Lollipop, Jason Convict Johnson, Brittany, Cameron Hammond Jr. AKA Red Freedom, Fleeta and Jacob of For Life Riders. The first female to read my book, Tasha Mickens, Joe, New York Jay, Juan, and any brother, that I may have missed who was there when I first started. Peace and thanks for all of your support.

Rest in peace to all of my fallen soldiers in PLFD 5150 rise and shine 95

Special Acknowledgement

To Papaya Wagstaff for all your help in the progression of making this happen, know that I Shine You Shine Red Diamond will always be a brother to Sistahs on Lit. You are truly a blessing to work with

Her Love

Demented, tormented illusions, confusions seducing my existence, the resistance to this lady's seductive personality can be the end of me. The enemy befriending me in an orgy of lusts intimacy, as poison as it may be, I swim through her sea lustfully, fulfilling misery, she's killing me.

Raping my pure flesh, taking my last breath, no more innocence is left. Empty is my steps, molesting the breasts of evil sex, dripping in sensual sweat.
Her body of regret sighs in the high of sinister passion, as we connect, the friction gets faster. She clinches my soul tighter, I excite her.
This beast, she feasts upon orgasmic release, my salvation now decease.
To the point of no return, the biblical burn of physical sin, ashes buried within a woman's virtue, a blessing and a curse too, anguished and pained when she hurt you.
Rain has never rained so icy blue. Her love is a four letter word that never touched the truth. Her sex is

real, I can't turn it loose.

This is the strongest lust from the opposite up above,

but in my mind it's simply her love…

Peace

Lennie F. Mickey III

CHAPTER 1

"Ohh....uhh! Ohh...yesss! That's it! Deeper... oohh....deeperrr!"

The erotic cries of a woman, burning in the flames of forbidden passion echoed off of the walls of the large master bedroom. The air was seasoned with the spicy scent of sinful sex, as Cinnamon and her lover's body were glistening with sweat. On her elbows and knees on the king sized bed, she was being assaulted repeatedly from behind, by the power of her lover's affection.

Perspiration rained down her beautiful nakedness, as their moans and groans filled the room. Her voluptuous, plump, ebony-brown ass shook with vigor, and rotated meeting the maximum force of his hips, as he slammed into it over and over again. She clinched the sheets from the intense friction of their fiery connection, as she felt the build of her second explosion happening.

They were so locked in the lustful embrace neither had heard the sound of the front door of the home opening, as her man entered.

Home at last. Supreme thought to himself….six and a half long years away from my family. I can't wait to see the smile on my little girl's face and hear the joy in my son's voice, once they see their daddy's home. Finally, I'll be able to hold the soft, sweet curves of my Cinnamon in my arms. It's been too long since that honey-brown body has been next to mine." Supreme could feel his blood rushing from the all of the excitement. Just thinking of the long, overdue, powerful love session that was soon to come with his woman, set him on fire.

"Oohh God!"

"What the fuck was that?" Supreme yelled out loud, talking to no one but himself, knowing he'd just heard something. He looked at the clock on the wall and saw it was too early for his children to be home, and he knew Cinnamon was supposed to be at work.

Still, he knew what he'd just heard sounded like the bumping and tapping of his bed, plus the sound of unfamiliar voices coming from upstairs.

He dropped his bags and ran up the steps. At that moment and with each step they seemed to go on forever, as the sounds of love making or just hardcore fuckin' burned the drums of his ears.

"Oohh…uhh…make me cum…."

The sounds of his woman's voice filled with cries of desire, put air in his Jordan's, as he ran faster to the top of the steps, fueled with anger and rage in his heart. When he reached the gateway to his betrayal, he stood faced with a huge pulsating door.

"Aaaah…oooh…aaah….yess!"

Supreme was standing at this door that seemed to be breathing with each scream and moan. He reached for the latch then lifted the door knob, but the door slowly opened before he could even touch it.

The first thing he saw was his heart's death facing him, looking him dead into his eyes on the bed, his bed. She was on all fours like the dog she was, and she never stopped her movements; even as she looked at the hurt in his eyes. It was as if she loved the pain she was seeing in him, as he watched her getting fucked in their bed, their home.

"Harder, push that big dick in harder, don't stop!" She moaned, while licking her lips, looking Supreme deep into his eyes.

His heart was crushed, as he turned to see who was behind his woman. She pushed her face in the bed and arched her ass high in the air, as he started smashing faster and faster into her, as if he were about to climax.

When Supreme locked in on who was giving his woman this pleasure, he lost it as he realized it was an unbelievable 3 foot midget with a big ass light bulb head pounding into his wife for life.

He jumped with the rage of a mad dog, ready to rip the big head off of the midget and shove it up his midget ass.

The midget noticed Supreme standing beside the bed, and they locked eyes. The midget smiled then winked, as Cinnamon yelled out, "I'm cummin'!!"

Boom! Bing! Bang!

"What the fuck! Supreme, what the fuck you doin' divin' off of the fuckin' top bunk of the motherfuckin' bed?" yelled Black who was pissed that Supreme scared the living shit out of him, as he'd come crashing off the top of the bunk beds.

Black was Supreme's cellmate, and he had 3 life sentences for the murder of some police officers. He was a black, powerful brother who hated white people and white America. He had done over 30 years behind the walls of cold, hard steel and raw stone; but the time had never broken him. He refused to let the white man take his soul, and he planned to out-live his sentences and help every young black brother out who were stuck and had to come learn the law. He'd taught them how to do time and not let the time do them.

He and Supreme had been cellmates for almost four and a half years. They were close; more like father and son if anything. They never talked about the outside world, that way, they could both keep their heads clear on what was going on inside around them.

Supreme had 10 years, and his time would be up in just a few more days. He was only given 6 years and 8 months out of the ten to max out. He would've been home sooner but he'd fucked up big time.

He was now on the floor, as Black was talking to him, but he'd hit the floor so hard, all he could hear was blah, blah, blah.

"My bad big bro…..I just had a fucked up dream," Supreme said, as he stood up, trying to get his head back in the game.

"What kind of fucked up dream could you be havin' when you about to hit the bricks?"

"Man, it's this midget."

"A motherfuckin' midget? What the fuck you drea-min' about midgets for? What you scared of them or somethin'?"

"No, it's nothin' like that, it's a long story man, and you don't wanna hear the kind of bullshit it is. It's a long story, brother." Supreme replied shaking his head.

"I ain't got nothin' but time, and how long have you known me, man?" Black asked, showing his concern.

"A minute."

"So you know you can tell me anything that's on your mind. I got your back 100% right?"

"Yeah, but…." Supreme said not sure. He was a little skeptical to share his dream, even with Black.

"Yeah, but what? You don't want me to know you like getting' freaky with the little people? It's okay. Some of those midget bitches got some phat asses," Black said with added humor.

"Nah, Black, ain't no shit like that, but they do got some big asses."

"Then let's build my young brother, let's find out why midgets got you flyin' out of the bed at night."

"Ha-ha, you funny. Okay, you hook the hot pot up for two cups of coffee, and we'll talk. What time you think it is?"

Black looked at his watch. "It's 4 o'clock in the morning man. Almost count time. I was about to get up anyway," Black said, as he put water in the hot pot and plugged it into the wall's socket.

Supreme went over to his locker and pulled out the coffee, sugar and the creamer. Black didn't take cream or sugar; he liked his coffee just like his women.... hot and black, mixed with nothin'.

Supreme sat up on the pillow that he'd put up against the steel locker. He was trying to figure out where to start with his story.

"Well, young blood, what's on ya' mind? Whatever it is, it's written all over your face." Black asked curiously.

"It's about Cinnamon.....one of my kids mother."

"What about her?"

"Well, she's gone, but I heard she was fucking with this dude."

Black cut him off. "Man I know you not worryin' 'bout who she been fuckin' the last 6 years? You gotta be fuckin' with me? You know a 10 year sentence is a long time and a woman gets lonely. Shit, she was fuckin' before you and you didn't care, now you in prison and you can't fulfill her needs, so it's not like she's cheatin' on you. You understand where I'm co-min' from, little brother?"

"I know that shit, and I ain't no sucker for love. Like I said, she's gone, but my love for her will never change because of some bullshit like that. It's deeper than that. In order for you to truly understand, I gotta take it from point A to B, then and only then, will you get to point C and clearly understand what's going on." Supreme stated.

"The midget thing and everything, you can make clear to me?" Black asked still confused.

"True."

"Then, my good friend, I'm all ears." Black said, as he handed Supreme the hot cup of coffee and sat on his bed, ready to hear what was troubling his best friend.

Supreme took a sip from his cup, after adding the sugar and cream then took a deep breath and started. "Well, it was back in 2003…"

If I ruled the world…. imagine that…. I'd free all my sons….I love them, love them, baby…. Nas and Lauryn Hill blasted from the speakers of my sound system. The song sounded out from the windows of my '04, money-green, 745I, with tan leather seats, while I rode with my sunroof open. I rolled down the streets of Plainfield, New Jersey living ghetto-fabulous, chrome 20 inch rims, shining in the summer sunlight.

I, Supreme Divine, was only 19 years old and already, me and my right hand man, A.G. a.k.a. American Gangster, was close to the top of the dope game. We had one of the biggest teams, Stick and Stab Clinton Ave.

The most feared block in Plainfield, full of young, black niggas that didn't give a fuck about nothin' but that paper. Our only motto was one of all gangsters, money over bitches and death to all snitches.

There were only two heads, just me and A.G. We started out with just a $50 flip, and now we had more money than we could count. Isis kept us stacked with the best coke and dope in the city. She was the Connect and the queen pin of all queen pins. She had a team of the most beautiful women you could've ever seen. All of them were dykes their only loyalty was to her.

"Hold up, what that got to do with you and your baby mother or you jumpin' out of bed in your sleep?" Black asked wanting to know where all of this was headed.

"Hold on Black. I'm gonna have to take you where I was at in my life, so you can get the full picture." Supreme said.

"Alright go 'head."

"I was riding down the street on my way to my grandmother's house. I always stopped by on Wednesdays to bring her some bingo money, plus I had to holler at my cousin Philly who owed me a little bread. I knew he didn't have it because he'd started smoking that rock.

Philly was once a big dog in the game, but a bitch broke his heart and he turned to rock to hide from the pain. He lost it all, his money, dignity and respect. You wouldn't know it by looking at him, 'cause he still stayed dressed to the tee. I used to look up to him, but now I had no choice but to look down on him. He showed me damn near everything I know, so I still looked out for him, everybody did. The love of my hood was real.

I pulled up in front of my grandmother's house and looked in my rearview mirror checking my dreads to be sure everything was in the right place. Philly was standing in front of the house on his cell phone, so I stepped outside my ride."

"Yo, 'Preme, I been lookin' all over for you. I need to holler at you on some real shit! I need to hold $100 dollars. I got something big goin' down, and it could double your money, man. I was just on the phone with my peoples, so we gotta act fast."

I could see he was high and the bullshit was comin' out of his mouth so fast I don't think he even knew what he was talkin' about. To give you a good mental picture, think of Bernie Mac high as hell on crack, and then you got Philly.

"Hold up! Philly, you already owe me $400 dollars now, and you want me to give you some more money? Nigga you must think I'm super stupid, or do I look like dolly- doughnut with a hole in my fuckin' head?" Supreme had asked Philly.

"Come on cuz, we family. I use to look out for you. Now I need you to look out for me. I'm tryna make a come up, man."

"Nigga, I don't want none of that chewed up grass you tryin' to feed me."

"What cuz?" Philly asked with a stupid look on his face.

"Bullshit nigga! Bullshit! That shit ain't nothin' but

chewed up grass," 'Preme replied, but before I could get in his ass, my cell phone rang, it was my personal phone so I had to answer it.

"What's good?"

"Money and spendin' it."

"Nah, you wrong nigga. Money and stackin' it!"

"I hear that shit! Still, I hope you comin' to A.G's birthday block-party; it started already."

"Yea, Pooh, you know I'm comin' through for my dawg."

"Where you at my nigga?"

"I'm at my people house tryna get my bread."

"Who? Philly?"

"Who else?"

"Put that nigga on the phone, he owe me $150."

When I turn to give Philly the phone he was already out.

"That nigga gone just that quick man," Supreme replied.

"I ain't worried 'bout it. I just wanted to fuck with him."

"Me too."

"Yo' ma, that ass too grown for that frame!" the caller yelled out.

"Man, fuck them bitches, where the money at?" Supreme asked.

"Man, its bitches and money everywhere!"

"Say no more, I'm on my way. One," he replied and hung up.

I put my cell phone back in the clip on my hip and made my way inside of the house up to my grand-mother's room. She was watching her 72 inch H.D. flat screen I had gotten for her. I stood in front of it, "Hey Grammy-Gram. I stopped by to bring you some money, you need anything else?"

"No, get out the way of my story boy." She was watching The Bold and the Beautiful soap opera.

"I know you not gonna talk to me right now, so I'll see you later."

I went in my pocket, pulled out my large bank roll, peeled off 3 one hundred dollar bills, put them in her hand and kissed her on the cheek.

"Thank you for my bingo money baby. I'll see you later."

"Okay Grammy," I said.

In no time, I was back outside in the warm sunlight at the driver side door of my car. My platinum, dia-mond Rolex was glowing in the sun's bright light. I looked like a million and felt like a million more. Life was good was the thought that ran through my mind, as I pushed the button on the key to unlock the doors.

"Damn daddy, can I ride on you?" I knew the voice before I even turned around. It was my cousin, Fugee's fine, freaky ass, sitting in her white Q45. I turned to respond.

"Girl, you so crazy, you know damn well you my cousin, so you can't take this big ride baby girl."

"You didn't care when we use to play house."

"Who is this?" I asked, as I saw her sitting in the passenger seat. She was so breathtaking, and at that moment she had stolen my heart.

"Who stole your heart nigga, your baby mother?" Black asked to be sure Supreme wasn't talking about his cousin.

"Yeah, it was her."

"Now, we getting somewhere, you talking about the first day you met her?"

"Yeah, Black, what did you think I was talking about?"

"I thought you was talking about hustling and getting money."

"All of that is a part of it too. I'm talking about

true, passion and pain that real shit, my nigga. You know… the kind of love you find in the madness of the streets, and in the arms of a ghetto queen? Seems like the only place you can find peace."

"I feel that little brother."

"Count time, stand up and give your name and number when I pass your door!" The C.O. yelled down the wing. Black didn't stand but Supreme stood as the C.O. passed the door."

"Name and number bottom bunk?" The C.O. asked.

"You know my name you motherfuckin' cracker and you know my fuckin' number, stank-ass pig, so don't ask me shit, your slave driven ass already know and the only reason I started to stand to come to the door is so I can say fuck you and that stank pussy you came out of, you sorry piece of poor white bird shit," Black spit out at the C.O. who knew Black for over 15 years and just marked him down, as for Supreme he had to give his name and number.

"Supreme Divine 43681."

The C.O. marked him down and continued to do his count.

"I get a kick out of this shit, every morning you tell

him that same shit and he just eat it."

"Fuck them cracker-ass pigs. Let's get back to your ghetto love story it was starting to get good."

"Where was I?"

"You had just met your baby momma."

"Who is this?"

"Oh, you tryna ignore me now, but back in the day your hand didn't ignore my ass, when we played house, Mr. Big Time," Fugee said jokingly.

"What's your name lil' ma?" I asked as I bent over to her window, not paying Fugee any mind.

"Cinnamon," she said looking me in my eyes.

"Naw, what's the name your momma gave you?"

"I told you Cinnamon, nigga." She spoke still looking me in my eyes.

Her eyes were gray without contacts, natural. Her skin was honey brown. She looked like Free from 106 and Park on BET. She was beautiful and I knew I had to have her. Plus, given the fact that I hadn't seen her before, or so I thought….

"What's that supposed to mean?" Black asked, as he was fixing two more cups of coffee.

"It means sit back and listen, and I'll tell you," Supreme said taking the cup from Black.

"Go ahead, I ain't gonna ask you nothin' else."

Supreme knew that was a stone cold lie. Black couldn't help himself. He had to ask questions, it was in his nature.

"That's her name, stop giving her the 3rd degree," Fugee said, speaking up for her home girl.

I paid Fugee no mind. I just couldn't take my eyes off of Cinnamon.

"Where you ladies on y'all way to?"

"We were going to hit up the liquor store."

"Good then. I'm riding with y'all. I was on my way there too."

With that being said, I pushed the button on my key pad, locking my car door then jumped in the back of Fugee's whip.

"Drive Fugee," I ordered jokingly.

"Nigga, I know if I'm driving drinks are on you."

"Money ain't a thing baby girl. Can't you tell by my bling?"

"Well, Mr. Bling-Bling, I know you got some good smoke," she replied.

Fugee was the type of girl who always wanted more than you offered, but still, you had to love her.

"Fugee, you know I don't bring none of that in

Gram's house. I got some in the car though. I'll give you some of the good purp when we get back."

"I'ma hold your sexy ass to that 'cause me and my girl got some stress on our brain."

"Oh yeah, what you got to stress about Lil' Ma?" I asked Cinnamon.

"Nothing I can't handle," she said looking at my reflection in the mirror.

"I'm sure you can handle anything that comes your way, but I know together, we can handle all things. Two heads are always better than one. What you think about that? Can you handle telling me where you from? I know I haven't seen you before or it would already be a done deal."

"What's that?" Cinnamon asked, still looking me in my eyes.

"Your problem, tell me about it?" I said in a smooth tone.

"Ooh girl, I can tell he feelin' you! It's on and poppin' in here!" Fugee said.

"DRIVE FUGEE!" we said in unison and all burst out in laughter.

Fugee pulled off and we were on our way. She had the radio playing low so we wouldn't have to strain our ears to hear one another speaking, but you could still here Avant and Kee-Kee Wyatt in the background as they harmonized, My First Love.

"No, I don't think I've met or seen you before. I didn't grow up out here. I'm from New York. I just got back in town, but it's a long story and not enough time to tell it." She spoke while breaking eye contact then started looking out of the window. I knew then she had something heavy on her mind, plus her voice was filled with sadness.

"Well, let me bring a little joy to your life. I'm going to my right hand man's block party slash birthday bash then we doing the grown and sexy thing at club Malibu. I would more than love to take you as my personal guest. V.I.P. all the way, drinks on me and anything you want is free."

"No thanks, I'm really not in a partying mood. I don't want to be around a lot of happy people, maybe next time."

"She got some real shit on her mind Preme," Fugee said, looking me in my eyes from the mirror, letting me know shit was real.

"Then how about this, you and me get together later and you can start telling me that long story after my man sees me at his block party. I'll skip the club and I'll bring all the time in the world so you can run down that long story of yours."

"Be my guest. If you wanna miss your party and get an earful of stress, that's on you."

"Hold up Lil Ma, it's not my party. My party is private, with just us. You and me, so, it'll feel like it's my birthday because of the gift of the time I get to spend with just you"

With those last remarks, for the first time, a smile broke across her full lips. We rode talking and joking all the way to the liquor store. The chemistry between us was starting to mix. I was feeling her and she was feeling me. I got out of the car and opened the door for Cinnamon as I talked on my cell phone.

Me, Fugee and Cinnamon walked inside the store. I was talking, taking care of business and looking Cinnamon up and down.

Cinnamon was short, about 5' 2", golden-honey brown, looking like Free's twin. Her long braids were to the back like Alicia Keys, and they dropped to the small of her back. The way those Apple Bottoms gripped her ass when she walked had a nigga feenin'. She had so much ass that it busted out of the sides, bouncing to its own hypnotizing beat. She had on heels that showed her beautiful little toes peeking out; the red on her toe nails matched her red and white outfit. The Apple Bottom tank top showed off her sexy breasts, which looked to be a mouthful. I don't know if it was the cool air of the A.C. in the store or if she could feel how hard I was eye fucking her, but her nipples were hard. I thought they were going to poke a hole in her shirt. I had to grab and fix myself. Lil Ma had me like a dog in heat. I didn't want the store man to think that I was shoplifting. The way she had the front of my pants on point, definitely looked like I was hiding something, in which I was.

"Preme, you gonna bring me the work or what?" My thoughts of lust were broken by the voice in the phone.

"Yeah KB, I got you later. I'm at the store now then I'm on my way to you."

"OK then, that's what's up."

"One."

"One."

I placed my phone back in my clip and grabbed the biggest box of Hennessy they had. The bottle in the box was huge, the largest I'd ever seen. I knew it would be perfect for my right-hand-man being that Hennessy was his favorite drink. I got me a bottle of Remy V.S.O.P. and placed them on the counter. Fugee had gotten her big bottle of Goose and orange juice but Cinnamon didn't touch a thing.

"Come on Ma, don't be shy. Get what you want, it's all on me."

"It's not like that, trust me. I got my own bread. I just don't feel like drinking.

"Well, let me ask you this, if you felt like drinking which of these bottles in this store would be blessed with your lips?"

"Remy Red."

I grabbed 2 bottles of Remy Red and put them on the counter along with another bottle of Remy V.S.O.P.

"Now, one bottle is for when you feel like drinking, the other is for when I come pick you up. Is that cool with you?"

"Like ice," she replied with a smirk on her face.

Fugee, not wanting to be left out grabbed another bottle of Goose and some orange juice then put them both on the counter.

"Preme, is there anything else?" The man asked

behind the counter.

"Yeah, let me get a box of White Owls and 2 packs of Blacks, Kep."

"That's it?" He asked. I looked at Fugee then at Cinnamon to see if everybody had what they wanted.

"Yeah, Kep, that's it."

"That will be $385.79"

I started patting my pockets. "Oh shit, I forgot my bread."

'Hell naw, nigga I know you trippin', you better take that chain off or something, you ain't going to have me up here looking stupid," Fugee said crossing her arms across her chest in protest. She was looking at me like she was ready to fuck me up. But Cinnamon didn't trip, she went into her Coach bag that I didn't notice before because I was looking at everything else, she pulled out a gold card, placed it on the counter and said, "Drinks on me," with a smile that I was looking for the whole time. I winked at Kep, the man behind the counter and he said, "No, Miss Lady, your money is no good here. Preme is good for anything in my store."

"Oh shit cuz, I didn't know it was like that," Fugee said glad that she didn't have to spend any money.

Cinnamon picked her card up off the counter, "Excuse me, Mr. Supreme."

"Excuse me hell, that's what you get for trying to make me out of a liar. Didn't I say drinks on me?" Then I went in my pocket, pulled out a big bank roll of all hundred dollar bills. I put 5 crispy hundred dollar bills on the counter. "Keep the change," I said as I grabbed the bags.

"Thanks Preme," Kep said as he picked the money up.

Fugee dropped me back to my car and she hit me up for a yard.

"Yo, nigga, I didn't forget. That money ain't got shit to do with what you said you was going to give me."

"What girl?"

"My weed nigga, I told you we had stress."

"Oh shit yeah, hold up," I said then went to my car and went in my hidden box behind the T.V. in the head rest and pulled out a big zip lock bag. I dip my hand in the bag, grabbed 3 thick buds. "Here don't hurt yourself, that's that purp not that backyard bullshit you be smoking." I said as I handed the weed to Fugee and she put it in her purse.

"Nigga, please, I always smoke the best, I'm Fugee' La."

"So tonight my Lil Cinnamon candy, me you, and all that stress right?"

"It is what it's supposed to be," She said looking me in my eyes.

"Don't pop the last bottle until I pick you up from Fugee's."

"Alright, nigga she heard you. Now let the pussy breathe."

"Fugee, what's up with your cousin?"

"What you mean?"

"You know what I mean girl. What's good, what's really good with him?"

"Hold up, how you know she said that? Where they at anyway? In the car? And if you was in your car how you know what they're talking about?" Black asked once again interrupting the story.

"Because, after we got together she told me everything that happened that night, before I picked her up."

"Why? And what Fugee look like?"

"Fugee, put you in the mind of Nia Long in the face but she got an ass like she belongs in one of those bubble butt pornos. And if you sit back and let me tell you the story you would know why she told me everything that happened."

"My bad, go ahead."

"So anyway, where was I at?"

"She was asking Fugee about you, I don't know if they was in the car or what but she was asking about you.""Oh yeah, that's right, well they was at Fugee's house then.".

"What's good with him?"

"Shit, Preme is Preme, I use to panty pump with him when we was little, I never fucked him, but sometimes I want to. I know that I am a sick slut because that's my cousin but he won't let me, even though I know he be looking at my ass. I can't tell too much but he know how to panty pump good," Fugee spoke as she lit the blunt she just rolled.

"Fugee, you are truly sick, I didn't ask for your nasty sexual fantasies about your cousin or y'all dry humping history. I want to know who he fucks with now."

"Supreme don't have no main chick, the streets is his whore but I know he can fuck any hot in the ass bitch in Plainfield, he about his money. 'Preme and

A.G. on the come up fast, nobody fuck with 'Preme and A.G. crazy asses."

"Why you say that? 'Preme seem cool to me."

"Yeah, he cool but even ice melts, he was nice because he likes you and he takes my shit because I'm family, plus you don't have on a bra either that got you some brownie points. 'Preme's name holds a lot of weight, people fear him because he is about his shit. He did a lil' time when he was little."

"How long? Cinnamon asked as she pulled the blunt smoke deep into her lungs. She started coughing and choking.

"Damn girl, don't kill ya'self, shit take ya' time, do baby steps,"Fugee said patting Cinnamon on the back.

"That's some good as shit." Cinnamon said catching her breath. Fugee got up once she saw that Cinnamon was okay. Fugee turned the stereo on full blast.

"Fuck around and got locked up, they won't let me out, no, they won't let Akon Locked up played through the speakers.

"How long bitch?"

"What?"

"How long?"

"His dick? I don't know I ain't seen it since we

was kids, it looked big to me then," Fugee said and turned down the stereo.

"I'm not talking about that, with your sick, twisted, crazy ass, I'm talking about how long he did in prison."

"I don't know, year or 2 maybe. I smoke weed. I can't remember my name sometimes, shit."

"Fugee, somebody here for you!" Fugee mother yelled down the steps.

"Alright Ma, I'm coming!"...

"A.G. this party is off the motherfuckin' chain, I'm feeling gooder than a motherfucker."

"Man, the night just starting 'Preme, I know you goin' to the after party."

"No-can-do playboy, I got a date."

"A date? I know you fucked up! All this fresh ass bouncing around here any you talking about a fucking date! I need some of that shit you popped or smokin'."

"Naw my nigga, I'm feeling nice but word, I met this new chick today."

"What's her name?"

"Cinnamon, she was with Fugee earlier."

"Cinnamon? You better off getting one of these bitches out here if you plan on fucking something tonight."

"Nigga, you act like you know her or something."

"I do and she ain't no gold-diggin' chicken-head looking for a silly ass nigga to come up on. Every baller in the city tried to get that ass last time she was around here, and each one got shot down like a battle-ship. I hate to say it but even me."

"Even you, nigga? I'm motherfuckin' Supreme Divine! Ain't never been turned down, plus I'm so fly I make the fuckin' clouds jealous! Jesus got to step his game up when fuckin' with me, who you playin' with?"

"Yeah, I hear that sugar sweet shit. That's because them broke bitches you been fucking with know you got that money, but she was born with money so that shit ain't nothing to her player, player."

"Nigga, I don't pay for the pussy, pussy pay me," I said, as I put the bottle of Remy to my lips and sipped.

"Then put 5 stacks on it."

"Get the bag nigga."

"What's the bag?" Black asked, as he lit a ciga-rette.

"Oh, that's just a leather bag we had with sucker on it. Me and A.G. had been betting each other since we was kids. It used to be $5 dollars but now we was getting that real money on the come up, it turned to 5 stacks. We would put the money in the bag and a third party would hold the money until they found out who won the bet."

"Alright, I understand now."

"So anyway, I told him to get the bag, but back at Fugee's."

Bash was smoking the blunt Fugee had just passed him. Fugee got up and said to him, "You want a drink? I got some Goose upstairs."

"Yeah, put some ice in it." Bash watched Fugee walk to the steps as her big ass made the flower on her short sundress quiver, that ass too loose. I know she got a thong on. She might not have anything on under that dress, he thought to himself. Then he turned around to see Cinnamon who was bent over in her own little world looking through CD's. Her Apple Bottom shorts were resting in the gap of her perfectly round spread ass. Her cheeks were busting out of the side and the way she was bent, he swore he'd seen the imprint of her pussy lips. He walked up behind her, and she felt the hardness of his dick in between her ass cheek.

"Let me help you."

"What the fuck nigga! You must have lost your fucking mind," she yelled cutting him off and pushing him back, as she noticed the bump in front of his jeans.

"My bad, I just wanted to help you, and pass you your weed," Bush said grabbing himself so she could get a good look.

"That's not my weed. That's my man shit and I don't think he'll like you trying to get free feels with your little dick, of his wifey, you better understand little nigga."

"Who the fuck is your man?"

"Preme!"

"Preme?"

"Yeah, little dick, Supreme Divine!"

"Oh shit, she was calling you her man already?" shouted Black, with excitement in his voice.

"Yeah, Yeah, now listen…..."

"Now, Poppadoc, hold this bread until tomorrow, me and 'Preme got another bet going on."

"Now what you boys bet on?" Poppadoc asked.

"Don't you worry about that with your Mr. Big looking ass. You better keep R. Kelly out your house, and don't worry about us. You know the rules. Don't give the money up until both say who won," I said to make sure everything was in the clear.

"Nigga, I know you boys do this shit almost every day and R. Kelly won't fuck nothin' I like, because I like them over 20 and fuck Mr. Big, I'm the vigor king and you little bastards are going to start paying me for this middle man shit," Poppadoc said, walking off with the bag.

"I'll see you in the morning to get my paper nigga," I said getting in my car.

"Bullshit, you'll see me in the morning spending your paper my nigga."

"Let the games begin, I'm out, happy b-day." I gave him dap out the window and was on my way....

"Yeah, you do know him and Fugee cousins, right?" Bash' face got so tight she knew 'Preme's name was one he didn't want to hear.

"My bad, ma, no disrespect. I just seen something I liked and went for it."

The whole time he was thinking fuck 'Preme that nigga ain't shit. I can't wait to catch that nigga slipping for shooting my people, Smooth. He lucky my uncle said no beef, get money, or I would slap the bitch for thinking he bullet proof.

"That's okay, little dick, let's just go back to what we was doing and act like none of this happened. I'm still bent over and looking for CD's and you can still look at my ass, which you can't have, and let your little dick get hard until it pop from your little day dream okay?" Cinnamon said then turned her back to him again bent over looking for more CD's.

"Many men wish death upon me, blood in my eyes. Lord and I can't see, these niggas trying to take my life away, many men, many, many, many men wish death on me," 50 cents' Many Men was playing, as I pulled up the 5 T.V.s I had playing the video. The car was lit up like a Christmas tree, as I parked in front of Fugee's house.

I saw Bash's blue Lexus GS 300 in her driveway. Fugee love them soft ass wanna-be-hugged ass niggas, I thought to myself as I was getting the music and the T.V.'s right for when we got back in the car.

"Yeah, that's how you get 'em. A yellow rose on the passenger seat.

"Where would I be without you, I only think about you, every thug needs a lady," Ja' Rule and Vita's Every Thug Needs a Lady was the sound in the room, with Cinnamon, Fugee, and Bash.

"What's in the bag?" Bash said looking at Cinnamon who was sitting lost in her own thoughts. Where is this nigga at? I hope he didn't get drunk and forget about me. I'm tired of playing third wheel with Fugee and this slack ass nigga.

"Yo!"

She looked at Bash as his yell broke her train of thought.

"Excuse me," she said with an attitude.

"What's in the bag?" Bash asked, now wound high and drunk from the 6 cups of Goose he'd drank.

"None of your fuckin' business!" Fugee snapped.

"Leave her the fuck alone!"

"I didn't ask you Fugee. I'm just playing with her, what's in the bag?"

"Drinks, little nigga," Cinnamon replied.

"I like to drink, who those drinks for?"

"Me and my man."

Just as I was coming down the steps, I heard Cinnamon saying I was her man.

"Ya' man? Ya' man not here so let me have a sip."

"Nah, he'll be here," she said with confidence. In her heart she wasn't 100% sure.

"That nigga ain't coming. He at that block party fuckin' some other bitch right now. Can't you hear them moanin'?."

"I told you, Bash, leave her alone before…"

"BEFORE WHAT?"

"Before 'Preme beat the fuckin' brakes off your ass," Fugee said with a voice full of anger.

Bash stood up, "Fuck Preme!"

I walked all the way down the step then Bash' drunken ass didn't see me or the ass whipping behind him coming so he kept running his mouth. Bash stood in front of the glass table and put his cup of Goose down on it.

"Fuck that punk-ass, dread-having ass Preme! When I see 'im I'm gonna bust a cap in his ass any-way! He might have seen my Lexus outside and was scared to come in, soft ass nigga."

Fugee put her head down because she knew what was about to happen. Cinnamon smiled. Bash thought it was because of what he was saying but when she pointed behind him, Bash' heart dropped to his knees. His high was gone and his drunkenness ran off and left him high and dry. He turned around only to see me towering over his 5'9 frame. My fist locked tight, my dreads hung long like a lion's main, and my eyes were the color of fire.

"Oh shit Preme…"

Boop! Bipp! Bash went flying through the air crashing unbelievably hard into the glass table, shattering it into a million pieces. I was on top of him with all 205 pounds, knocking him out and waking him up with another blow. I was speaking in tongues like a preacher with the Holy Ghost. Cinnamon was scared and turned on at the same time. She didn't know if she was going to run or play with herself. Being that I was 6'2, it looked like a 6th grader beating on a 3rd grader in the school yard.

"That's enough Preme, you going to kill him! Jay, help!" Fugee yelled calling her brother who came running down stairs.

"What's going on, what the fuck!" Jay said as he saw me on top of Bash in a bed of glass. He ran over to us and started stomping Bash. Now, Cinnamon was laughing.

"Oh shit, this is not my night," Fugee yelled out with her head in her hands.

I stood, then went in my belt and pulled out my .45. I had lost it for a minute.

"What the fuck y'all doing in my house? Preme don't you do that shit in my house, you nappy headed motherfucker!" I looked up from standing over Bash, gun cocked and pointing at his head. My eyes were blood shot red and I saw my aunt standing there with her robe wide open, hands in the air with nothing on underneath her robe but her complexion. That cooled things off with the shock of seeing her like that.

"Look, Auntie, you might want to close your robe."

"Yeah, Ma, shit," Jay said turning his head.

"What? Y'all act like y'all ain't seen tits and ass before," she said as she closed her robe. "Now, who's going to pay for my broken shit? I don't want to hear shit but money hitting my hands." She reached out to me. I put my gun back in my belt and kicked Bash again.

"This one on me nigga and this shit ain't over," I said as I pulled the money out of my pocket, counted out a stack for disrespecting her house like I did. "You still want to take a ride and talk Lil ma?" I turned to Cinnamon who eyes were locked on me the whole time. She grabbed up her things then told everybody bye and she made her way up the steps and outside with me. I opened the passenger side for her and she saw the yellow rose on the seat.

"For me?" she asked as she picked it up off the seat smiling.

"Naw, I was just giving it a ride but since it has no place to go but your hands, I guess you can have it," I said then walked around to the driver side. My peoples, Jay, came outside calling me. "Wait a minute," I said opening the door and giving her my keys.

"Don't go back in there fighting," she said as she smiled at me.

"Fighting? What fight? I just beat that silly nigga's ass."

"Well, don't go in there beating no more asses."

"Don't worry Lil Ma, just take these keys, listen to some music and look at a little T.V. I'm going to get that nigga another time, it's over for now."

"It better be." She warned me, with a smile on her face.

I closed the door and went to see what Jay wanted.

"Yo man, help me get this punk ass nigga out the house," Jay said. I turned to Cinnamon who was looking me dead in my eyes. I winked and went in the house with Jay. Cinnamon stuck the key in the ignition.

"Didn't I tell you I love you, that don't mean I wouldn't cheat on you, cupid doesn't lie," 112, Cupid's song brought the car to life. The video was on all 5 of the T.V.'s lighting the car up in the darkness of the night.

"That's my song," she screamed.

I picked Bash up out of his bed of glass and helped him to his feet. "My bad, Preme. I was just bullshitting around." Bash was talking all out his ass. I don't think he knew what he really was saying.

"Fugee, help this nigga to his car. I gotta wash my hands."

She and Jay helped Bash up the steps and out the door to his car. I went to the bathroom and washed my hands and face. I looked in the mirror to make sure everything was in the right place. I saw I was still bling-blingin'.

"Time to make it happen," I said to myself in the mirror before I walked out of the bathroom to my car.

When I came outside, Bash was gone and Jay was nowhere in sight.

Fugee was bent over the passenger side window of my car talking to Cinnamon. Fugee had a phat, apple shaped bubble-ass that no man could help touching it.

SMACK!

"SHIT!" Fugee yelled, as the pain of my hand crashed into her ass, setting her cheeks on fire, "Stop playing unless you going to put something in it."

"You crazy and we family girl, get you some help," I said, as I jumped in the driver side of my car.

"You know Bash gon' start some shit," Fugee said. "You should already know what I told her."

"Fuck that nigga and that bitch he came from! I'll see you later. Me and Cinnamon got to go on with our private party."

"Whatever, I'll see you girl, do everything you know I would do, twice."

"Girl, you so crazy," Cinnamon said to Fugee as we pulled off...

CHAPTER 2

"Going to make your body wet, uh uh." Buster and Janet Jackson were playing, as I pulled into the gate of a park that was blocked. I got out, moved the block then got back in the car.

"Nigga, we going to jail, can't you see this park is closed?"

"Yeah, it's close to everybody else but me and you, we're special."

"Special? We'll be specially locked up if the police come," Cinnamon spoke with concern as I pulled in the park.

"Read this sign, what does it say?" I asked, as I pointed to the sign my headlight was shining on.

"Star Point Park, and?"

"Well, how can they lock me up when I'm bringing my star to its point of happiness?" All she could do was smile at my compliment.

"What if another person needs to find this point?" she asked.

"They better see that the park is closed before I call the cops."

"Boy, you crazy," she spoke as she laughed.

We pulled up on top of the hill where the waterfall was. The full moon and stars seemed to mirror off of the water. It was like there were 2 skies in one night. It was the most beautiful sight I'd seen. By the look on her face, she had never seen such peacefulness either. She had no idea that I would bring her here. She thought I would take her to a hotel or maybe my place and beg for some ass like any other nigga, but Supreme Divine wasn't like no other nigga. I took it to the next level at all times. I got out of the car, opened the door then went in the seat and got my star point kit.

"What's a star point kit?" Black asked inquisitively.

"Oh, that's just something I keep in the car for them hard-to-get women; a bag with candles, wine glasses and big ass picnic blanket. Star Point Park is the best place to get a woman to feel like she could tell you anything because it's so peaceful and when it's just you and the stars, the sky's the limit."

"What you think you a real player now or something? I have to give it to you for that park thing, that's old school all the way," Black spoke giving

Preme dap.

"Naw, big homie, I'm just born with an old soul of a Mack."

"Okay Goldy, what happened next?"

"Well, we were at the park and…."

I grabbed the bag, found a nice place in the grass laid out the blanket, put candles at each corner and lit them. She just stood there in pure amazement, as I set the scene of our night for communication and maybe even a little physical stimulation. I removed the bag she held in her arms with the drinks, as I looked her in her eyes.

"Do you care to join me and relax, so you can free the stress that's on your brain? My time and attention is all yours," I said as I lay back after pouring her a glass of Remy Red.

"All this for me? I don't know what to say. I wasn't expecting this."

"Just tell me what's on your mind so maybe I can help you work out your problem."

She took her seat facing me, I stood and went to my car to get my boom box out of the trunk and press play so the CD could really set the mood.

"As I stand here contemplating on the right thing

to decide, will I take the wrong direction, all my life, who can I run to, when I need love." Excape's Who Can I Run To song caressed the night and our ears.

"Who can I run to, to share this empty space, who can I run to, when I need love." The song played, as I sat down facing her once again, the candlelight danced off her complexion.

She was a truly beautiful, honey colored, black goddess and I really wanted her, not just for her sex. I saw something in her eyes that touched me deep within.

"So, what's going on with you?" I asked looking in her eyes, lost in everything that made her a woman.

"What you mean?" she said as she sipped her glass trying to stay away from my temptation.

"I mean what's all the stress on your chest?"

"I told you. It's a long story but not enough time to tell it."

"Look ma," I said showing her my watch.

"That's a nice iced-out Rolex."

"Baby girl this watch has more than ice, look at it."

"What, the Platinum? I said it's a nice watch. I know you spent a lot of money on it," she said with a little attitude, thinking I was trying to floss on her.

That's what I wanted her to think so I could break her down.

"Girl, I don't know what you looking at. Something must be wrong with your eyes. Can't you see this watch is magic?"

"Magic? Nigga, please, what I look like I'm 5 years old? You must have had too much to drink at that party or you hit your head coming out the car. Now I get it, you on ex."

"Alright, if you done. What time is it?"

"It's 1:32am."

"Now watch this." I pulled the pin out, the watch stopped. "See."

"See what?"

"See, I stopped time, for you. So, now you have all the time in the world to clear your heart and mind."

Once she realized what I was doing I saw her face light up brighter than the full moon.

"Magic? Most men told me they would give me the world, all lies, but no man has ever stopped time just to get to know me. What's wrong with me? Hell, nobody ever stopped time, period! I truly don't know what to say." She spoke as she looked deeply into my eyes, seeing my soul that I couldn't hide even if I wanted to.

I looked back into her eyes, and all I saw was myself, and I felt something turn inside of me that I'd never felt before. I questioned myself, is this love?

"Just tell me what's on your mind. All you have to say is what's wrong," I said softly, she took a deep breath before she started to speak.

"Well, you remember when I told you I just got back in town?"

"Yeah."

"Well, I had just left my ex down south just the day before."

"Why? Did that nigga put his hands on you?" Out of nowhere the blood in my veins start racing and turned into fire. Just the thought of a man hitting her, putting her in pain made me want to kill, and I really didn't know why.

"No, he ain't that big of a fool. I can hold my own."

"Then why you leave your man? What? You fell out of love, or did you cheat on him?"

"No and no."

"What? You didn't like being with a country boy?"

"He's not from the South, his family is.'"

"Then where he's from?"

"Plainfield."

"Plainfield?" I said with a little shock in my voice because A.G. told me earlier that nobody could pull her.

"Yeah, Plainfield."

"What Block?"

"Clinton Ave."

"Get the fuck out of here! Whose from Clinton Ave?" She really had my full attention now.

"Joe-Joe."

"Joe-Joe?" I spit back in my Remy bottle.

"Yeah, you know him?"

"Yeah I know his, his….. soft ass, but he ain't nobody. Why in the hell would somebody like you fuck with a punk ass, wanna-be down-ass nigga like that? I'm not hating, but that nigga is a real duck. He just had no hustle with him, a can't-get-right type of nigga. All he wanna do is trick and that's real. Plus, niggas use to play him out take his shit and beat his ass, he kept a black eye more that any boxer I know."

"I heard about all that but the past was the past and that's not why I talked to him. Joe-Joe was sweet and nice to me and he cared about my feelings, made me feel like I was his queen."

"Then if it was all that good, why you leave him on route 66 and why are you sitting here making me stop time?"

"Because once we got down south he found some new friends, you know how them country niggas is, they thought he was cool because he was from here. Once everybody started kissing his ass and them silly fast ass country chicken heads wanted to give this slow nigga some pussy, he played me to the left. I worked hard every day. My real father died left me a nice piece of change but I still worked. He did nothing because he knew what I had in the bank. I paid all the bills and didn't cheat on his 2 minute ass but for all my hard work love and loyalty what do this nigga do to me (me) the one that asked him for nothing but his love and honesty. This no good nigga cheated on me with some flat ass big titty tall ass country bitch. Then this sorry motherfucker tried to play me in my face, talking about let's have a threesome. I stayed for 2 years before that trying to work things out but when I got to the point that my new name began to be Bitch and he came home to change clothes or just to get a nut off, I couldn't take it anymore, my heart was broken and pain was so real." Tears began to fall from her eyes and I knew she was still hurting. I didn't say a word, I just listened and let her clean her soul. "I stood by his side when people from Clinton Ave played him out. They use to walk up to me in his face and grab my ass, then tell me I should leave his punk ass alone. You know Mike-Mike?" I shook my head in agreement. "Mike-Mike punched him in his face just to show me that Joe-Joe was soft. He didn't do shit but look stupid, so I bust Mike-Mike in the head with a bottle and knocked his ass out.

"I started laughing hard."

"What's so funny?"

"I heard about that shit, I was locked down when it happened, I didn't know you did that shit, nobody gave me a name."

"I was being a real woman, holding my man down and now all I got from his ass was pregnant and his ass to kiss."

"Pregnant?" my eyes got big, the joke was over now, she shook her head, stood and walked by the lake, her back to me. She started crying looking at the moon and the stars that rested on the water. I quickly came up behind her, without missing a beat to console her.

"Don't worry, I'm going to get rid of it, just like I got rid of him. My own mother don't even know I'm pregnant, only Fugee and now you."

"Why do you want to kill the child that's apart of you and may be the best part of him." I never believed in abortions and since I was feeling her story I couldn't see her ending it so sad, with the death of her first child.

"I'm not going to raise no fatherless ghetto story. I got a little money but a child need more than cash, my child needs a father but his slack ass is not around." I don't know if it was the moment or what but I said without thinking,

"You got me." She turned to face me looking me in my eyes even with the tears in her eyes she still had me under some type of spell.

"This is not your child."

"I can fix that, watch this." I picked up a rock threw it and it skipped three times. Then I told her to read the sign carved in the big rock. It said skip a rock 3 times across the water and make one wish.

"So, what's your wish?"

"I wish that you bless me with fatherhood of your

child." Before she could answer, I kissed her with all I had…

"Hold up, you mean to tell me your baby mothers, well one of your baby mothers had another kid that wasn't yours?"

"Yea, I never told anyone this, not even my own flesh and blood."

"Which one ain't yours the boy or one of the girls? I saw your pictures."

"The boy."

"Get the fuck out of here, he look like your twin." Black, shocked, and couldn't believe the bomb that was just dropped on him.

"You heard the saying, 'feed a child 'til they look like you' but only the love I have for him makes him mine. I'll die to protect him or try to feed him, you feel me?"

"One, 100% little brother."

"So anyway me and her was at the park starting our love story but while we was doing that.".

"There's that little nigga Jay right there." Bash said to his brother as they pulled up to the chicken and pizza. Jay was getting out the car with his girlfriend, not really paying attention. His back was to them when they pulled up. Bash and his brother jumped out the car.

"Yo, Jay," Bash said. Jay turned around to see who called him only to be punched dead in his face, taking him by surprise, knocking him on the ground. Bash and his brother started to kick Jay to sleep, stumping him like he was on fire and they was trying to put him out. His girl was still in the car, she called 911 and begged the boys to stop. She jumped out the car trying to help her man, only to be next to him getting her ass kicked too, just like him. They didn't stop beating them until they heard the sound of the police. But, before Bash left he grabbed Jay and spit in his face. "Tell that bitch ass Supreme he's next," then, kicked him in the face and his brother kicked Jay girl in her shit. Rhonda and Jay lay on the ground as Bash and his brother sped off. Rhonda made it to her feet before Jay but he was worse off. The cops came, Rhonda said she didn't know the guy who jumped them. She did but snitching is a no -no. Jay had to be rushed to the hospital, Rhonda followed the ambulance to the emergency room. There she called Fugee and told her what had happened….

"I belong to you, I belong, I give all my love to

you, every time I see your face, makes me what to sing." Rome's hit song from back in the day "I Belong" played as we 2-stepped in each other arms. Then my personal cell phone started to ring. I broke our embrace reluctantly to answer it.

"What's good?" I said into the phone looking in Cinnamon beautiful eyes.

"Preme, they jumped Jay, he's in the hospital all fucked up. They even beat his girl." Fugee yelled in the phone crying.

"Who jumped him?" I said turning my back to Cinnamon so she couldn't see the anger in my face.

"Bash and his people, they fucked his face up bad, my mother is going off."

"Don't worry about it, I'ma take care of it."

"Preme, don't go out and kill nobody, Jay not dead he just got fucked up but he going to live, just fuck that bitch ass nigga up."

"I told you, I'll take care of it."

"Preme, you don't need no heat."

"I'm not going to kill 'em but I'm going to get his bitch ass."

"Give me your word, you not going to kill nobody."

"Word." Then I hung up my cell phone and turned to Cinnamon. "We have to go."

"What happened?" She said with concern in her voice.

"Bash jumped Jay and fucked him up, don't worry he's okay but we got to ride." I said as I started making my way to the car.

"What about the stuff on the ground?" She asked following me to the car.

"Fuck it." I said dryly as I opened the door for her to get in. She got in, I took my place at the driver seat and we were off…

"Mess out! Mess out! Time to eat, get it while it's hot. Mess out!" The C.O. yelled as the locks popped on the doors and the once quiet prison halls now came alive. The inmates came out their doors talking and bullshitting on their way to the mess hall. Supreme and Black been talking so long that the sun had come up on them.

"You going to eat?" Black asked not moving out his spot.

"What they got up there today?"

"What's today?"

"Tuesday."

"Then it's shit on a shingle, sloppy gravy or burnt toast." Black said with a smile on his face knowing Preme hated that meal.

"Fuck that, I'm not going, I'll wait for Good Brother to come through selling them breakfast trays.'"

"Yeah, me too, I don't feel like walking down there for Bayside State Prison's best today."

"Let me get my money ready now, you know how Good Brother be acting."

"Yeah, money on the wood makes it all good, money out of sight something aint right."

"Yeah, that's him," Supreme said, taking 2 packs of Newport's out his locker. "Today, breakfast is on me, my old friend, for giving me your ear."

"Well shit, I should be paying you I haven't felt this free in years."

Knock. Knock.

"Come in!" Black yelled. The cell door opened.

"What's up Big Black and what's going on Supreme?" The tall slim inmate said as he walked in the small cell.

"Everything is everything but it's all in the hands of time my brother." Black said as he gave him dap.

"What's good with you slim shady?" Preme said to the man also dapping him.

"Preme, Slim Goody needs your help again, I need a poem for my girl, I fucked up and I have to make it up. I need one of those special apology ones."

"Slim Goody, I don't know how you got that name as much shit you stay in brother." Black spoke as he sat up in his bunk so his friend could have a seat. As Slim Goody took his seat next to Black he started to tell his story. "Naw, on the phone."

"What did you say?" Preme asked so he could know what to give him. Supreme was a great poet, he had a way with words that was a gift from the Gods. Black told Supreme he should go on Apollo, or write a book of spoken word. Supreme started the book and plan on putting his art on CD's.

"Well, it's like this she started talking about her sister told her that I called her begging for phone sex."

"I know you did that shit Slim Goody," Black said.

"Yeah, I did but the bitch wasn't supposed to tell it. She didn't tell when I use to hit her off when I was home," Slim said.

"So what happened?" Preme asked knowing it was more to the story.

"I tried to back out of it and turn it around, so I told her that she was fucking."

"Man you know better than that shit!" Black and Preme spoke in unison.

"I know, I know but it's too late now. I need you to help me fix it, I got 2 packs of Newport's right now." Slim Goody said as he pulled out the packs from his pocket and handed them to Preme.

"I got just the thing for that, I just wrote it last week for my girl, I know if it worked on her it'll work for you." Preme looked through the papers he took from is locker then found the piece of paper he was looking for. "That's it! This is perfect for what you going through."

"What's it called?" Slim Goody asked.

"My Apology," Preme answered as he sat back on his locker.

"Spit it for me let me see if that's what I need." Slim Goody said to make sure he was getting what he was paying for.

Preme took a deep breath then begin to recite the words of the poem. "My Apology...Let my apologies, read like a eulogy in the cemetery of misery, burying the confusion between you and me, listen to the sweet symphony, of the resurrection of our unity, playing beautifully, together we supposed to be, you're not my enemy or an entity that can't find understanding with me, you're a part of thee; like the Earth to the trees, A blunt to my weed, A breeze to the leaves, Air to the birds and bees, the cold to zero degrees, let's put our anger on freeze and stop and breathe…Inhale, exhale who know me well? Locked away in a prison cell, my emotion rebel, a personal hell. Looking in the eyes of Satan, questioning your dedication, is you loving me or running the streets with him, having relations? With all this pressure and time I'm facing, Baby, it's you I can't see replacing, just in casing you romantically with this poetry. Even in our darkest of fights, our love shine amazingly bright, there is nothing wrong only (us) and that's the only thing that makes my life right…Peace…"

"That's it, man that's that shit right there!" Slim Goody spoke as his face lit up like the Empire State Building, knowing that his girl would love the poetic communication of words. Black just chilled knowing Supreme was a master with word play, so it didn't amaze him one bit that Preme had what Slim Goody needed.

Tap. Tap. Tap.

"Come in!" Black yelled from the bed. The door slid open.

"As' salaam, Alikum, my brothers in bondage, I see that you have not made it to the mess hall but you are very much in luck, I have with me 5 breakfast trays. Hand cooked by yours truly. The best cook on the compound"...

"Cut the bullshit, Good Brother, what do you got? We already hungry so you don't have to give no sales pitch. Preme got the money right there." Black said cutting him off as he knew Good Brothers' song and dance.

"Well, in that case, I got bacon, eggs with cheese plus 4 big buttermilk pancakes with maple syrup on the side. Each of those trays, 5 in all, are full to the top and is going for the low price I called (I got my brothers back) cost of 4 penitentiary dollars apiece,: Muhammad A.K.A. Good Brother spoke as he showed off the white trays of food.

"Now look at this shit, you came in here with that as' salaam alaikum shit dressed in all white, wearing your magic half of hat, selling pork bacon, you should say as'salama bacon." Black said opening his tray. His comment made everybody laugh, even Good Brother.

"I don't eat pork, Allah said don't eat it but he didn't say nothing about selling it." Good Brother replied.

"I hear that shit, make that money." Preme said as he gave Good Brother his payment for the trays. They had a little small talk, then, Black kicked everybody out the cell. He said it was because he wanted to eat in peace but in fact, he wanted Preme to finish the story.

"Good looking out Preme, with the poem." Slim Goody said as he followed Good Brother out the door.

"It's all good homie, thanks for my bread." Preme said giving Slim Goody dap.

"Peace, Blackman." With that Slim was out the door and slid it close behind him.

"So now them story blocking motherfuckers is out of here, what happened when you found out about your people getting jumped?" Black asked, putting a piece of crispy bacon into his mouth.

"Well after we went to the hospital to check on Jay, just make sure he's okay/ he was a little fucked up, broke nose, black eyes, and bruised ribs but he was going to live. Jay been fucked up worse than that but now it was time for the big pay back"…

"I aint no killer, just don't push me, revenge is the sweetest joy next to getting pussy." Tupac's Hail Mary played as we road down the street not saying a word. She knew I wanted Bash, she also knew I was going to get him but what she didn't know was where we were going to be next"…

"Stop…Hold up! You mean to tell me, you went to handle your business with shorty in the car? Man, I know you was slipping. You just met her, what if shit got ugly and you had to put that punk ass nigger where he belongs, 6 feet in the dirt?" Black asked.

"I wasn't slipping, well maybe a little but I was pissed that this fag ass nigger fucked with my people. I didn't care about the fact that we jumped him earlier and that it was only his get back. Fuck that! I'm Supreme Divine. But, I took shorty for 3 reasons. One she never asked me to take her home, which showed me she was a rider until we die type of woman. Two, I knew if I had her there I would not likely kill him and three, the sun had not come up yet and she was still earth 5 stacks."

"Money over bullshit."

"You know it."

"I hear that shit little brother so what happened next?"

"Well, we pulled up in front of that nigger house, I turned the music down then"…

"What's in the bag?" Cinnamon asked breaking the silence in the car.

"It's payback, I want you to hold this." I said taking off my chains and rings, plus my watch and gave them all to her. She looked at it as I opened the car door. I knew she wanted to stop me but she left it alone because she also knew anything she tried would have been pure vain. I took my 45 out my belt, gave it to her, she took my gun. "If anybody comes out that house with a gun or there is more than one, shoot to kill." I told her before closing the car door without giving her time to say a word. I took my gun off me because I knew in the heat of the moment I would've killed him. It still was dark but I could tell morning was coming to run the darkness away. I slipped the brass knuckles on each hand that I had in the bag then knocked on the door.

Knock. Knock.

"Who is it?" The bad sleepy voice came from the other side of the door.

"It's me Smooth, open the door." I knew his soft ass would think I was one of his punk ass cousins that I put four hot ones in his ass at the club for flashing a gun in his pants that he wasn't going to use, like he was Ice Cube in Boyz in the Hood. But, anyway thus dumb motherfucker opened the door without even looking to see who it was.

"She kicked ya ass out again." Crack. Wap. Bup. Bip. I start punching him in the face, time the door opened. The first punch hit him dead in the mouth breaking his jaw instantly. I then hooked him in the eye, which started to blow up like a balloon. He was already snoring by the third punch but I kept on beating his face into a bloody mess. I would've beaten him to death if Cinnamon didn't scream.

"That's enough Preme, stop, don't kill him, I need you!" I don't know if she had a spell on me or what but even in blind rage, the sound of her voice made me stop. It was like she pushed the off button or something. I was covered in his blood, my hand and face. I stood, kicked his ass in the head one more time before we made our way to the car. When we got in the car I saw she had my gun in her hand.

"What you was going to do shoot me if I didn't

stop?" I asked as I pulled off.

"No, I was going to shoot him so you would stop." She said handing me my gun back.

"Man, that girl was a real rider. I don't know too many women that would stand by your side after seeing you almost kill the same guy twice in one night. Plus that was the first time she ever met you. She had to be feeling the same thing you was feeling."

"I know Black, that's what got me to feel her more but if you stop talking I can tell you what happened."

"My bad little brother, I just dig how little momma held it down, go 'head with your story."

"So anyway, we pulled up to my apartment and I don't know what I was thinking, I took her to my real place. I had 3 places I took bitches I just wanted to fuck, or just show niggas I didn't know like that, or didn't trust like that, to let them know where I lay my head. Only A.G., my Grandmother, Tangy A.G. girl and Fugee knew where I really laid my head so anyway....

"Your love is a one in a million it goes on and on, love ya baby," Aaliyah's One in a Million bombed as I parked the car, I got out, opened the door for her, then popped the trunk and pulled out my hot pink polka dot car cover and put it over my car. She looked at me like I was crazy.

"Why you putting that ugly ass car cover on that nice ass car?"

"You really want to know?"

"I asked you didn't I?" She replied with a sexy smirk on her lips as we made our way up the steps to my door.

"I put that ugly shit on my car so people won't know that's my car. Nobody would ever stop and think that under that ugly thing is my car."

"That's smart, you full of surprises when you not beating people up."

"I don't start shit, I finish it, I am a man that stands for something, that means I aint going to fall for anything. Nor am I going to let anybody knock me down without a fight. That's the same thing I'm going to teach our baby." I said as I opened the door to my place.

"You really mean the things you said at the lake?" she asked still unsure. I turned to face her, cutting on the lights to my studio apartment looking her in her eyes, those beautiful gray eyes.

"I don't say things I don't mean." I wanted to kiss

her after I spoke but I had that punk ass nigger blood on me, so a shower was calling my name. "Make yourself at home, sorry it's only one bed but then again I never bring anybody here. There aint nothing but beer in the fridge, if you hungry I'll take you to get something to eat after I take a shower."

"I'm cool, go wash your ass."

I walked pass my leather L shaped couch where I had my 72 inch Plasma hanging on the wall in front of my red oak glass tables that matched the red oak hard wood floors. I had a huge fish tank full of exotic salt water fish, all types of tropical colors in the water, that was in the living room part, my bedroom part had another 72 inch Plasma Flat Screen sitting in a stand with a surround sound system. I also had my stereo hooked up in the system. My bed was king sized, with pillows black and gold, black and gold comforter and under that, black silk sheets. I had hundreds of D.V.D.'s and C.D.'s in a stand next to the T.V.

"Make yourself comfortable while I hit this water." I said pulling my gun from my pants then taking the clip out and the one in the need, then placing every-thing on my nightstand that matched my bed.

"You have a nice place, who all those people on

the wall?"

"That's me and my family and most of them are me, Tangy and my brother from another mother A.G."

"Tangy is my girl, I haven't seen her in a while, nice to hear she still with A.G. cheating ass. He tried to holler at me, you know?"

"Naw, I didn't know that but thanks for telling me though." I really knew but didn't want her to think we were talking about her. I pulled out some weed I had in my nightstand and some blunts. "Do you know how to roll?"

"Do burning wood smoke?"

"Girl, you got a smart mouth, you keep talking like that I'm going to have to put something hard in it to see where your brain really at."

"We'll see if you can handle what's on my mind one day."

I had to admit she was on point and had a jazzy two step about herself. I went in to the shower. I heard music but couldn't make it out. I was in the shower about 10 minutes when I felt her hand on my back. "Oh shit, what the fuck! Girl, you shocked the shit out of me." She wasn't in the shower just her head and with a rag.

"I just wanted to wash your back, where your soap at?" I handed her the Burberry body wash, I seen her eyes take a trip across my body. She came in just on time because I was hard as hell thinking of her mouth on my dick, so I know I was giving her a good show. I turned as she washed my back.

"I can tell you never had a real woman by your side or to back you up."

"Why you say that?"

"Look at this rag, a real woman got her mans' back so it should never get dirty. I'ma make sure it don't ever look like this again, get under that water, you should be good now." She said then left without another word. The funny thing about it, her words rang true, she was totally right. I was a Mack, I had no real woman, I had some chicks I fucked, some more than others but no real wifey. I spent most of my time at A.G. and Tangy's because I didn't like being alone in fact this was the first time I've been home in weeks. I truly only came here when A.G. and Tangy was doing the romantic thing or I just wanted to escape from everybody...

"Preme, I don't mean to cut your wisdom but I got to say this, that girl is deep. That shit she did and said with the rag was real. I don't think I ever had a woman come at me like that. I guess that's why my back stayed dirty."

"Yeah Black, I guess that's why my back stay dirty now that she's gone but let me finish."

"Go ahead, I just had to say shorty was on point with her shit."

"Well, I got out the shower, oiled up and put my Burberry smell good cologne on. I had my dreads hanging down on my shoulders. I wrapped a towel around my waste then walked in the room"…

"Time on my hand since you been away boy, I can't stop these tears from falling from my eyes, I'm so sorry, sorry." Mary J's I'm Going Down was blasting from the sound system. She was watching B.E.T. late night video soul. I walk in with fresh towel and wash rag in my hand then handed them to her, I also pulled out a pair of boxers and a T-shirt for her to put on after her shower. She thanked me and went into the bathroom and closed the door. On my bed was 4 perfectly rolled blunts. I picked one up and lit it, I slid on some black silk boxers then walked to my kitchen where Tangy left me some smell good candles, and it was about 7 of them so I took them in the bedroom part. I'm just in my silk boxers I seen she put my jewelry on my dresser. I didn't bother to put it on because of everything play right then these boxers was coming off soon. The only thing I would have on is a smile as I am beating the brakes out that pussy. I set the candles where I wanted them to be, smoking my weed. I walked in the bathroom with a fresh rag did the same shit to her but I turned it up, took it to the next level.

"Boy, you scared the shit out of me!" She screamed as she felt my hand on her back.

"First off, baby, I'm not a boy. That was the last nigga you was with, that's why y'all not together now because grownups don't play with other people kids. I am all man and as your man I will always have your back and front." I said then I stepped in the shower with my boxers on and put the blunt she had rolled in my mouth, rag in hand as the shower water rained down, hot and steamy.

"Man, you're crazy!" She said as I soaped her back enjoying her soft beautiful body. The bubbles slid down her back to her ass that looked like heaven in brown flesh. I washed her from head to toe without trying anything sexual, even though she moaned when my hand went across her breast, and when I went between her legs. She knew I wanted her, my dick was sticking out my boxers. There was no way to hide the fact my body was screaming for her sex. Neither could she, her nipples was so hard they looked like Hershey Kisses.

"Now, you should be good, a man always get the job done." I said as I stepped out the shower, wet blunt in mouth.

"Wait." She said.

"I'll see you in the room." I said stepping all the way out the shower. I could hear it in her voice she was on fire but I wanted to play the game she tried to play, plus show her that my dick don't think for me. I can be with her in the shower and still don't fuck even if I wanted to. I'm not going to lie it took everything in my power not to fuck her right then but I had bigger plans on how I was going to cook this chicken. I wanted to make a memory.

"You wrong for what you started." She said sticking her head out the shower, as I put another towel around me and threw the wet half blunt in the toilet.

"I know." I told her then flushed the toilet on that ass."

"Oh, shit, that's cold!" She screamed as the water went from hot to freezing fast. I laughed as I ran out the bathroom. "I'ma get you back she yelled as I closed the door.

I had to light me another blunt because I fucked up the other one in the shower. I lit all the candles that I had all around the room, then turned the light off. I found my sex CD which is full of all types of love songs then put it in the CD player. I laid on the bed with nothing on but oil and a smooth pulling blunt. I set music to the song I wanted and held the remote until I heard her cut the water off, she stayed in there for a minute, I knew she wasn't dressing because all her clothes were now in here with me, the only thing was in there was oil and a towel, I set it up that way.

The reason I got in the shower with her was to let her get over the shock of me seeing her naked, plus to show her my game was sharper than hers. I took the clothes when I was in there because I wanted to see her nakedness in candle light as it danced off the oil on her body. I truly wanted to make love to her. I didn't want it to be a fuck. I wanted it to be a night to remember, not just for her but for me too.

She opened the bathroom door I pressed play. "All you got to do is say yes, open up your mind and let's do this." Floetry song Say Yes gave life to the romantic scene of candlelight. She had the towel on her head, her body sparkling with the glow of the light that was riding her curves. It was a sight to behold, pure African poetry in the flesh. I was at a loss for words, the whole time my eyes was locked on her, I knew she had a nice body but now my heart was like the song you yes.

"you took my clothes and I can't believe you did all this for me."

"I didn't," I said as I was standing now face to face our bodies lightly touching, she looked up at me in those soul taking eyes.

"Then who you did this for?"

"I did it for us, now let's make a love scene as will make a porn star jealous." I said as I kissed her soft lips with all my passion, removing her towel from her head, I put her soft angelic body down in the edge of the bed. Our lips were locked tasting each other lust. I positioned myself between her parted legs, her body was trembling I don't know if it was me or music that filled her with so much excitement, I went on kissing, nurturing the fire of our desire. I found myself sucking on her hard dark chocolate nipples, like a baby getting his last meal. "Put it in, I need to feel you inside me, please, baby, give it to me." She moaned her request of longing. I slowly eased all 10 and a half inches I had to offer inside her ebony, she was so wet and tight it was like I was taking a virginity instead of a mother to be. I looked down and enjoyed the candles light showing her face full of ecstasy. I was loss in the wetness of her hot pussy. I teased her by pushing deep inside her powerfully until I hit the bottom, keeping up with the flow of the song then pulling out halfway, rotating with each thrust as I slowly pumped in and out. It took everything in my power not to cum. My mind was racing trying together it felt as if our souls were locked together. The way she was acting I could tell she was about to climax. Our bodies now covered in sweat, she came with the powers of a thunderstorm as it ran down on my hard excitement. She started to cry out.

"Preme, what you doing to meee?" As she shook uncontrollably then her body starts to just quiver after her climax spent. I then picked her up and put her all the way on the bed, I still haven't gotten mine yet. The song changed, "Take your time, work it slowly, work it, work it." Excapes Work it Slow now filled the ears of our burning desire. I laid beside her and the next thing I knew she rolled me over and was on top of me, kissing my lips and guiding me back into her hot drippings ebony fire.

"Preme, I want you to cum for me daddy. Show me it's good to you." She moaned in my ear, her voice sound sweeter than music. She was working the hell out of my dick, placing her hand on my chest. She was sliding up and down, moving her hips in a circular motion. Each time she came down I pushed up making sure I hit all 4 corners of her walls, her creamy juices flowed as she rose, flexing her inner muscles around my throbbing dick that was pounding up deep in her with raw aggression. "Oh God Preme!" She screamed as she leaned forward digging her nails in my chest. "I can feel that dick in my stomach!" She yelled out in ecstasy.

"Take this dick girl, make me cum." I demanded as I smacked and gripped her bouncing ass so I could pull her deeper on to me.

"Oooh, sshit, I can't hold it I'm cccc AAAh." She screamed quickening her rhythm and started really bouncing that ass up and down hard and fast. I couldn't take it anymore the way that pussy of hers was gripping my dick every time she pulled up I lost it, she was better and tighter than me jerking my own dick. Once she felt me unleash my excitement up inside her, unloading in her with a powerful force, her body start jerking, gyrating her hips when she slammed down meeting my last thrust of lust. Our lips locked and her cum ran down on me like her water broke and she wasn't 2 months yet. We both were dripping in sweat kissing still connected to one another, we kissed with so much passion that she had another orgasm. We fell asleep in each other arms.

I woke up to a hot wet great feeling between my legs. I opened my eyes and looked down to see what was going on and Cinnamon was giving more brain then with a smart head. Her hot mouth was so wet I couldn't help but fall into deep euphoria from the feeling. She was bobbing her head up and down, her hands massaging and sliding in perfect motion up and down my shaft as she deep throated my dick. I was on cloud 109 watching her suck my dick as if it was the sweetest thing on Earth. She tried to take all I had to offer but gagged halfway down, her lips slid up and down, kiss, sucking, her hands working in unison covering her spit, her head started bobbing faster and faster as I felt myself about to cum….

Knock. Knock. Knock.

"What the fuck!" I said as I pushed her away and jump up quickly. I'm not going to be slipping like Bash, I grabbed my 45 from the nightstand, put the clip in, cocked it back putting one in the head, then went to the door, wearing nothing but a hard dick and my gun. I look through the peep hole and seen it was safe, it was A.G. girl, Tangy. I opened the door, Cinnamon still laid in the bed but she covered herself with the covers.

"Nigga, put some clothes on come to the door with your dick all hard sticking out like that, don't you know you're not in Africa anymore and I know you wasn't jacking your dick coming out the door like a porn star all hard and shit." She said, the whole time she was talking her eyes was on my dick.

"My eyes are up here, stop talking to my dick like that and hell no, I wasn't jacking my dick. You broke up something me and my company was doing since last night."

"Nigga please, I seen you naked more than your mother and hold up damn nigga, what you on Viagra? It's 2 in the afternoon." She said coming in as I turned away.

"No, I'm just that damn good at what I do." I said, putting my gun in the living room table and making my way back to the bedroom, she was right behind me.

"You right to come to the door with that gun after that shit y'all pulled last night."

"Y'all?"

"Yeah, you and those six niggas you took to Bash house and jumped him with."

"Cinnamon, you hear that shit? This nigger said I jumped him with 6 niggas."

"Hey Cinnamon, I didn't know you and Preme messed around. When you got back? Tangy asked, standing at the end of the bed.

"Oh, I been back, I knew Preme for a second." I could tell that she was embarrassed that Tangy saw her there with her pants down, well, in this case pants, panties, bra, everything gone, somewhere on the floor of a nigga apartment she didn't really know.

Tangy knew Cinnamon was lying because she knew everything about me. That wasn't the first time she saw me naked, with her fine ass, she done seen my dick more than me, we was just cool like that, we slept in the same bed and never fucked, never nothing sexual, she was one of my best friends. I saw her sexy ass naked too, she got a nice phat ass and she would put you in the mind of Melissa Moore. The only thing that kept me from trying to fuck her was that she was my right hand man girl, if she was anybody else, I would have been knocked it down. I never came at her like that and he knew I never would, the trust we had was real.

"So, where did y'all meet?" Tangy asked trying to be funny I knew what she was doing, so before Cinnamon could answer, I saved the day.

"Come on now, time to go, I told you we was doing something. You want to play 21 questions it's time to go." I had her hand taking her to the door, dick still swinging in the wind. All I wanted was Cinnamon in my bed, I knew Tangy was going to tell A.G. how I came to the door and how I had Cinnamon naked in the bed, talking about we been at it all night. I knew my 5 stacks were as good as gold.

"I just stopped by to let you know that the police looking for you."

"The police."

"Yeah, that snitch ass nigga took out a report on

you, y'all broke his jaw in 3 places."

"Stop saying y'all, I beat that nigga ass, it felt like 6 niggas, I aint worried about him, snitch nigger, ditch nigger, I'll take care of his ass later, right now I got something I need to be working on." I told her, as she went to the door.

"Ok be safe, I'm just giving you the heads up, you wouldn't pick up your phone. But I see now you got other things that need to get up." She said pointing down at my dick.

"You got jokes but when this door close duck because I don't want you to hit your head going down the steps. My cell must be dead, aint been on the charger. I'll see you later." I kissed her on the cheek and told her good-bye then closed the door and locked it. Cinnamon came out the shower wrapped in a towel. I walked over to my dresser, "I'll be down there, one," then ended the call. At the dresser, I went in it and gave her a tank top and sweat pants Fugee left last time she spent the night. She got on her cell phone and talked to whomever. I was hungry so I jumped in the shower, she came in again and washed my back. I got out threw on some sweats and a tank top too. We left to get something to eat at IHOP. She gave me her cell number and I dropped her back off at Fugee's, I didn't go in, I called A.G. and told him to meet me at Poppadoc's house.

When I pulled up his black 745I BMW was parked in the driveway, he was sitting on the step with the bag in his hand and a blunt in his mouth. I stepped out of my car after I pulled in behind his.

"I told you, nigga, that I was going to beat that pussy up." I said taking my money out of his hand.

"Yeah, you got that, I'll get you next time but now we got to beef with Dollar and his boys over that shit y'all did last night."

"Like I told Tangy, I fucked that punk ass nigger up, do you care about beef with Dollar? Who the fuck is he?

"Fuck Dollar that's what guns for, I love this street shit. It is what it is my nigga"…

***

"I feel you and your home boy but what happened to you and Cinnamon after that night." Black asked wanting to get to the point.

"Well, Black, aint shit happened that night. I didn't see her until 2 weeks later. I never called her."

"What?! What happened to all that shit you was talking about her eyes and you wanted to be the baby daddy? What the fuck? Was that game because if it was then the game is ice cold."

"Then call me Mr. Freeze. Naw, I'm just bullshittin'. I'm not going to lie and play like that and say I was running game. I really was feeling her but a lot of shit popped off after that night. I'm not talking about Bash and Dollar either."

"Who is Dollar?"

"Dollar is one of the old school niggas on the west side of town. He's really called Big Dollar because he's fat as hell but his pocket matched his size. He was Bash uncle so that's where he came in with the beef. But that nigga wasn't hitting on shit fucking with us. The real shit was the Feds and Flash."

"Who Flash?"

"I didn't tell you about Flash."

"No, you think I would ask you about something you told me, I got a lot time but you know old Black don't waste time asking questions I already know."

"I know, I feel you on that shit. But Flash was the white dude everybody got their cars from. I don't care what kind of car it was, he had you for 10% of what the car cost. He would get it for you, papers and all. I just got the car I had from him only 3 months earlier. Then come to find out the Feds had tracking devices and cameras in the whips. The way we found out was one of our homies on the other side of town got knocked and he had his lawyer tell us about Flash, my homie sold out his car. The Feds had everything, I didn't really do shit in my whip. I always had rental cars but every now and then I'll slip up."

"Damn, they can do that shit?"

"Man, them motherfuckers can do anything nowadays. Shit you can be watching T.V. and a camera can be in it and the T.V. is watching you."

"Man, shit real out there."

"Black, you just don't know the half of it."

Tap. Tap. Tap.

"Come in, you story blocking motherfucker." Black yelled from his bed, sitting up as the door opened.

"Yo! Black, we need you at the card table the pot is up to $750 cash money and it's like taking candy from a white baby, these young cats don't know shit about spades." Tex said, standing in the door, Tex was Black partner in crime at the card table. He knew no matter what time of the day it was Black was coming to get that money.

"Pardon me Tex, Preme, I need to get at you on some personal shit. You know I need one of those things." Rick said, standing by Tex at the door.

"Well, Preme, let me get my ass up and get this money with Tex and you get that money from Rick sucker for love ass." Black said, as he dapped Preme and left the cell with Tex. Rick came in.

"What's the problem homie." Preme said.

"It's my baby mother, she stopped writing and taking my calls, she won't even let me write my own children. I need something to let her know that I'm still their father and no matter what when this shit is over I'ma be there for my children. I just want her to understand what I'm going through. Man don't laugh I know I sound like some sucker for love ass nigga but I really miss my kids and I've done ran out of things to say." Rick voice was full of sadness, he was only 21 years old and he had 20 years for armed robbery trying to pay the rent for the same sour ass bitch that stopped writing.

"I got just what you need homie, there's no need to hold your head down. A man love who he love, no matter what evil the woman do, we can't help the fact that our hearts still cling to the wrong person but it may just be the wrong time in their life. Feel me."

"Yeah, the wrong time is 20 years in prison." Rick said as Preme went in his locker, pulled out a piece of paper.

"This will do it, I wrote this to my own baby mother when she pulled the same shit. How many kids you have with her?

"2, a boy and a girl."

"Then this will work perfectly."

"Spit it for me, I got 3 packs for you if it's what I need."

"I know this is what you need and you better not tell nobody but this one is on the house because I understand your pain. Now listen, it took me 2 weeks to put these words together." Preme said then took a deep breath then started to let the spoken words be spoken. "I call this Miss Bryant a Father in Prison... A father mind, lost in his incarceration, burned down bridges of communication, leaves broken hearted sensations, miss pieces with no replacement, feeling lower than hells' basement. Love makes no sense, the left side of my chest I clinch from the pain and agony of my children not knowing I'm the other half of their family, not looking for your sympathy, just empathy, picture yourself being me and you'll see, that penitentiary is truly misery, for you lose everyone that you hold closes to thee, locked doors, no keys, angers me, listening to the devils ha ha and hee hees makes me feel lower than underground feces. My fatherhood, I send with all dedication but it's tossed in the trash like a woman menstruation on a maxi pad, my children without their dad makes my emotion feel deeper than sad, those who come in their life and play dad to them it's just a fad, punk ass fags, just use and abuse their mother, just sex they don't really love her. Then leave when they get mad and my children are left with had, instead of a dad. This is what I see but too far for my hands to grab. So out of reach, like water to a dried up beach, your tongue spit flames of lies and deceit, ashes my soul, makes my knees weak of the buckling pain, worry and grief of if I ever see my children again. Miss Bryant, just listen as my heart cries out to our children through the walls and gates of this prison, my darkest vision, haunts me like no other, my daughter and her brother calling to another saying Daddy! Daddy! And it's not even me, how the fuck could you let this be, this piracy taking love from our children that's truly fatherly, this is a robbery that will be prosecuted once the day I'm free, shine thy light on my seeds, so they can grow fruitfully, baby momma hear this holy scripture that's written, a father love from prison, shine brighter than the sun once it has risen… peace"

"Man Preme you need to go to Apollo or something, you got a way with words that move people."

CHAPTER 3

Toya pulled up in a candy apple red Lincoln Navigator, sitting on 28 inch chrome Giovanni rims Pirelli tires looking ghetto fabulous, she park in front of the building where the person she was looking for was standing, she hit the horn to get his attention. Leakey looked up to see Toya fine ass calling him. He walked over to the driver side window.

"What's good sexy?" Toya said with a sexy smile.

"Everything, momma, what you need?" Leakey said leaning in the window.

"Money, my nigga, cold hard cash." Toya said liking her lips.

"You mean to tell me that bitch trickin' on chrome now?"

"No my silly little ghetto, small time nigga, the money you owe Isis, I came to pick it up. Being that your cell phone must be broke and your whip is not working to bring her the paper. I came down to your level of the world to collect the money and go back up to my place back on top looking down on small time niggas like you, little daddy." Toya spoke in her most sexiest voice almost moaning her words.

Leakey backed away from the window and was pissed off instantly; she hadn't planned on paying Isis anyway for the 3 bricks he got from her on the face. "Shit, everybody respect this bitch, for what? She aint killed nobody I heard about but even if the bitch did I got guns and niggas that would ride on these bitches and take everything." All those thoughts was playing in Leakey head when he said, "Fuck Isis, tell that pussy eating bitch, I said if she want her money she got to let me fuck that tight ass pussy of hers and suck my dick and if it's good and she let me cum in your face, I'll give her half."

"Is that all you like me to tell her, Mr. Big Bad Gangster." Toya was pissed but didn't lose her cool and stayed in the same sexy tone.

"Naw, tell the bitch I need 4 more bricks before she get some of this dick." Leakey said while grabbing his dick in his pants.

"I'll be sure to let her know your request Big Daddy." Toya spoke as she pulled off picking up her cell phone, dialed, the phone rang once and was answered by Isis.

"What happened, Toya?" Isis asked.

"Isis he said fuck you and suck his dick."

"Okay then plan B is now in the works."

"Isis, you shouldn't get your hands dirty baby, that's what goons and money is for."

"If I don't do it personally niggas will think that they can fuck me out my money and play me for cheap and goons would try me but if I put the work in myself, plus I have the best coke, that gives me the power and fear gives me the respect. That in all makes me the almighty queen."

"Okay baby, I'm with you 100%, I'm going to the spot and set everything up."

"Peace sweet thing."

With that Toya hangs up the cell and dialed again, 2 rings and answered.

"Hello." Gemini said into her cell phone waiting to hear what the next move was going to be. Toya just dropped her off before she pulled in front of Leakey building.

"Yeah, it's a go, go get him girl."

"I'm on it."

"Love ya, be safe."

"I got this."

"One."

As Leakey stood on the corner, he felt like he was the king of the world, especially after playing Isis and getting the bricks.

"Ya girl aint whoa, C.O.'s aint whoa, P.O.'s aint whoa." Black Rob's back in the day hit Whoa screamed from the speakers of the black escalade sitting on dubs.

"What's good with you Leakey Leek?" A.G. stopped and turned the music down as he spoke to his homie.

"Everything's everything Big Homie." Leakey said looking at A.G.'s whip sizing the whole thing up counting the money as he spoke.

"I hear that shit but what's up with that business out here we talked about. You want to get down or what?" A.G. said hoping that his homeboy take the easy way and get down, if not Leakey was going to have to lay down. Supreme was coming home and they was going to take over the city.

"Man, I'm good. I got this on smash, under lock and key. I just told that pussy sucking bitch Isis who run the shit."

"You told Isis you run this?" A.G. said thinking to himself (Shit Isis will take this slow ass nigga out for me, I know the nigga aint pay her for that work and he talking shit, I can count the money now from this spot.)

"Hell yeah, this is my hood and I been holding this shit down, Isis can eat a dick."

"I feel you homie but you might want to keep peace with the connect so your hood can eat."

"Fuck that bitch. It's more than one connection, in this world."

"The world is yours homie but make that money, be smart, don't let the money you make pay for your funeral."

"I'ma get with you later, right now that ass over there is calling my name." Leakey said pointing at the girl walking in front of the building.

"Damn, who is that? She looks like Kim Kardashian with a loose Buffy the Body ass. Look at that thing jiggling." A.G. said eyes locked on the movement of the girl ass cheeks that was walking.

"I don't know but my block, my bitch. I'll holler at you later." Leakey said making his way from the truck.

"What happened to money over bitches?"

"I got money, now I'm going to spend it tricking

off with this bitch." Leakey said with his back turned on his way after the girl with the phat ass. She had white shorts that looked like they were painted on. "Yo, Ma, hold that ass up!" He yelled after her but she didn't answer him, she paid him no mind as she walked swaying her hips around the building. Leakey eyes were locked on her pumping ass that seemed to have its own rhythm with each click of her heels. When he caught up with her she was standing in the mirror of a big black van putting on lip gloss. She was slightly bent over and the way the shorts hugged her perfect round, basketball ass he couldn't help but picture himself drilling her from the back. He eased up on her playfully, smacking her on that loose ass making it vibrate from his touch. "What's up ma?" He said like he knew her. She turned around to see who just popped her on her ass.

"Do I know you?" she asked in a sexy voice, licking her lips see Leakey had his gear together and was blinging like he was from Cash Money.

"No, my bad, I thought I knew you from the back you look like somebody I knew but from the front I see you look like someone I would like to get to know."

"Is that right, then you know it's time to pay up playboy if you really, really want to know all this."

"Baby, I am willing to pay whatever it cost to fuck that big soft ass, what do they call you my date to-night?"

"Gemini but this ass, your money nor your dick is long enough but playboy it's time to pay my girl Isis."

"Isis! Fuck Isis. That dike bitch can suck my dick like I said if she let me fuck her and now you then I might pay half of the money, Miss Gemini." Time the last word left Leakey lips the van door slid opened and Isis and 3 more of her beautiful crew was stand-ing there with guns pointing at Leakey. Isis chrome A.K. 47 trimmed in pearl white with a Rambo knife at the tip. The gun had a 120 round banana clip hanging as it pointed in Leakey face.

"So you want to fuck me? You want to stick your little dirty dick in my pussy?" As Isis talked she point-ed the gun, now at Leakey's dick, making the point of the knife touch it lightly, sending chills down Leakey spine. "Then you want me to suck your nasty ass dick, or is it the other way around, tell me little daddy what you like so I can get some of my money?" Isis asked in a deadly tone. Leakey was at a loss for words for a

second. He just stood, trying to get his thoughts together. "What's wrong little daddy, is that not what
you said, you bitch ass nigga."

"Fuck you bitch! What the fuck your cum drinking ass going to do, let that A.K. rip in broad daylight?
Who fuck you think you playing with? This aint no
motherfucking movie and yeah I wouldn't mind fucking that pussy and sticking this dick down your cum
drinking throat to wash my dick off afterward. Bitch
maybe I'll bring you back from between your momma
legs." Leakey said. He felt safe because he was in his
hood and there's no way in hell she could bust her gun
and make it out alive.

"No, nigga, I got your bitch, put your motherfuckin' nickel and dime hands up to God because all you
got here is hell bitch ass nigga." Then she clicked the
A.K. making it ready for action. The look in her eyes
told Leakey death was knocking on his door if he said
anymore bullshit. He did the smart nigga thing and put
his hands up. "Gemini, run his pockets." Isis ordered.
Gemini patted Leakey down and found his Gluck 40
in the lining of his pants plus a large amount of cash
in his pockets. "So this why you talk like your dick so
big, you got yourself a little gun. Now let's see how

big it is now that it's gone. Cuff this bitch before I kill him, we going for a ride." The girls in the van, never saying a word, jumped out cuffed Leakey and threw him in the van. Gemini took her place in the driver seat and pulled off, like nothing ever happened. Isis pulled out a needle. "Go to sleep bitch." She said as she shot Leakey up with the drop in his arm, knocking him out almost instantly...

He awoke to the smell and pain of his own flesh burning as his face stuck to the hot radiator. He had no pants or underwear on. "Now, bitch ass nigga, you wanted to fuck me out of my money, and you wanted me to suck your little piece of dick right bitch?" Isis said as she walked facing him.

Leakey was chained to the radiator helpless. He had no choice but to give in.

"Alright bitch, you win, I'll pay you your shit now let me fuckin' go." Leakey pleaded while still trying to sound like a man.

"Fuck that nigga, too late, if I let you pay me when you want to then everybody will think they can fuck me around but I don't get fucked. I fuck bitches and now bitch ass niggas like, nobody sick dick in me, understand, my silly little bitch ass nigga." Isis spoke as she came up behind him putting both her hands on his naked ass cheeks and parting them then rammed 2 of her dry fingers roughly in his virgin asshole.

"What the fffuck bitchhh! Are you crazy? What the fuck you doing? " He yelled trying to move burned himself each time he moved on the radiator. The girls started laughing at his struggle.

"Cut the camera on Gemini, it's time to make ghetto porn." Gemini started taping the show as it played out, pointing the camera at Leakey and Isis. Isis started unbuttoning her pants as she stood behind Leakey.

"I told you I'll pay you your money, you don't have to do this, I didn't mean what I said, it was the pills, weed, I was drink," Lucky cried out not knowing what she was doing behind him, Isis just was getting more turned on by his begging, to her it was like a virgin asking to take it in easy, she loved the power she had over him and the fear in his voice gave more excitement.

Once her pants hit the floor you could see she wore a 12 and a half inch strap on. She kicked Leakey's legs apart as if she was the police about to do a search, Leakey feel the huge mushroom shape head of the large thick strap on ripping in to his dry asshole.

"NOOOO!" He screamed in agonizing pain but Isis ignore his cries of pain and grabbed his hip as if he was a bitch and started ramming all 12 and a half into Leakey asshole. "Helllp, AAAAH!" Leakey yelled out. Isis smacked his ass cheeks like he was her bitch.

"Take this dick bitch, this is what you wanted, you wanted to fuck me." She said pumping him hard in and out his ass with the strap on, killing his manhood, you could hear it in his screams and cries. She was fucking the man out of him, pushing his virgin asshole like he was a seasoned whore. She was turned on so much that her nipples, harder than crack rocks, pointed through her shirt, sweat started to bead on her forehead. "Oh shit bitch, this ass is good I am about to cum." She moaned as she smacked his ass that was now making sounds, letting the room know it was no longer virgin. She slammed into him filling his asshole with all 12 and a half inches as she shook with her climax. Leakey had long since passed out. The girls watched in amazement. Isis kissed Leakey on the side of his face as she was still deep within him. "Now bitch, that wasn't so bad, you tries to fuck me, so I fucked you. We even, keep the money, that ass was worth it." She whispered in his ear as she pulled out of Leakey's shitty, bloody asshole. The room smelled of shit and sex, as her strap on hang bloody from her raping Leakey ass.

Gemini came with a wet soapy rag and wiped Isis strap on clean. Isis gave Gemini a deep passionate kiss then pushed her head down to lick up her cum that was dripping between her legs under the fake balls of her strap on. She gripped Gemini head and grinded her on her face as she had another orgasm. Gemini lapped up every drop of sweet nectar like a thirsty dog....

Leakey woke up, this time no chains and no pants or underwear, he was in so much pain, on the floor next to him played a DVD player playing his rape over and over again, next to that, Leakey saw his Gluck with one bullet. After seeing his manhood taken by a woman he put the gun to his head. POW! His brains went one way and his body went the other.

CHAPTER 4

"Now, I'm glad it's count. We got about 2 hours and a half before they open the door again. By that time I should have gotten most of the story." Black said as he lit up a Newport.

"Let me get one of them, I don't feel like going in my locker." Preme then lit the cigarette that Black passed him.

"Now, where was I?"

"You was talking about Flash working with the Feds."

"Oh yeah, Flash was selling cars that the Feds had tricked out to bust those who was big time and build a case on those on their way to being at the top of the game. I was glad I didn't give him 10 stacks up front or they would have got me for the tax aviation. I sold my 745I ASAP, me and A.G.

We always got the same car different color. This time we got '05 Chrysler 300c Hemi, we put a Bentley kit on them. I had cocaine white with suicide doors, tan leather seats, cherry oak gut sitting on 24 inch chrome dubs. A.G.'s was black on black, black leather gut. We both had 5 T.V.'s, everything, the cars was super loaded, bullet proof, the works. It looked like we had 2 Bentley's, was sitting on our block. We just got out our cars our out Poppadoc shop, I was flossing hard, summertime dressed in a white linen and iced out, dreads hanging."

"4, 5, 6, niggas Seeloe, pay me my shit and shut the fuck up, all you side betting motherfuckers." Pooh yelled as the money hit the ground next to the dice. I was sitting on my car talking to Sacaria, sexy red ass, when a white '04 Yukon pulled bumping Me, Myself and I by Beyoncé. I was sipping on a grape soda, my favorite, when the truck pulled up. The doors opened, Cinnamon got out the driver side, then Fugee, Tangy, Guchh, Big T and Wizzy, some of Clinton Ave's finest jump out the truck. I kept my cool as Cinnamon and the girls walked my way with that nigga you aint shit look on their face, all of them looking like sexy balls of fire. Cinnamon who lead the crew of girls was dressed in a tight Baby Phat outfit red with her long hair cornrowed to the back like she was ready to fight.

"Preme, who the fuck you think I am nigga?" She said time she saw me. She started marching up to me. Sacoria punk ass didn't stand her ground, when she saw her coming with Guchh and all them she just moved out the way. Sacoria didn't want problems with Cinnamon and them bitches. I stood face to face, she only stood to my chin, I had to bend my head so we could be facing each other but, by the way she was talking you would think she was 10 feet tall.

"What's the problem Little Momma?" I said with a smirk on my face.

"What's the problem? Nigga, you got that stupid ass monkey looking smirk on your face asking what's the problem. Nigga, you got me fucked up, you must think I am one of these stank ass hood rat, chicken heads that you can run that bullshit game on because you think you the shit , nigga, you got the game fucked up, all the way up. Don't think I'm sweating you, I'm just checking you, so next time you step to a real woman make sure all your shit is in order with you little dick ass, if you had 3 or 4 more inches then maybe I would be sweating you, you better off fucking these little nothing ass ghetto want to be super whores, stank pussy bitches." She said the last remark looking and pointing as Sacoria, daring her to make a move but she didn't open her mouth. Now everybody stopped what they were doing and started looking at the show she was putting on.

"Bitch. Little. You wasn't saying that bullshit when you was calling out my motherfucking name."

"Nigga, I was calling you name so you could put the little motherfucker in but I guess you couldn't hear me because you started screaming, 'I'm Cumming', you 3 second little dick motherfucker."

"Look here little miss thing, you better take your little sick sucking nut drinking ass under that rock you came from before I have one of these crack head bitches beat a spark plug out your little hot ass." Then I tried to take a sip of my soda.

SMACK.

"Under a rock? Nigga, who the fuck you think I am nigga, I'll kick your ass and any rock smoking bitch out this motherfucker, I aint scared of you nigga, let's do this," she said after she smacked my grape soda on my $600 outfit.

Everybody start oohing and aahing like a bunch of little kids at a playground fight.

At the very moment I became enraged. "Bitch!" I shouted as I jumped up and stood right in her face; everyone knew I was about to knock the living shit out of her ass. She jumped her little ass back at me, and as

I looked in her eyes I saw no fear, but I could tell she was hurt, and I was the cause of her hurting. I was lost in her eyes. My anger was no more, and all I wanted to do was take every drop of hurt out of her beautiful eyes.

"Look ma, we don't have to take it there, let me make it up to you," I offered. My boy, A.G. put his head down.

"Make it up nigga? I ain't heard from you in 3 weeks now you talking about making it up? What happened to the rock you wanted me to go under? Fuck you nigga! I don't need you or this bullshit." She turned to walk away. My heart started racing as I saw her turn her back to me. I reached out and grabbed her hand and did the unthinkable. I dropped to one knee like captain sucker for love.

"Look ma, let's start over, the hands of time work like this. I can't change the past, that's gone, lost in the world of yesterday but I can learn from my mistakes in the past and be a man to you and apologize for what I've done or didn't do yesterday. There was a lot going on but trust me none of it was more important than you so today and now on let me make things right with you, things between us." She looked down at me covered in soda and she knew for me in front of all of those people to be down on one knee I had to mean what I was saying.

"How you going to make this up Preme?" she said with no more anger in her voice.

"Let me take you to dinner tonight and a movie, how does that sound? Let's just take it nice and slow." I said still looking up at her as if she was my goddess.

"That sounds good, call me."

"I lost that last cell phone I had your number in, I need it again."

"Okay but you can stand up now, I forgive you." She said smiling knowing she had her victory.

"Yeah, tender dick, stand up, be a man and stop begging, playboy playing in the dirt." A.G. yelled and everybody started laughing, everybody but Sacoria. I stood up and walked her to her truck. Fugee hit me up for some money and Tangy told me I did the right thing. Before they pulled off, Cinnamon gave me a deep kiss. Everybody said "awe". A.G., Pooh, Rocky, Big Shawn, and Goldy, the rest of them niggas held it on my ass.

"Nigga, give me your player card so I can burn it, I never thought I'd ever see my nigga turn into a suck a duck for love ass nigga."

"A.G. I aint no suck a duck, you know me better than that shit."

"I can't tell, you let her punk slap fire out you in front of everybody, you know you should have slapped the shit out of her for disrespect, you going to have problems later with her hand watch."

"I know but man I couldn't, I'm really feeling her."

"Man, that girl must have some super pussy, for Mr. Supreme Divine to talking about feelings after one night."

"Fuck this shit, it's not going to be on me, I'm going home to shower and change and get right."

"Yeah, you better change, right back into a man, my nigga."

"I hear that shit. I'm out."

"See that's a strong sister, she reminds me of the black women we had back in the day. Thy stood for something, they didn't take no shit, unlike these Lil Kim wannabe's today. If you step on the women of my day toes they'll cut your ass from sugar to shit. But they was real women that always stood by their man side, never let him fall short. I can't see nothing wrong with her yet. The only problem I see is you."

Black said to Preme, looking at him.

"Black, you don't see nothing wrong because I didn't get to that part yet. I'm just letting you know how and why I feel the way I do for her." Preme spoke letting Black know it was a lot more to the story if he just sit back and listen.

"Okay, did you take her out that night?"

"Yeah, let me tell you what happened, if you keep cutting me off, you will never know, I'll have to write you a letter to end the story."

"My bad, go ahead."

"Well, I called her, we talked. She told me where she lived and her mother didn't like drug dealers. I didn't care because I wasn't a drug dealer, I was a hustler, I had vending machines all over town, plus I owned a rooming house where I also had workers pumping for me. I dressed in a nice Gucci button up, Gucci shades, LRG jeans and belt and Gucci shoes. Around my neck was a platinum chain with yellow diamonds and matching cross with matching bracelet, watch plus iced out platinum pink ring all the ice was cool lemonade. The yellow diamonds went with the light yellow that was in the shirt. I splashed on some Burberry smell good and was out the door on my way to make it happen...

"I can feel it in the air, I can hear it in your voice," Beanie Sigel's I Can Feel it came from my speakers and T.V.'s as I pulled in her town house complex, this was top shelf, all the way, nothing was parked outside but BMW's Lexus' and Range's. It was about 7:30p.m, late summer, young people were still outside, black, some of the white. They all stopped to look at me like they never seen a car sitting on chrome before. I saw a bad ass chocolate chick work that ass off beat to the music. I guess she just wanted me to see that her ass was phat. I pimped by and made my way to the town house marked 247 Hidden Park Drive. I pulled in the driveway behind a Mercedes 600 next to it was a '05 Cadillac STS, red, the Mercedes was white. I parked next to the '04 Yukon. I popped my door up so I could get out my car, with the flowers I got from Plainfield Flowers on Park Ave. I called her to let her know I was outside, she told me to come ring the doorbell. I made it to the door, rang the doorbell and a boys voice answered.

"Who is it?"

"Supreme." I answered. Then the door opened, standing before me was a boy who looked no older

117

than 14 or 15 years old. Big T-shirt, baggy jeans, you know the fake hip hop look that want to be down.

"What's up man? You must be Preme, come on in, my sister will be down in a minute, you know how girls are."

"Yeah, I know what you mean, Little Daddy."

"Y'all going to the movies?" he asked.

"Yeah, that's the plan Little Daddy, since you questioning me, what's your name little man." I asked him, wanting to know who was giving me the 3rd degree.

"My bad, my name is Charles but everybody call me Chuck."

"Nice to meet you Chuck" I said giving him dap with my free hand.

"What are you and her going to see?"

"Monsters Ball, or something like that."

"Yeah man, I wanted to see that, I heard Halle Berry getting her freak on, can I come?"

I didn't know little dude but I got to say he was cool, he had a good vibe about him. "I don't care if it's okay with your sister and mother, it's fine with me."

His face lit up like the Kool-Aid man as he thanked me and ran up the steps. I looked around the place it was nice, a fireplace and everything. A little girl popped out of nowhere, she was pretty with her 2 long pig tails in her hair.

"What's your name Little Momma?"

"Brandy." She said. "What's your name?" She asked in a baby voice that was good for her age.

"Supreme, how old are you Little Momma?

She put up 4 fingers and said "I am 5 years old see."

"You are? Then let me show you how to make 5." I said then went in my pocket, pulled out some money, counted out 5 one-dollar bills. Then told her for each dollar put one finger up. She did. "See, that's 5 years and that's your money."

"My money? Why?"

"Because you're 5 years old and you're very pretty."

"Prettier than my sister?" She asked looking up at me with the same eyes as her sister, only hers were light brown.

"Yes, but don't tell nobody." I said, she smiled.

"Do you like Mike-a-Mike candy?" she asked.

"Yeah, they okay, why?"

"Because I like them a lot and I want you to get me

some but don't tell my sister or my mommy okay." She spoke this time on a whisper.

"Okay, I got you." I said in the same tone.

"Thank you, I'ma go get my sister for you right now." Brandy said then ran up the steps. Two down, a mother to go, this is easy. I was thinking to myself, then her mother was coming down the steps in a red silk robe, it was short, I could've swore on a hundred bibles I seen her pussy when she was coming down the steps. Her robe opened a little, it could have been black panties but I felt all the blood in my body rush to my dick. Her mother was sexy, too sexy, and beautiful, she looked like Halle Berry better half with a phatter ass plus she had green eyes.

"How are you? Supreme, is it?" she asked in a let's get to the business tone.

"Yes it's Supreme Divine and these are for you, I handed her the orchids.

"Thank you, you shouldn't have. Excuse me while I put these beautiful flowers in water." She said as she walked to the kitchen, her ass made that robe disappear, and the fact that she had no bra on made that silk even more sexier. I had to fix myself quickly because mom had it going on. When she came back in the room I had already been sitting down. She sat across from me, as we were facing each other, she crossed her legs and I took a deep breath. I know she knew she had an effect on me and how hard her nipples were let me know she getting her rocks off.

"So, Mr. Divine, what are your plans with my children tonight?"

"Well, Ms. Bryant, I plan on taking them to the movies and then a bite to eat."

"I see, tell me a little about yourself, what do you do for a living?"

"I own a rooming house that has 6 bedrooms, plus I have 11 vending machines all over the city Plainfield. I'm working on trying to open a Laundromat called Supreme Wash once I get the building." I said with my head up because I knew I had it going on.

"Your family must be well off, giving you all those businesses."

"No ma'am, I grew up dirt poor, I didn't have a pot to piss in, to be real with you, I don't even have the piss, my mom died when I was young, never knew my father, all I ever had and got is my grandmother. Nobody ever gave me anything, not even a cold." I said telling her my ghetto story.

"Then you must have good credit to start all those things yourself." She said looking to see if I was going to hide anything. I'm from the hood. I know when a motherfucker is fishing for info, trying to run game. That's how I stay ahead of them pigs, who the fuck she thought she was playing with?

"Let's not beat around the bush, I know what you are getting at Ms. Bryant, I'm a man and I'm not ashamed of nothing I do or did. I made my way through school, I sold drugs the whole time, I saved my money and now it's paying off. My money is hustling for me." I said to put her in her place so we could stop this cat and mouse game.

"Well, I must say, I am impressed with your honesty. I know you had or were selling drugs by the way you are dressed. But that's neither here or there, would you please stand by the fireplace so I could take your picture." She said as she picked a little digital camera off the coffee table.

I was thinking, I must have that pussy on fire, she needed a picture of me to play with that wild fire while I'm gone. I stood by the fireplace, the flash went off as she quickly took the picture.

"This picture is for the police if you don't bring my

baby back safe and sound, do you understand where I'm coming from, Mr. Divine?" She said looking me in the eye.

"Yes ma'am." I said. She quickly killed the fantasy I was having of her getting rocks off thinking about me.

"Cinnamon, and Charles, don't keep Mr. Divine waiting," she yelled up the steps. "Good night Mr. Divine and don't forget what I said." She shook my hand and went up the stairs. I still was looking at that ass and if she had any panties on they had to be thongs the way her ass was shaking going up the steps. Charles came down first then Cinnamon. She was dressed in a fly Dolce and Cabana tennis outfit, her skirt was short and sexy, and it showed off her honey brown legs. She was breath taking, like a good blunt of purp, the thoughts of her mother were long gone once I saw her.

"Sorry I took so long." She said looking me up and down.

"Don't worry, trust me, it was worth the wait, like anything worth really having is." I said in a smooth tone. She smiled. Her little sister came downstairs.

"Bye-bye Supreme, don't forget me." Brandy spoke with a smile. I winked to let her know that it was good, her candy was in the bag. We, Charles and Cinnamon, made our way out the door and to my car.

"Wow, that's your car? You got a Bentley? What does S.D. stand for?" he asked with wide eyes.

"My name, Supreme Divine." I answered as I unlocked the door by hitting the alarm.

"Wow, you got a Bentley, with your name on it." He said.

"If you want to call it that, it's the closes thing to one in the hood." I said as I popped up the door for Cinnamon. Her brother lifted his door up in amazement as he got in the back seat. I took my place as captain of the ship. I started the car, the T.V.'s came on and Beanie Sigel was back on again. I turned the music down.

"Yo, Chuck, you can play the playstation if you want to, the games are in the armrest it's over a hundred back there. I'm sure there is something you would like." I said, looking at him in the rearview mirror.

"Thanks man, I never played in a car before." He said with excitement in his voice.

"It's the same as in the house but only you're going somewhere."

We made it to the movies in no time, me and Cinnamon talked like we was long time lovers all the way there. The vibe was good, her brother just played the game, that's all I really wanted him to do anyway.
I found a parking spot, her brother was so into the game, he didn't want to go in.

"Don't move my car." I spoke as I reached under the seat and stuck my 45 in the belt of my pants. I saw the look on his face and I knew my point had been made.

"I won't, I just want to chill and play the game, I'll see that movie on D.V.D." He said. I went in my pocket and gave him a 50 dollar bill.

"That's if you get hungry or want to come in." I said as I handed him the money.

"Thanks man good lookin'."

"Chuck, don't move his car, this is not mommy car." Cinnamon told him.

"I'm not, shit, I know who car it is." He fired back at her.

Me and Cinnamon got out tickets, popcorn and drinks. I got me some Mike-n-Mikes to eat too. We sat in the back, we didn't pay the movie no mind.

"So, how's my baby doing?" I asked.

"I'm fine." She replied sipping her soda.

"I am not talking about you, silly, I'm talking about my other baby, in your belly."

"I got rid of the little bastard when you didn't call and"…

"What the fuck you do that shit for, I told you I was going to be there. You don't get a call so you killed my child like some chicken head bitch, I thought you were better than that shit." I said cutting, I was super pissed and loud, I didn't care who heard me.

"What are you mad for?" She said like nothing in the world was wrong.

"What I'm mad for? Bitch you killed my baby." I said with anger and hurt in my voice. I really felt like she killed my child but I really was saying to myself, if only I called her that baby would have made it.

"Are you for real? You really meant what you said at the lake?" She said in amazement.

"Every last word, if you wouldn't have killed it I would have taken care of that baby with all I have." I said with sincerity.

"I thought you changed your mind."

"Stop thinking so motherfuckin' much."

"Well, I was just bullshitting, I go for my first check up next week."

"Don't ever play with me like that again and you're wrong, we go for our first check up next week."

"Don't try to play big daddy now, I'm still mad at you for making me cry. I thought you played me just to get the pussy."

"Thanks for reminding me, I do got to make something up to you." I said putting my popcorn and candy in the empty seat next to me. I got on my knee in front of her, in between her legs then I put my hand up her shirt.

"What are you doing, its people in here?" She spoke as she put her hands on mine.

"Don't worry about them, this is about me and you so sit back and relax, let me make this up to you, the best way I know how." She slowly let my hand go and I kissed her legs and thighs as she opened them. I ripped her thong from her body and put them in my pocket, she really opened her legs and put them on my shoulders, she fell back in the seat, her skirt rested above her hips, as my mouth went to feast on her nectar, between her thighs. I started tasting her creamy essence as she released it in my mouth. It was like she started to cum instantly once my tongue entered her swollen lips of desire. I kissed and sucked on her wet opening. She grabbed my head with both of her hands and started rotating her hips in a circular motion, = her juice on my fingers.

"Ooooh Prrreeeme, ssheee looooking aaat meeee, oooh Preeme I'm cummmming." She screamed as she grinded her pussy on my tongue, as I worked now 4 of my fingers in her with the skill of a lesbian trying to turn a girl out. Sucking and licking her erect clit. "Prreeme it Cumming, Daddy, I can't take it, oooh ssssshittt!" She yelled as she shook uncontrollably pulling my face deeper within her thighs, I couldn't breathe, she came so hard I felt like she was pissing on my face. After her orgasm was done she released her might grip. I sucked up every drop before letting her legs down, we kissed soulfully. She licked and sucked some of her cum off my lips and face, then whispered in my ear that the lady, 2 seats beside her, was looking at us the whole time. I looked in the light of the darkness and had eye contact with her, my lips were glistening still like I just ate a big ass glazed doughnut. She turned her head when she realized I was watching her watch me. I kissed Cinnamon once more then returned to my seat. I knew my job was done.

"Preme, let's go, I don't want to be here anymore."

"Why?"

"Because it feels like everybody is looking at me."

"You're beautiful, they're supposed to look at you."

"You know what I mean, they looking at me because of what you did."

"So what, if I want to eat your pussy that's sweeter than candy in the movie, to make you happy, so the fuck what, as long as you was able to cum that's all that matter to me. Fuck them." I spoke loud putting her on the spot because I was enjoying her embarrassment.

"Please Preme, let's go so we can finish what you started."

"That's all you had to say the first time, we out."

We left everything and went out the movie. On our way to the car, I stopped and turned around to get the candy for Brandy. When she saw me with the 5 big boxes of candy she knew off back who I got them for.

"Brandy told you to get them didn't she?"

"Now what, you trying to make me into a snitch." I said. Cinnamon couldn't help but to laugh as we walked to my car. When we got there her brother was in the driver seat getting head. All we could see from the back window was the girl bobbing her head up and down the way he had the seat back. Cinnamon was pissed and wanted to open the door but I stopped her.

"Leave him alone, you wouldn't want nobody stopping you from busting your nut in the movies."

"But that's different, I'm grown."

"So you meant to tell me when you was his age you was a virgin and was not trying to have sex?"

"Why are you taking his side? What, it's a guy thing right?"

"Don't come at me with that cheap ass 2 cent psychology, you know what I just asked you."

"Now you trying to turn me into a snitch." She said and started laughing.

"I hear the shit, I see you like to play baseball."

"Why you say that?"

"Because you like pitching shit back at people."

"Preme, you so crazy?" She said. We had a little small talk until they were done. The butterfly doors popped up open and the little chick he had giving him the brain work came out. She was alright, she had a nice little shape with her. She was dressed in fake Baby Phat shit, I seen that type of bitch over a million times, I knew from the look in her eyes she was a gold digging hustler.

"Okay Chucky, give me a call baby. That's my number, now it's your number anytime you need me." She said as she hugged him and gave him a piece of paper.

"I'ma hit you up tomorrow but now I got to take my people home." He said, so I played along. If the little nigga wanted to play big shot caller I wasn't going to put salt in his game. Supreme Divine is not a player hater, in fact, I helped him out and played along.

"Thanks man for letting me rock your chain, watch and bracelet and here is your money." I took off my jewels and gave it all to him, even my bread. The little gold digger bitch eyes lit up when she saw the money hit his hand.

He looked at me shocked at me, thinking I would be mad. "Yeah, it cool, y'all ready to go, I'll take y'all to get something to eat." In a tone that was cool as ice.

"Yeah, Big Chuck, can I drive this time, your car is so fly." I asked like I was the biggest clown in the circus or the sucker of the year. That made Cinnamon pissed that the little bitch looked at her as if she had the shitty end of the stick and needed to step her game up but she kept it cool and let her little brother get his shine on.

"Yeah, you can drive but don't go too fast in a ride like mine you got to take your time." He said as he threw me the keys.

"I understand Big Chuck, I won't." I said with fake ass excitement.

I closed the door down for Cinnamon as she was in the back to the driver side. We sat in the car as he talked to the little ghetto hustler, then she kissed his cheek and was on her way. Chuck got in the car thanking me for not blowing his spot up.

"Man, this was the best night of my life." He said voice full of pure joy.

"Where you know that girl from Chuck? Cinnamon cut into him like a knife into butter.

"I just met her, I was sitting in the driver seat listening to that song Put it in Your Mouth. She tapped on the window and said "that's what you want me to do?" I said "what?" she was like "put it in my mouth" I said hell yeah and unlocked the doors she lifted up the door and jumped in, from then on there were no words she went to work. I don't know why but I was glad she did." He said confused to why she really did it.

"I know why little homie." I said backing out the parking spot and making my way out the parking lot only to see the same girl getting in the passenger side of a BMW M5.

"Why?" he asked exquisitely.

"Because she thought you was a baller and she want to ball too." I told him.

"She was a whore?" he asked.

"Naw, little homie, she is a hustler, she use what she got to get what she really want." I answered him.

"If she fuck and suck for money she is nothing but a whore, right Cinnamon?" He asked her like he had me in a corner.

"He got you there Preme, sound like a whore to me." She said

"Okay then, how much you paid her for that blow job?" I asked him.

"Nothing, I aint no trick!" He yelled.

"How much did she ask you for?" I asked him again.

"Nothing, the only thing she asked for was my number then she said it would be better if I took hers." He said still not knowing where I was going with my line of questioning.

"Now, you see what I'm talking about? A whore would get paid, not your number and name. One shot, one kill. But a true hustler see the big picture, like them people at the food court in the mall that give free samples, she shower you a little of what she was working with just enough to make you want to chase her to see what's next because after the first nut she know you'll pay for the second one later. Trust me, with that little gap she had, little momma would take you for everything you got. She's what you call a baller's weakness," I said with wisdom, trying to school the little brother on game in the cold streets.

"What can she do to hustle me?" he said, thinking he was now on point.

"She's a stone cold freak! You can fuck her any-where, anytime, and any way you want to. You could fuck her in the ass or even in front of her momma, and she'd turn around and ask her mama to suck her juices off your dick if you told her to. She the type of bitch that baby mommas want to kill, as she brings their baby daddy to his knees," I said hoping he got a clear understanding.

"So that's your weakness huh, Mr. Baller?" Cinnamon asked looking at me like I was so suck for good pussy.

"Hell no, I said that's a ballers weakness, I aint no fucking duck ass baller. I'm the motherfuckin' man that made the ball. Feel me? I said putting her back in check.

"That's some real shit you dropped on her little brother, not many people know the difference between a whore and a hustler" Black said dapping Preme.

"Black, the streets raised me, I learned the game from pimps, players, and hustlers, both male and female. They showed me the hard lesson the street teach a long time ago. But, you want to talk about my education or what happened that night?" Preme asked.

"Shit, you know I want to know what happened."

"Well then let me finish the story."

"Go ahead, I was just digging the way you was schooling little bro."

"Alright, we stopped to get something to eat at

Chicken and Pizza"…

"I'm in to having sex, not making love." 50 Cents In Da Club made my speakers bump as I pulled in at the spot, in the parking lot of the Chicken and Pizza. I got out and lifted the door open for Cinnamon so she could get out of the car.

"Take a picture make the moment last forever, only cost you a little cheddar." Chad, the picture and everything hustler said to us with the camera in his hand. The parking lot was packed, this was the hot spot after the club, movie, or whatever to grab something to eat.

"Come on let's take a picture Preme." Cinnamon said in a baby voice.

"Yeah, Big Preme, make memory with the pretty lady." Chad said getting up the background on the wall of the building. All the girls from my block was up there with niggas from other hoods, they saw me and Cinnamon taking flicks and how I was all over her that she was my girl. I put my hand up her skirt on one of the pictures the she realized she wasn't wearing panties. Chad got a free look at her candy shop.

"Preme, stop, I don't have panties on!" She said pulling her skirt back down. Her brother was already in the place. Me and Cinnamon walked to the doors she was under my arm like my wife. Easy B was standing at the door rapping 2Pac. He is A.G. cousin, he used to have all the bricks, he was Isis' connect. He held the whole Jersey down before some bitch slipped something in his drink and fucked him up. He went from being one of the most powerful richest nigga in the hood, to standing by waiting on a check from SSI.

"What's good with you Easy B?" I said giving him dap.

"Everything's, everything but I got to do this track real quick?" he said again as he gave me dap. He started looking at Cinnamon then started rapping Brenda Got a Baby by Tupac. We walked in I was thinking to myself how the fuck did he know. I didn't pay it too much mind. Cinnamon was locked under my arm, everybody giving her respect, the respect of a ghetto queen because she was under the arm of a ghetto king. We made our orders. Her brother was getting his mack on. He still had my chains on but I didn't care, I liked watching the little nigga do his thing. After we got our food we went back to the car, chilling ready to go. I walked to my side and stopped to talk to some nigga I knew about some money in his hood, when K Gee, Bash older brother and 3 other niggas was getting out a Black BMW 528I.

"Look at this motherfucker right here, where your homeboys at now nigga?" K-Gee said walking with his boys my way.

"They at your momma house fucking the dog shit out of her, if you hurry you and your little buddies can get next, bitch ass nigga!" I said in a what the fuck you going to do voice.

The chicks from my hood seen what was about to go down and left their niggas they were with and came outside and jumped in front of me. "Hell no niggas, this is stick and stab Clinton Ave, aint shit poppin' off over here." The girl yelled.

I saw Cinnamon and her brother about to get out the car so I pushed the locks on my keychain and gave her a look that let her know I was good.

"Oh, you want to hide behind these dick sucking chicken head bitches, they can get it too." K-Gee said standing his ground.

I went in my belt under my shirt and pulled out my 45, cocked it, ready for action. "What you say nigga? Tonight, you ready to die and bring your duck ass homeboys with you because I'm damn sure about to help ya bitch ass." I spoke as I pushed my way through the girls making it to K-Gee. We were face to face, well he was faced with his life in my hand, and His face froze like it was zero degrees outside. This bitch ass nigga didn't have his pistol and by the look in his homeboy's eyes, none of those clowns did either. I guess he felt a little safe when he started to open his mouth.

"Ffuc..!" POW! Before he could get the words out his mouth I chopped him upside the head with the gun. I hit him so hard the gun went off and I fucked around and shot the nigga that was behind him, in the arm. K-Gee was on the ground, the other 2 niggas was standing there with their hands in the air. I stood over K-Gee crying punk ass.

"You ready to die nigga? I said in a voice full of rage.

"Please, Please don't kill me, I got kids, Preme. I'm not a gangster, I'm a dad." K-Gee cried out looking up at me, seeing that his time was about to be over. He knew the only game I play was for keeps and he fucked up half stepping. I was about to pull the trigger and give that bitch nigga soul some much needed peace. I was in the murder zone, I forgot there was about a hundred witnesses that was out there, until Cinnamon hit the horn of my car and called my name.

"Preme, the cops coming," she screamed.

I kicked him in his face. "I'll see your ass, next time make sure you kiss those ugly kids." I said as I went running, like everybody else, to my car because nobody felt like being questioned all night by Plainfield P.D.I pulled out the parking lot like I didn't just shoot a nigga and was about to kill another one. As we rode I acted like nothing happened, to me it was the same old street story, when there is beef in the hood but to them it was something out of another world.

"I would have gotten out and helped you but my sister locked the door on me." Chuck said breaking the silence as we rode around.

"Naw, that was okay, I had them bitch niggas, they wasn't hitting on shit, I could've let them girls beat their asses." I said.

"Man, I can't lie I was scared when that gun went off, you didn't hear Cinnamon scream?" he asked.

"Aah, you was scared of the big loud gun baby girl?" I asked Cinnamon like a father take to his child that thinks it's a monster under the bed.

"No, it wasn't the gun that put the fear of God in

me, it was the fact that I thought you shot him in the head in front of everybody. That's why I screamed for you, the fear that you was going to prison forever." She said, trying to give me understanding.

"Nobody up there would have told on me if I would have killed them fag ass niggas."

"Preme, a snitch is in every hatin' ass nigga heart and if you didn't see the hate in them niggas eyes when we was getting our food, they was dapping you out of respect but in their hearts they was praying for your downfall. Did you see any of them niggas that was dapping you breaking their necks to help you when that shit jumped off? When them other niggas pulled up to jump you, them fag ass niggas didn't bust a move. Them same niggas that was dapping you, showing you that fake ass love was watching hoping that you get fucked up or killed. I watched them snitch ass niggas when the gun went off, they jumped dead on their cell phone. Now who do you think they was calling?" She spoke with nothing but real sincerity.

I had to admit she made a strong point. None of the clowns was out there, even when their own bitches was rolling with me.

"I felt that, that's why I didn't count on no nigga, I

don't trust them. I suspect them when it comes down to war, the only thing I trust is my gun and that's only if its full of bullets and in my hand, you feel me?"

"All I am saying is, Preme, I know you are a man and you got to do what you got to do but baby be careful." She said with so much heart, I had no choice but to let the words sink in.

"I got you baby, I'll work on taking it easy," was all I could say.

"Yo! Man, where is we going now, it's only 12 o'clock the night is still young, lets hit the club up." Chuck said with excitement.

"Yeah, the night and you is young and we taking you home and you better not tell what took place tonight or you will never come out with us again." Cinnamon said to her brother.

"Girl, are you crazy, I'll never tell, I aint no hating ass snitch nigga. I wouldn't say shit about tonight or any other night with my big brother Preme." Chuck said thinking about the next time I took him out with us.

When we pulled up to her mother house Chuck gave me back my jewels and him and Cinnamon got out the car.

"I'm just going to walk him in," she said.

"Grab an overnight bag," I told her.

"Why? I never said I was spending the night with you." Cinnamon said standing at my window.

"Who said anything about spending the night? You did that already, it's after 12 now, and I'm talking about spending the day." I said letting her know my game was always on point.

"Okay, smart ass." She said then kissed me and I gave Chuck dap. They went in the house and my cell phone started ringing.

"Yo! What's good?" I answered.

"Man, you must've lost your mind. Shoot people at the Chicken and Pizza. We came down there deeper than Wu-Tang, to burn that shit down because Roxy called me and said that you was getting jumped, so me and the goons packed up, six cars, trucks and shut shop on the block down. But, when we pulled up all we seen was police talking about somebody got shot. You know with all them pigs out there we had to keep it moving, so I called Roxy and she gave me the rundown of your cowboy shit." A.G. said in a joking tone.

"My nigga, them niggas had my back against the

wall, I had no choice, it was just me and my 45. You know aint no way in hell I was going to let them niggas do me like they did my peoples. I really didn't mean to shoot that nigga, the damn gun went off." I said laughing.

"But you know now, the beef is at the next level, it's all gun play, from here on out."

"It's always been gun play in these streets, that's why are cars are bulletproof and we stay strapped. Shit, if you going to play the game, play hard." I said

"That's the only way to play, all the way. But where you at?" A.G. asked.

"Cinnamons."

"Then I'ma let you go, I just called to make sure your tender dick ass was still breathing. I don't think that nigga snitched on you like that punk Bash. Tangy said tell Cinnamon what's up with your soft ass nigga." A.G. said.

"Tell Tangy she got a ghetto soft ass." I shot back.

"Watch your mouth nigga," A.G. said laughing.

"I'm good, I'll hit you up later."

"One." A.G. said ending the call.

I saw the bag of candy I got for Brandy on the floor so I called Cinnamon.

"Come out her and get this candy for your sister."

"Alright, give me a minute."

"One." I hung up the phone, played some music, she came outside just to grab the candy and went back in the house.

"You're more than wonderful, more than amazing, irreplaceable love of my life." Brian McKnight song, Wonderful, kept me company as I waited for Cinnamon. I love R&B, when I'm stressed to the max all I listen to his old school R&B, it clears my head, and I guess I picked it up from my grandmother.

My cell phone wouldn't stop ringing, people calling me asking what happened. Cinnamon was getting in the car as I hung up with my homie Crazy Lenny. She had changed her clothes, she looked like she took a shower, and she had a nice little sundress on.

"I got panties on now nigga." She said lifting up her dress, showing me the black silk that was wrapped around her muffin between her legs. Before I pulled off I took her thong that I ripped from her body at the movies and put them on my rearview mirror.

"I got your panties on my car. Shit you was in the house so long, you could have made those you got on yourself."

"You going to leave them thongs up there like that?"

"Yeah."

"You crazy," she said, then kissed me on the cheek. "That's from Brandy, you know she waited up for her candy. Time you called she was just asking about it but she told me to tell you thank you and give you that kiss"…

I took her to the Loop Inn, we got the heart room, everything in the room is red and shaped like a heart, the hot tub, everything, even the king size bed. The room was nothing but mirrors even the ceiling. I forgot my weed in the car so I went back outside to get it. When I was coming back to my room I saw this pretty boy, older nigga from my block named Mook, he was the x-man and real heavy in the game. That nigga had a real Bentley GT and a house on the hill. He was older, he ran with Philly. I came up under him. I can't lie, I really looked up to this nigga, and he had every bitch in the city on his dick. The nigga kept an exotic chick, I really wanted to be like this dude when I was younger. The only thing I didn't like was the nigga was soft as wet dog shit. He couldn't or wouldn't fight to save his life but he would put that change on your head, so that's what made him dangerous.

"Mook! What's good with you?" I asked dapping him.

"Aint shit, just taking care of a little business." He asked as we was dapping each other. He looked a little nervous.

"I bet, who is she?" Where she from China?" I asked.

"Naw, I aint got no pussy this time, just my people." He said.

"You got any of them things with you?" I asked him talking about the x-pills.

"Yeah, why, what's good?"

"You know why, I got me a nice little thing in the room that I want to beat the you know what I'm saying off that pussy."

"I got you, hold up, and let me get them out the room." He said, then turned his back and opened the door and left the door cracked as he went in his room. So I took that as a sign to come on in. I walked in his room and I saw Patches sitting at the table with over 10,000 x-pills. Patches is a fag that hangs out with Fugee every now and then. He look like Mike Tyson with long ass hair and finger nails plus make up.

(Super fucked up.) Patches talk like a little bitch but he is a 5 time golden glove winner. He would beat that ass if you tried to play him fucked up. He had respect, I just didn't understand why he was in a heart shaped room with Mook alone.

"Mook, what the fuck is up with this? You and Patches? Hell naw homie, I know you not playing in shit." I said with rage in my voice.

"Don't knock it until you tried it Preme." Patches said putting pills in a bag.

"Don't play with me Patches if you want to keep your brains in your head." I fired back.

"Stop that shit Patches, that's how shit get started. Nigga, I don't play in shit, I am the shit, you got this all fucked up, Patches is my motherfuckin' cousin. The only reason he's in here is because he's family and I trust him. He also been working for me for the longest. I got this $500 room because I don't have to worry about the police or getting ribbed like at those cheap crack head hotels... you feel me?" Mook said.

"I understand but Patches, don't ever come at me with that fag shit again, you dig?" I said letting him know that I would kill his stupid ass for that gay shit.

"Boy, I was just playing with you, how is Fugee?"

Patches said talking like he was a female.

"Fugee is still Fugee and a boy is that slack nigga sticking dick in your ass, I aint no motherfuckin' boy!" As I spoke my cell phone rang, it was Cinnamon wondering what I was doing. I told her I was coming and hung up the phone. Hearing how horny she was made me forget the little beef that was starting with Patches.

"That was my little hot thing now, wanting me to come put that fire out. She was letting me know she can't wait, you know how it is," I said, now talking to Mook paying Patches no mind.

"Yeah, you know I know how it is when a fire get started. Here, take these don't worry about it, this one's on me, just don't tell nobody what you seen here. I don't want nobody knowing how I move and try to rob a nigga." Mook said as he handed me a bag full of pills, I know it was about a hundred or more in the bag.

"You good, I got you , I aint seen shit, good lookin', I'll see you later," I said and dapped him on my way out the door.

"Bye Preme." Patches fag ass said.

"Fuck you Patches." I said on my way out the

door, across the hall to my room, I popped 2 pills. I didn't understand why he gave me so many pills. He knew we were homeboys and I wasn't the type to run my mouth. Cinnamon didn't waste no time when I entered the room. Time I closed the door, she started kissing me like I just came home from prison. She had nothing on but her heart's desire and in no time my clothes were nothing but a memory.

She dropped to her knees and started sucking the life out of my dick. She was really putting in work. She was sucking my dick better than a crack whore trying to get a $20 rock. I put my hands on her head and started pumping her bobbing head that was going back and forth off of my throbbing dick. I was so excited, the X was starting to kick in. I started to make her gag as I pushed as much of my dick as she could take down her throat. She was letting me fuck her face until she knew I was hard as steel. She pulled my dick out of her mouth and turned away, then stood to her feet. I still was looking crazy, my dick head feeling like it wanted to pop off and she stopped.

"Now you know how you left me feeling in the movies?" She said while walking with her back to me going to the heart shaped bed, putting nothing but action in that ass, as her cheeks were bouncing with each step. I felt that X hit me full blast and I was now king ding a ling.

"You want to play games with my dick, okay." I said as I got on the bed with her. She laid on her back, I was standing on my knees on the bed, looked down on her and smiled. "You think this is a game, look at my dick." I said, with my dick hard as a brick over her as I was between her legs.

"Why would I think of doing that Big Daddy when this pussy need that dick?" She said as she started playing in that pussy and started moaning. I guess she was turned on by the way I was watching her. So I flipped her hot ass over on her stomach to give her what she was looking for.

"Wait, Daddy, I'ma make this pussy cum for you." She moaned so sweetly.

"I put my own work in baby girl." I spoke, voice full of that heat and desire as her beautiful plum round honey brown ass cheeks were spread and her pussy dripping like a leaky roof. I grabbed hold of her hip, got my dick in that dripping opening and began to commit a murder in the first degree, killing her from the back, doggy style. This wasn't like the first time, we fucked this time. I wanted to punish that pussy as I slammed in and out off from the back, making that ass shake like Jell-O.

"Preme, you fuck this pussy. Oooh shit." She screamed out.

Smack. "Work this pussy girl." I yelled smacking her ass cheeks. Smack. "Work this dick with that pussy girl, you want to play motherfuckin' games, make me nut." Smack. Smack. The slapping sound of her ass cheeks rang in the room.

"Oooh Preme, AAAAH ooo God." She moaned and screamed.

Smack. She started throwing her ass back on me in a fever working her pussy muscles on my dick that was covered in her wetness that I was smacking out over her. Smack. "Is it a game?" I asked with force, as I pounded in and out of her. Smack. Smack. I stuck 2 fingers in her asshole as she was working, with my body in perfect rhythm, not missing a beat.

"Oooh, Preme, I'm cummin' again Daddy, can you feel it, it's coming." She screamed, slamming back on my dick and the 2 fingers I had up her ass hard.

I pulled my fingers out of her wet clinging asshole and pound her deep as she released a powerful orgasm that had her ass shaking and jiggling like a water bed in an earthquake. Her cum was thick and leave running down my balls. I turned her over on her back to drink up her womanhood, her juice was dripping from her as my tongue was flicking thoroughly like a dog lapping up water across her clit, while pushing 2 fingers gently in her asshole. She screamed, "Preme," as she came again. As she was cumming I slid on her, pushed my dick between those thighs. She dug her nails in my back when she felt the strong force of my exploding climax unloading inside of her, making her cum now, with me grinding her pussy on my dick, releasing for the last time. We both were covered in sweat. I just laid on top of her, still inside her, trying to catch my breath.

"Preme, I think…I'm…never mind. Forget I even said anything." Cinnamon said under me. I pulled out of her so I could face her on my side.

"What? You're thinking what? You can tell me anything and more, my ears are always yours." I said feeling that X and relaxed because of that good nut.

"No, you not supposed to say what's on my mind after sex, especially if it's for the first time." She said.

"Say What?"

"I think I'm in love with you Preme, you been on my mind since we met and I know by me saying that after what we just did you going to think that now I'm just dick whipped."

"Yeah I know I beat that pussy, I knocked the love in that pussy." I said jokingly.

"See." She spoke like she wanted to cry.

"Naw, I'm just playing because the truth is I must be pussy whipped more than you because you just think, I know I'm in love with you. I felt that thing called love the first day I looked into your eyes. The fact that you got some good pussy is just icing on the cake."

"Preme, you don't have to lie to me, it sounds nice and everything but"…

"Shh" I kissed her. "Okay, there was this one girl that fucked like a porno star."

"Stop, you know what I mean." She said, hitting me playfully on my shoulder.

"Look baby, I love you and I shouldn't have to say nothing I don't mean, look in my eyes. I love you, you are my first love." As I spoke she started to tear when she heard the words leave my lips.

"I love you too." She said. I kissed her again then

worked my way down her neck, her breast, then stopped at her belly. I kissed all over her stomach.

"I love you too baby, Daddy is out here waiting on you, the world will be too, you're my son." I said to her belly.

"How you know it's a boy? It don't even have feet yet," she said, with a sweet sexy smile on her lips.

"I am a man, I know my child." I said warmly. We enjoyed each other bodies all night long, until day break, it was perfect to me.

The morning came, we went to IHOP on 22nd, had breakfast. That night, like I said before, it was so perfect, it couldn't get any better. That's when I felt something was going to happen. I dropped her off at her mother house and was on my way back home. I get pulled over, blunt in the ashtray, then they locked me up for a bench warrant for aggravated assault on Bash. I told Cinnamon to hold my pills because I had a gut feeling. My gut never lies but I still got a weed charge. I got a $100,000 bail for the assault and $500 bail for the weed. I called A.G. but I didn't get an answer so I called Cinnamon and told her to call him so he could come bail me out.

"I got you baby, don't drop the soap." Cinnamon

said jokingly.

"If I did, aint shit going to happen, you know that your man can hold it down for the home team." I said in a pissed tone, I hate gay jokes.

"I'm just playing. I love you."

"I love you too and tell my baby I love him too."

"We love you back, bye, let me do this." She said.

"One." I hung up the stank ass jail pay phone, went back to my cell laid down on my bunk, knowing A.G. would be there any minute to bail me out. It was 10 in the morning, the way Union county work I'll be out by midnight if they bail me out in the next hour. I met this nigga named Leakey, he was a stick up kid plus he had hustle with him. We build a little, I liked his go getter attitude, that's when I asked him did he want to get down with my team. He was only locked up for some bullshit tickets and stupid shit like that so as soon as I got out I was going to bail him out too. He had his own hood plus where he lived was nothing but money. All he really needed was a connect, that's where I was going to come in. I didn't worry about him robbing me, my respect was real in the hood and he knew I put that work in. I went to sleep after bullshitting with him.

"Divine, pack it up! Bag and baggage, you made bail." The C.O. yelled and the lock popped, I gave my cellmate dap.

"Call me now, I got you." I told him.

"I'ma hit you in the morning, it's late now." He said as we dapped.

I was out the door to my freedom. I stood at the big steel doors outside waiting for it to rise so I could see my right hand man and get ready to go to Knockers for a cold one and see some tits and ass bouncing at the bar like we always did but this time it was different. When the door came up, there she was, standing next to her white Yukon in Baby Phat sweats, looking like a ride or die with a red rag on her head.

"Where is A.G.?" I asked as I took her in my arms.

"I don't know, he is Tangy problem." She said, then gave me a kiss.

"Then how you bailed me out?" I asked.

"I told you, I got my own money and don't need A.G. to bail my man out. I told you I got your back.'

"I'ma give you your money back when we get to my crib."

"I don't need your money, I need you home with me and I'ma do whatever it takes to keep you there"…

"Count clear! Count Clear! Mess out! Mess out! The C.O. yelled and the cell doors lock popped, now all the inmates filled the hall.

"Man that Cinnamon was a real chick, she paid your bond, how much you think she kicked out?" Black asked sitting up off his bed.

"About 10 stacks and some change." Preme told him.

"Damn, if that's not love, I don't know what the fuck it is. You only been with her twice and she kicked out 10 of them things."

"Yeah, that's why I fell so hard for her it was all peaches and cream in the beginning. I told everybody she was having my baby and the hood really opened their arms to her. Me and her mother got cool and I met her step-father, he and his wife were in to real estate. They had their own agency. They owned four town houses in the complex where they live. I got one for me and Cinnamon when she was about 4 months. We stayed 2 houses from her mother and them. Everything was going good. I let Fugee have my main spot where I used to live. Cinnamons step-father, whose name was Robert Bryant, sold me my Laundromat. I was putting Supreme Wash into works. A.G. started a dog farm and opened 2 candy stores that he got for a good deal from Mr. Bryant. Things were looking good until my grandmother passed. I found out Cinnamon was 5 months, I'll never forget that day.

Tap. Tap.Tap.

"Come in and it better be good!" Black yelled.

"Yo Preme, here is your cell phone, good looking last night. What's good with you Black, man?" Skip said as he dapped Black up and gave Supreme his cell phone.

"So, what's up with your homeboy that got hit up? How did it play out?" Supreme asked within his most concerned tone.

"Excuse me, I'ma take a walk to the mess hall to check on some bread. Preme, We'll finish up later have a seat, Skip." Black spoke as he dapped Skip and Preme and left the cell, closing the door behind him.

"So, what's up? Did he make it or what?" Preme asked.

"Naw, he died this morning, I didn't have your charger and your phone went dead. But what do I owe you, for last night, for using it?"

"Nothing man, how you holding up?"

"I don't know I loved Rah-Rah like he was my brother. I wanted to be there for him but life is a dirty game. Me and him grew up together. I go home next year and I can't believe he won't be there. Do you have anything that I can send to his sister that she can read at the funeral for me? I'm not good with words but you might don't write stuff like that. All you do is love things right?" Skip spoke with pain in his voice.

"Wrong, man, my name is Supreme, that means I am Supreme at everything I do. I got just what you need. Hold up, let me go in my x-file." Preme said as he went into his locker and pulled out a black folder.

"These are things I sent to my fallin' homies over the years. I got one in here just for you, it's called Holding On." Preme said with joy, knowing he could help his friend out.

"Holding On, what does that mean?" Skip asked looking up at Preme with the papers in his hand.

"You'll see I am about to spit it for you, let me first put this phone on the charger." Preme spoke as he hooked his phone to be charged and hid it on the side of the steel toilet. "Now, you ready."

"Go 'head Preme, I'm all ears, do ya thing."

"Holding On...Look at these streets, mothers dying of grief, murderers took their sons like thieves, ashes to ashes dust to dust in the grave as you lay them to sleep, summer feeling the heat, bloody war and beef, screams of peace, aint none of this is land of the Shaton, 8 years old with a gun, pimpin' lady heroin, first to second street, every block got a nigga in their memory, pouring out the Remy and Hennessy, flash backs of ghetto tragedies bring on the strength in one, the youngest casualty bring the strongest man to his knees, Jesus please, only God himself can save us from our enemies, pain sting like bees, burned down family trees, at the hottest degree, the smoke makes an asthmatic wheeze. Love is all lies, crack open the skies. Look at the streets of heaven, all my niggas died, murdered from weapons, 357's, Mac 11's, no matter what it was, we still stressing, all this hell I'm catching, every day isn't promised, God truest confession. Niggas droppin' like flies, men aint supposed to cry, I can't stop the flow from my eyes, hard to strive, son where is your daddy? Standing in back of a Caddy, aint seen me once since he had me. The world is too cold, it shivers me, mothers too young having babies at deliveries, I look at my city and ask the Lord to have pity, for the niggas that no longer with me, that I don't forget, see, I tap the cap and let it pour, give thanks that you aint hurtin' no more, as the bloody Remy hit the floor, that's what the first sip is for, thought of us growing up in locked doors, them niggas that hit you up, my 44's will stop them breathing for sure, make even the score, pain and shame alone a new adventure but happiness consoles me in all of my grief. Holding on to your memory…. Peace…"

"Man Preme, that some powerful shit, I got tears in my eyes, that everything I wanted to say but you found the words to say it for me." Skip said wiping his eyes.

"Thanks, take it and copy it and bring it back, that's my only one. You don't owe me nothing but don't tell nobody." Preme said handing Skip the paper.

"Good looking, you got that homie but it's almost over for you aint it?"

"What?"

"You going to hit the bricks soon right?"

"Something like that, I did mine, now it's my time to shine.

"I'm right behind you next year Preme. Next time I see you it should be on T.V. or something and I'm not talking about America's Most Wanted."

"That's not going to happen, John Walsh won't be putting my mug shot on T.V. I got plans little homie and prison or an early grave is not one of them. Feel me?"

"Yeah, with both hands and my heart."

Tap. Tap. Tap.

"Come in." Preme yelled from his locker.

"Preme, can I have a word with you one on one?" Dray said walking in the small cell.

"Yeah, we good, Skip, that everything you need?" Preme asked turning to Skip.

"Everything's everything, I get at you later, good lookin' out again." Skip said standing up.

"You know what it is, anything homie, peace."

"Peace." Skip said dapping Preme and left never saying anything to Dray, who had just come in.

"What's good with you Dray?" Preme said putting down the rest of his paperwork.

"I need a little something, I don't need no credit, I got $50 in cash that I got off visit."

"That's cool but you know I only see 60 dollar bags of dope, if you don't need a 10 dollar credit then you must be bringing down my prices."

"No but Preme, I'm a little sick, I understand that's your price but you of all people can cut me a break. I spent plenty of money with you over the years. Cash, I never came up short and I always pay when I said I was going to pay, all I'm asking for is a break, 50 dollars is all my girl had on her and the bank was closed Sunday. You know my money is good. I can't stand to be sick in here." Dray said holding his stomach.

"Alright, I got you but I want 3 packs of smokes and I'm talkin' Newport's and I'm giving you this last bag I got, give me that money." Preme said. He didn't need the money but he loved laying down the law when it came down to business. If Dray wanted to get high he had to pay for what he wanted. Aint shit free.

Dray went in his state pants pocket and pulled out a folded 50 dollar bill and handed it to Preme. Preme took the money and gave him the bag of heroin.

"Now, go get the rest of my shit out that full ass locker of yours."

"I got you Preme, thank you, thank you, good lookin'!" Dray said as his face lit up time the bag hit his hands. Dray left. Preme put the money in his hiding place. He made a lot of money in prison over the years, he and A.G. Shit, the prison yard was the safest to hustle and the drugs was six times the value. He had four C.O.'s on the team, plus girls from his hood brought the work in. The whole prison yard was his personal drug kingdom. Every hustler on the yard got all their drugs from Preme. Life isn't so bad, he thought to himself as he put a block on the window of his cell door. Then, he dialed a number on his cell phone that was now charged.

"Who is this?" A.G. said in the phone as he rode down the street.

"Nigga, you know who this is or you wouldn't have answered the phone." Preme said laying back against the wall, sitting on his locker.

"You know that's right homie, what's good with you?"

"Everything moving slow motion, everybody money hit like it was supposed to?"

"Yeah, everybody but that nigga Kung Fu, this is the second week his money been funny but don't worry about it you got today and a wake up then you home. Don't be no fool and let that nigga, Kung Fu, fuck you up from coming home."

"Shit, aint no nigga going to fuck me up, when it comes down to me coming home but no nigga going to fuck me out of my paper either. I'm going to take care of his ass before it's all over."

"Just be careful. Oh yeah, you know Leakey died the other day. I tried to call you last night but your phone must have been off."

"How he die?"

"He killed himself."

"Over a bitch?"

"Something like that."

"Who pussy was that good and fucked his head up?"

"Isis."

"Isis? How the fuck he kill himself over Isis? She don't fuck with niggas, do she?"

"Bullshit, I got the D.V.D., hell, the whole hood got the D.V.D. Leakey owed Isis for some work and try to play her for it. In other words he tried to fuck her out her money, so she kidnapped that nigga tied him up and raped him. She took the nigga manhood in the worse way and not only that she put it all in D.V.D."

"How the fuck she do that?"

"Very, very, painfully with a long ass strap on. She got them fine ass bitches of hers passing the movies out in the hood. The D.V.D. is called Fuck Me and I'll Fuck You."

"Man, Isis is wild, she on some other shit. Leakey should have known better, I know Taz is going to flip. What's up with Tangy?"

"She alright, I just pulled up on the block, do you want to holler at anybody?"

"Naw, did you hear anything on the situation yet?"

"Not yet homie but it's been over three years but I got people looking."

"Yeah alright, that's good. Why you and Tangy aint never had children yet?"

"I don't know, she don't want none right now, until this street thing is over with, I guess."

"Or maybe you shooting blanks."

"Nigga, fuck you, I know my balls bounce."

"Yeah, but can they score?" Preme said laughing in the phone.

"Fuck you!" A.G. shot back jokingly.

"Ok, who out there on the block?" Preme asked.

"Joker, that all I see right now." A.G. spoke as he looked out his driver side window.

"Tell Joker to come holler at me and give up that joke of the day."

"Joker come here, somebody on the phone want to get at you!" A.G. yelled at Joker who came running over to the truck. A.G. handed him the phone out the window.

"Yo, what's up?" Joker said after putting the phone to his ear.

"Joker, what's the joke of the day my nigga?" Preme asked.

"Preme, what's up my nigga? What's good with you man?"

"You know me trying to turn a dollar into a billion but what I need is that joke of the day, I know you got a good one in the stash."

"I got a good ass one for you. See, it was this Sunday school teacher and she asked the children in her class what's the first thing that goes to heaven from us? One of the kids raised his hand and said I know! I know! It's your head because when you talk to God you look up to him. That's very good the teacher said but that's not right. Another child raised his hand. I know! I know! It's your hands, the boy said. Why? The teacher asked. Because when we pray in church, we hold up our hands. That's very good but that's still not right the teacher said. None of the children would raise their hands. But right when the teacher was about to give the answer, out of the blue, one little girl put her hand in the air. Do you know what got to heaven first from us? Yes. She said, it's your feet. Feet? Why? The teacher asked with a puzzled look on her face. Because last night I heard my mommy praying and I opened the door, she was with my daddy and her feet was in the air and she screamed Oh God, I'm Cumming!

"Ha, ha, oh shit!" Preme laughed hard in the phone. "Joker, you stupid, Oh God, I'm Cumming." Preme said still laughing.

A.G. was lost in laughter.

"Good lookin' Joker, I needed that, let me holler back at A.G." Preme said.

"No problem, take care of yourself Preme, one." Joker said before passing the phone back to A.G.

"One." Preme said.

"Yo, man, Joker shot the fuck out."

"Yeah, A.G. that nigga should be on Def Comedy Jam. Let me go, I'll hit you back up later." Preme said.

"Alright, one."

"One"…

CHAPTER 5

"Naw, everything's good here Preme, I aint some little nigga that used to follow you around and spend the night over you and Cinnamon house all the time. I'm doing big things now. I can't wait until you see how I got this little town on smash. Roselle aint shit, these niggas soft as hell but the money come like a hot in the ass porno star."

"I hear that shit Jay, when was the last time you heard from Fugee?"

"Yesterday. She doing her thing at the hair salon. SHIT!" Jay yelled.

"What happened?" Preme asked.

"Talkin' to your ass, motherfucker, Wheels is beating me in Madden. The nigga just scored on me with those sorry ass Steelers and I got a stack on this game." Jay said.

"What team you got?" Preme asked.

"You know I got the mighty, mighty, motherfuckin' Cowboys."

"That's right but they about to take count and I got to talk to my nigga Black about some shit. I'll hit you up tomorrow. Win that money from Wheels, tell him I said what's up."

"Alright, I'll see you in a day or two, hold your head. One."

"One." Preme said.

Jay hung up his cell phone. "Now, I'm going to bust bullshit Steeler shit up, with your cheating ass." Jay said putting his cell phone on the table.

"How am I cheating? I'm higher than a mother-fucker and you still can't do shit with those Cow-girls." Wheels said.

"I can't tell I am about to score on that ass now." Jay said.

Knock. Knock. Knock. "Come on, open the door, it's me, Tasha!" Knock. Knock. Knock. "Come on shit, I got y'all food!?

"Hey Tasha, that ass looking too right in them shorts and all I need is a handful."

"How the fuck could you see my ass dark as it is Blue?" Tasha said, turning to Blue.

"Because, I seen that ass in the daylight, plus you got that type of ass, that shine in the night. It's a real life full moon that keeps this dog howling." Blue said looking Tasha up and down.

"I'm coming, hold your hot ass up, I'm about to score on that Steeler shit!" The voice yelled from the other side of the door.

"Blue, you better keep it moving, you know how Jay is but come up to my job and we can do something on my lunch break." Tasha said turning her back to him making her ass cheeks jiggle, giving him a quick show.

"Damn, I'll see you when I see you for lunch and I eat all my food little ma." Blue said walking down the street, just in time because the front door of the house started to come alive, she heard all the locks opening then the door opened, revealing a tall slim Jay, with a rose gold and diamond chain, with a huge globe that said the world is mine in all types of different colored diamonds.

"What's up, my little sexy Wendy's girl, the one I can't get enough of." Jay said looking at the two big bags in her hand.

"What the fuck you think is up? You got me standing out here in this darkness, somebody could've came and raped me, while you was too busy playing some fucking Madden. They do got a thing called pause, you know." She said, handing him one bag full of the food.

"Fuck pause, when money is on the line and if you got raped you would really like it anyway. The only thing that I need to know before I let you in is do you got my spicy chicken sandwich in the bag?" Jay spoke as he took the bag from her, then turned his back when she shook her head that his food was correct. "Lock all the locks behind you." He said and walked off.

She closed the door but never locked one lock and followed him in the living room of the small house, holding a bag in her hand. Wheels was sitting in his wheelchair.

Two years earlier Jay and William was at a club and they got into it with some niggas, William knocked one of the loud mouth dudes out with his long time boxing skills and Jay was beating down another one. When the guy's homeboy saw how nice William and Jay were with their hands, he didn't want any parts of that ass whipping, instead he pulled out a 9 millimeter. Pop. Pop. Pop. Shots rang out, William tried to run but his back was full of hot lead. Jay got hit in the arm and in the leg. Everybody ran out the club, even the shooter, leaving them on the dance floor for dead. They lived but only half of William made it. The doctor told William he would never walk again, he would have to spend the rest of his life in a wheelchair. That's when he changed his name to Wheels. He and Jay been ride until they die friends ever since. They were partners in crime, they sold X pills and the best smoke in town. They had Mook as the connect on the pills and a guy in Texas on the weed. They sold all weight before and after they got shot. This was their trap house. Tasha, they met 3 weeks ago, Jay paid her to bring him and Wheels food when she got off work. Jay fucked every now and then to make her think she was his girl but he knew she also used to give Wheels head. She was a super freak with a big soft ass. She could go for a twin sister of Meagan Good and that didn't hurt nothing either.

"Hey Wheels, baby, you going to take me for a ride?" She said as she walked in seeing him in his usual spot in his chair with the 357 sitting on his lap. He was in front of the 74 inch flat screen HDTV about half sleep, nodding from all the weed he has been smoking all day. He snapped out the nod just to get a piece of Tasha's bouncy ass when she passed him.

"Damn!.. Tasha, you didn't put no honey mustard

on my shit, if it was a dick you would've put mustard, cheese, ketchup, whatever it needed to go in your motherfuckin' mouth." Jay yelled as he got up and walked to the kitchen with his food in his hand, the same thing he did every night. Tasha didn't reply. She reached in the big Wendy's bag she had and pulled out a Gluck 44 with a silencer. Once Jay was out the room she walked up behind Wheels, who was now passed out sleep, put the gun in the back of his head and pulled the trigger.

Pink.

Wheels face opened up exploding all over the T.V. screen, the bullet went in cracking it. As Jay came in the room, still bitching about his sandwich... Pink. Pink. Pink. He was met with 3 shots, ripping through the flesh and bone of his chest, throwing him to the floor. He was dead before his body even hit the ground. Just then the front door opened and Face came in with his twin Gluck's, drawn, silencers in place...

Face got his nickname because he was at a part with his baby momma when she seen him bumping and grinding all on another chick, he was all drunk, humping the girl ass like they was in a hotel room fucking. She confronted him. Mike turned around and smacked the taste out her mouth. If he wasn't drunk, he wouldn't dare try to raise a hand to Kim because she was all hood about her shit. She busted a bottle on a table and damn near wrote her name on his face. Everybody was calling him Scarface but he cut it short to Face. Even though he was a stone cold killer he didn't touch one hair on Kim's head for what she did. He loved her and knew he was wrong, anybody else would've cut him would have been dead before his blood hit the floor. That was the last time Face ever got drunk.

Face walked in the living room and seen Tasha. "I took care of everything baby, let's get this money." Tasha said, greeting him with a smile.

Face put his guns back in his belt and gave her a kiss, "Fill these bags so we can get the fuck out of here." He said handing her some bags and playfully smacking her on her ass when she turned her back to him.

"Ok Daddy, but don't start a car unless you ready to take a ride." She said, putting an extra sway in her hips as she walked away.

Face walked over to the wheelchair, where Wheels

was slumped over and ran his pockets and took his money and jewels and put them in his bag then walked over to the fireplace where Tasha told him they kept their money stashed. He reached up in the chimney and pulled out a brick of cash wrapped in plastic, then another and another, 4 bricks in all. He took the jewelry box from off the top of the fireplace filled with all types of rings, chains, and dumped them in his bag.

Tasha had a bag full of money, weed and X pills. She handed the bag to Face then turned to get the chain from Jay's neck. She looked back and saw Face was watching her bending over to get the chain from Jay's neck. The blood rushed from his face to his dick like air out of a flat tire, leaving him with a sexual Euphoric high. He always got excited when he seen big money and bigger asses, that was his weakness and the way she was bending that ass was spread, he swore he had her pussy screaming "Fuck me! Fuck me!" he couldn't help it but want to trash that ass real quick. She had an ass that was nothing but amazing. He grabbed himself with his free hand without knowing. Tasha turned with the chain in her hand, saw Face holding his dick in his pant, she could tell he was excited by the bump in the front of his jeans.

"The world is yours Daddy, do you want me to fix it for you?" She said as she walked up to him, giving him the chain. She turned to him, undid her shorts, pulled down, she wore no panties she felt they only block things she need in, when it was time to fuck. She bent over, put her hands on the coffee table moving her hips from side to side, making her ass shake for him. Face came up behind her putting his hands on the hot flesh of her hips. Smack. His right hand went across her ass cheek.

"Oooh that's it, smack that ass, I been a bad girl, I need you to punish me with that big dick.: She moaned as she spread her legs then arching her ass up so he could easily penetrate her.

Face put his hand in his pants, pulled out one of the twin Gluck's. Pink. Pink. Shot her twice in the back of the head.

"Damn, what a waste of a good piece of pussy but I told you, you hot in the ass bitch not to let nobody see you and what your good dick sucking ass do? Try to be cute all up in a broke ass nigga face, I told you a million times if it don't make money it don't make sense, that makes it a dead issue. But you want to be hard headed, chasing hard dick. Now look at you. You're dead. I just had to get you before the police did. Real is real, I'll see you in hell, keep it real hot for me you dumb bitch." Face said, kicking her dead body with his last words. He put his gun back in his pants, picked up his bags, threw some pills and weed on the floor and carefully made his way out the door.

CHAPTER 6

"Alright, you done made all your calls and the door is locked for the night, so aint no more story blocking motherfuckers. You can finish the story. You got less than 48 hours now and I want to know what happened before you leave." Black said laying back on his bunk, relaxed and ready to take the ride down Preme memory lane.

"I got you but you know that nigga Kong Fu aint pay my money yet, he think because I'm about to be out that he can put me out my paper but he sadly mistaking. I'ma get my shit one way or the other." Preme said with a little anger in his voice.

"Kong Fu is a stupid nigga, we going to have to kill him, that motherfucker name aint Kong Fu for nothing." Black said letting Preme know what time it was.

"We don't have to do shit, I got this. I told you when I leave everything is on you but right now this one is still on me. I got a little plan for his ass tomorrow. But for now, where was I?"

"You was talking about when your grandmother

died."

"Oh yeah, that's when she was 5 months but shit before that she was about 3 or 4 months, we was at her checkup, me, Cinnamon, and her mom…

"Damn, he got a big ass Buzz Light Year head, it is a he right?" I asked looking at the ultrasound monitor.

"Preme, if he look like Buzz Light Year in his head, is that big, that's because it's your family, that don't run in my bloodline." Mrs. Bryant said, pointing at my head.

"Mrs. Bryant, you look kind of like Buzz yourself, hell Cinnamon got a big ass beach ball head." I spoke as I kissed Cinnamon on her head.

"Ha ha but you love my head." Cinnamon said smiling.

"You know I do. I raise, so nurse, what we having? A boy, right?" I asked the nurse who was looking at the monitor.

"That's what it look like to me, a healthy baby boy." The nurse answered pointing at the monitor.

"I told you we was having a little Preme." I said with excitement in my voice.

"You're not going to name my grandson after a sandwich." Mrs. Bryant said in protest.

"I'm not naming your grandson after a sandwich, I'm naming my son after his father." I said letting her know who was boss.

"Well, Supreme is a sandwich with everything on it."

"That's where you're wrong, now, ask your daughter, she call out my name more than enough to know what it means. I'm sure she could tell you what I'm named after."

"What was that?"

"The best, Supreme mean the best and that means your first grandchild is nothing more than the best." I said to Mrs. Bryant with a smile to end the debate.

"Well, Mr. Best, all the talk you and my mother had about sandwiches has made us hungry, why don't you go grab us something to eat from the cafeteria." Cinnamon asked me holding her belly.

"What do you want?" I asked her.

"Anything that's food, I'm hungry, I can eat a cow."

"I got you baby. I'm hungry as hell too, would you like anything Mrs. Bryant?"

"No thanks, I thought we were supposed to be going out for lunch?" Mrs. Bryant asked.

"We are, this is just a snack before lunch." I said walking to the door.

"I'm okay, just bring me any kind of soda." Mrs. Bryant said.

I stopped at the door then asked the nurse if she wanted anything but she respectfully declined. I walked in the hall and down the steps. At the end of the steps I saw a door open, in the room was a nurse and a girl sitting in the room. The girl looked so sad as she looked at the screen showing the life that was growing inside of her. I tapped on the open door.

"Do you mind if I see your baby?" I asked the girl sticking my head in the door.

"No, if that's what you want to do," she said with her voice full of sadness, as I walked in the room.

"Don't feel bad, my baby got a big ass Buzz Light Year head too, like his mother, I think it's a black thing," I said to her jokingly, trying to lighten up her mood. The girl started to smile, I guess she just wanted somebody to enjoy in the happiness she was feeling. "Where is your big head baby daddy at because I know he got the big head because yours is on the alright size, why is he missing all this fun?" I asked.

"He had to work but I told him I'll bring him pictures of the ultrasound." She said with a little more joy in her voice.

"What are you having?" I asked looking at the monitor.

"A little girl!" She said with the same excitement I had when I learned I was having a son.

"I'm having a boy, maybe you can hook my son up, put him ahead of the game because if she going to look anything like her momma I know she going to have to beat them off with a stick." After I said that her face lit up, it was the truth, the girl was pretty.

"Thank you but you are crazy, your son aint even born yet and you're trying to hook him up." She said looking me in my eyes with a smile.

"Shit, they do it in Africa, before the baby even come out the nuts, it's already married and everything. Like I said a pretty lady like you, I know you is going to have a beautiful baby, no matter how ugly the father is." My last comment made even the nurse laugh. I stayed in the room talking to the girl so long that Cinnamon and her mother passed by and must have heard my voice because they came in the room.

"There you are, I sent you to get food and you done got a whole other family." Cinnamon said jokingly.

"My bad baby, I lost track of time chilling with my friend, I don't even know your name." I said to the girl.

"Octavia." The girl said.

"My friend Octavia, I just met her, she having a girl with a big ass head, so I wanted to hook my son up, ahead of time. You know what they say, two big ass heads are better than one." I said.

"Preme, you don't care what come out your mouth. Hi, my name is Cinnamon Bryant and this is my mother, I hope he wasn't too much trouble."

"Naw, you have a good man, you are a very lucky woman. I was feeling down because my baby daddy couldn't make it and Preme came out of nowhere cracking on my baby head but it was all good anyway. To tell you the truth, he really made my day." She said with a smile.

"Supreme is a good man and it's nice to see that somebody understands how good I am plus see what a real man is worth. Some women are blind to that golden fact." I said looking at Cinnamon.

"Well, Mr. Good man, where is my good food you were supposed to get but no you was too busy being good to somebody else that you forgot to feed me and your child." Cinnamon said putting me in check mate. I walked over to her and gave her a kiss then kissed her belly.

"I'll make it up to you and the baby later. You ready?" I said.

"Yeah, it's been nice meeting you Octavia. Good luck with the baby." Cinnamon and her mother said.

"Yeah, you going to need all the luck in the world pushing that one out." I said as I walked out the door.

We was outside at our cars when her mother got a call telling her she had to go take care of something at her office.

"Preme, feed my grandchild and my daughter and stop trying to save the world." Mrs. Bryant said, getting in her car.

"I got you ma, they are about to eat right now." I said closing the door for her in her Cadillac STS.

Me and Cinnamon got in my whip and her mother went one way and we went the other.

"So, what you want to eat Baby Momma?" I asked her.

I got a taste for Mickey D's fries and a hot meatball sub from Subway."

"Damn, that does sound good."

We stopped at McDonalds drive thru, ordered 5 extra-large fries and 2 strawberry milk shakes. I paid at one window but when I got to the next window to get my food I saw that punk ass nigga Jason. This nigga been owing me money for almost 2 years. I gave this nigga some work and he stepped off with the shit. I am not talking a little bit of shit either and me and A.G. had to go in the black bag with the ski mask and Gluck to get right. I swore if I ever seen that nigga again I was going to get his ass. I wanted to kill him but where I was at it was not going to happen without getting a life sentence. It wasn't just the money, the nigga jacked us for, it was the fact the nigga was like our brother. We did everything together, he would be right where me and A.G. is if he didn't do that shady shit. My eyes turned red, my blood started racing. I put the car in park. Cinnamon was saying something but I didn't hear shit but kill this snake motherfucker, the next thing I knew, I was pulling Jason fag ass out the drive thru window. "Oh Shit. Preme. Wait. Preme." Boop. Boop. Stup. Stup.

"Shut the fuck up motherfucker! Sorry motherfucker!" I said through clinched teeth. Before I knew it, the police had me on the ground, cuffing me and putting Jason in the ambulance. I still was cursing, I didn't notice Cinnamon standing there holding her stomach crying until the police car was pulling off. For a moment my revenge made me forget she was even with me. But as I rode pass her, we locked eyes, she moved her lips as the tears ran down her face. She asked,

"What's wrong with you?" That was all I could make out. I'm not going to lie, I felt like 100% pure, uncut shit. The last thing I wanted to do was make her cry. She jumped in my car and followed us to the police station. I got an assault charge and a gun charge. I had most of the bail money on me, it was $80,000 for the assault and for the gun it was $60,000. She put up the other $1700, that's all I needed…

CHAPTER 7

"**D**amn brother, you got to have some control, how the hell you going to do something like that? Man, the girl was pregnant and you beating people up at McDonalds. That's the type of stress that could've hurt the baby." Black said shaking his head in disbelief.

"I know but that's one thing I can't stand and that's a snake ass motherfucker. If I let a person close to me and them motherfuckers cross me, it's like I cross myself, so I have to make them pay. I am a man before anything. I stand for something and if anybody get in the way of what I stand for then I'll knock them off their square before they knock me off mine." Preme said to Black pulling on a Cigarette.

"I feel you on that but it's a time and place. Don't get me wrong I am just talking about the stress on the baby, fuck that nigga, you should have got his sour ass but I still don't understand what the midget got to do with this."

"Do you want me to tell you that or do you want the whole story? I am trying to get you to understand why I fell so hard and she is in my dreams but you have to see everything that I did so you can maybe tell me or better yet help me understand why she did what she did."

"Okay, so far you acted like a pure asshole, was there any time you didn't act like an ass?"

"Now don't think she didn't act up because she cut up too. She was pregnant and all but she had a hand problem, she cut on me more than once, I think my temper was rubbing off on her."

"Naw, you can't say that, the sister was strong when you met her, remember when she smacked the shit out of you, on your own block."

"Yeah, you right on that note. I should've checked her then like my homie A.G. told me but her temper was why I was feeling her. After she bailed me again things was cool. The summer was ending and her sister and brother was about to go back to school so her mother and stepfather wanted me to take the kids to six flags before their class start"…

***

"You having fun sexy?" I asked Cinnamon as we walked through the park.

"Not really, I can't get on no rides and my belly is

sticking out like I'm the fattest girl in the world. Let's go play some of the games and see if you can win something for the big girl." She said as she held my hand.

"Sexy momma, I'll win whatever you want. What do you think Mr. Bryant? You want to win these beautiful ladies something?" I said, looking at Mr. Bryant who was hand in hand with Cinnamon's mother.

"Let's do it for the ladies." Was his reply.

When we made it over to the games, I slid the girl running the game a hundred dollar bill to make sure I win the biggest prize they had. I wanted to make my lady smile. We were out there all day and I was having a ball. Me and her brother was riding everything the park had to offer. Shit, one time I got on a ride with her little sister that I know I was too big for, hell, it's not every day I could break free and just have a good time. I never grew up with a family like this, doing things like this together as a family. It was all new and I was enjoying the feeling. I've been to six flags over a hundred times with A.G. and my homeboys but this was the first time I had clean fun. I didn't have any weed, pills, or alcohol in my system. My mind was clear. I wasn't worried about if something was going to jump off after we left. Me and her brother was having the time of our life, he made me feel like a kid again, or the kid I never got to be. This was the first time I was somewhere without my gun and wasn't worried about it. In fact, my gun was back at the house in my glove compartment of my car. I didn't even drive my bulletproof car. I rode with her mother and Mr. Bryant, in their new Cadillac Escalade. I bought one for Cinnamon to do the family thing when the baby got there. Cinnamon's Yukon I had tricked out chrome rims, T.V.'s, the works. I even put butterfly doors on the damn thing, bulletproof, plus a new cocaine white paint job to match my car. We were living ghetto fabulous but I didn't think the hood life would be healthy for the baby. I wanted my child to feel safe, like I was feeling that day. I felt more safe then, than with my whole click of goons. I guess it was because of the fact, when you with your homie, we be looking for something to happen and 9 times out of 10 it's something bad. We pray that something bad happen so we can show how gangster we are. But, when you doing the family thing, everybody in the family is looking for one thing and that's a good time. Just to have fun and enjoy each other smiles. Her brother, always use to tell me how much I had it going on because of the money. If he knew how much the money cost he would understand it was I that really envied him.

"A winner! We have a winner!" The girl yelled as I shot all 4 ducks in a row.

"Yeeeees!" Cinnamon screamed, clapping her hands and hugging me. "You did it baby! You did it." She's still yelling with excitement.

"What's my name?" I asked.

"Preme."

"No, what's my name when I give it to you good?"

"Supreme! Daddy Supreme!" She said with more excitement.

"So, you know I'll always do it for you!" I said in a smooth, you know I get the job done tone.

"Sir, pick your prize, you can have any of the big ones you want." The girl said, that was running the game.

"I want you to get the lion, Preme, please, please!" Cinnamon said, sounding like a child begging her daddy for candy from the store. She looked like she was in a better mood that's all the really mattered to me anyway. She wanted the lion because she was a Leo.

"I'll take the big ass lion, please!" I said to the girl. She grabbed the very huge lion and handed it to me. I turned around and handed it over to Cinnamon. The damn thing was almost as tall as her. I think her mother got jealous being a Leo herself. She ordered her husband to win her one. She didn't ask, she really wanted him to win it. He didn't want to be outclassed by me but when he shot he only hit 3, always miss the 4th one. I knew he was getting pissed because his wife told him to put on his glasses so that he could see what's going on. He dropped almost $300 trying to win the big prize. He won the little prizes but she was not happy with that, she wanted the big one. She even asked the girl if she could trade the 20 little small lions for one big one. The girl told her it wouldn't be fair. I slid the girl another yard.

"Would you like me to win you one?" I asked Mrs. Bryant.

"I don't think you could do it again, the first time was lucky, the 4th duck moves too damn fast. I bet you a hundred dollars plus dinner, that you can't do it on more time." Mr. Bryant said with his hating ass but I took the bet, all I did was pay for his wife's lion. I picked up the gun, shot four times, hitting all four ducks in a row.

"A winner! We have a winner, the sexy lucky man with the dreads is a winner! Claim your prize!" The girl said, giving me a wink to let me know it was all good.

"Mr. Bryant handed me the money but he had a look in his eyes that said I'm going to get you back, you showed me up in front of my wife, and I owe you one.

"Thank you Preme, you might be good for something after all." Mrs. Bryant said smiling, like she just won 10 million dollars.

We chilled at the park for a little longer then made our way back to the truck. As we were coming out the parking lot me and Mr. Bryant and her brother Chuck eyes were locked on the girls or shall I say full grown women that had their asses dancing in front of us. You know Six Flags also have a water park and I guess the women that was walking in front of us was coming from the water side of the park because they were wearing two piece bathing suits. One of their ass was so big, round and bouncy with each step. Don't get me wrong both of the women had picture perfect bodies to die for. One of them was a redbone with long hair in a nice slim 2 piece red thong bikini. She had a nice apple bottom jean ass, with a lot of shake to it. Like they say, the blacker the berry, the sweeter the juice. The other woman was dark, black, milk chocolate. I don't know if she was covered in baby oil or what but she had dark black skin that shined and seemed to glow. Well to me it looked like she was glowing. She had on a two piece like her friend but hers wasn't a thong, it was a lime green bikini. The way that ass swallowed the bikini the bottom could have been called a G-string. Cinnamon was talking to me but all I heard from her was 'blah, blah, blah'. My mind and ears was lost in the reality of that beautiful perfect jiggling ass that was making the front of my jeans want to go boom. The way her hips moved was making her ass cheek pop like she was dancing in the Go-Go club. I started to tip her. Mr. Bryant got busted first but he saw his time to pay me back for earlier so being the smart old school that he is pushed the weight off on me.

"Preme, stop looking at that girl like that and take a picture, it'll damn sure last longer." He said but I was so lost in God's black work of art in motion, I didn't even hear him. Cinnamon had no idea the women was in front of us until Mr. Bryant said something, then she looked at me. She said something but I still didn't pay her no attention. I was lost in my own lustful daydream. I was so gone that I had a hard on and didn't know it. I pictured the chocolate goddess bent over a hood of any car in the parking lot with that ass spread and…SMACK.

"Oh, shit! What the fuck?" I yelled as my face was on fire. She smacked the daydream out of me, she hit me so hard that the women in front stopped and turned around to see Cinnamon all in my face yelling at me for being all up their ass. The stank ass bitches smiled like they meant for that to happen and turned back around then made it clap harder.

"How dare you disrespect me like that? I'm talking to you and you lusting after some big booty stank ass whores." She said, hand on one hip and the other pointing in my face. I was angry as hell I wanted to smack the shit out of her for putting her hands on me like that, like I was some fucking child. The only thing that saved her was the fact that she was pregnant and her mother seen the anger in my eyes and jumped in between us and Mr. Bryant kept telling me that she was pregnant, that was just her hormones. I ignored him and his dumb ass shit, my eyes were looking dead at Cinnamon.

"Cinnamon, don't put your hands on me no more, I'm not nobody's child, don't chastise me like one. Don't put your fucking hands on me no more." I said in a deadly tone, everybody knew what I was saying; even Mr. Bryant knew it wasn't a game. Cinnamon, a hard head make a soft ass, she didn't give a fuck what I said or how I said it.

"Don't play me no more like I'm some chicken head and I won't have to smack you back in to reality." She snapped back.

"Look, keep that hand shit up and you going to get what you're asking for." I warned.

"What Preme? You going to hit me? You going to beat me down like some nigga in the street and I got your baby inside of me? You're that big and bad?"

"Fuck it, I don't want to talk no more, I said what I had to say." I then turned my back to her and went to the truck with Brandy asking me was I okay. I could hear her mother getting on her about her hands. Mr. Bryant and Chuck was talking to me, telling me I did the right thing. We rode in silence. We stopped to get something to eat, everything was on Mr. Bryant because of the bet earlier. I was on my cell phone with A.G. I told him I was doing the family thing.

"You know Nora was out here asking about you." A.G. said.

"What you tell her?" I asked.

"I told her you was taking care of some shit."

"Right, right, where was her girlfriend, she was anywhere around?" I asked.

"Naw, I didn't see Dona, just Nora, she said she be back to see you and she told me to hold you down until she came back."

"What was she driving?"

"That red Nissan 350z. Damn what you need to know all that for? Shit, aint you about to be a daddy nigga?"

"Yeah, I am about to be Nora's daddy when I see her?"

"Now I know you bugging, that gay bitch aint giving you no pussy. She want the same thing you want. How long I been taking your money every time we betted on her?"

"Nigga, I bet you double that, I'll get that ass if Donna not around." I said to A.G. in the phone but I knew that bet was lost before I even betted.

"You know I'ma have the bag when you get here, don't forget to bring my 10 stacks."

"No, fuck that you better have my 10 stacks on deck." I said to him knowing he was smiling from ear to ear counting my money that I didn't even give him yet.

"I hear that sweet shit, even bullshit makes the grass grow. I'll see you when you get here. I'll be at the spot."

"One." I hung up my phone and walked back to the table where everybody was eating, they was about done and was getting their things. Cinnamon tried to talk to me but I was still pissed.

"Baby, you still mad at me?" Cinnamon asked trying to sound as sweet as cotton candy.

"Naw, I just got something on my mind, there is some real shit I got to get into. A lot of money in on the line." I said dryly.

"Anything I can help you with?"

"No, this is a man thing, it aint got a damn thing to do with you."

"If you not mad then why are you talking like that and not looking at me?"

I turned and looked at her. Her mother and them

had left and went to the truck, now it was just me and her.

"Look, let me tell you something, I love you and the baby very much but don't get it fucked up. Next time you smack me in my face, like I'm some punk ass nigga, I'ma bust your motherfuckin' ass, baby or no baby. If I don't hit you that mean you keep your motherfuckin' hands to yourself but if you open the door, I'll start busting that ass every time you piss me off, understand me!" I said looking her in the eyes, letting her know shit was real.

"You would hit me?" "I'll bust that ass, try me. I love you but I aint going to be your punching bag. I'll beat the brakes off you first."

"I'm sorry, I just got so mad…"

"Shhh, I don't want to hear that sorry shit, just don't do it again or you will be sorry." I said and kissed her. We walked out to the truck, hand in hand.

"I see the love birds are back together." Her mother said as we got in the truck.

"You know my baby love me." Cinnamon replied.

We all had a little small talk then next thing you know we were back at the house. I helped Cinnamon bring her things in the house. She told me she was going to call Fugee and Jay to come over to stay the night because she knew I was leaving. I told her I might be gone all night. I took her Yukon because I didn't feel like moving the cars around. I went to my little duck off apartment, changed and got fresh for Nora and my cell phone rang. Speak of the devil, it was her.

"What's good? Who is this?" I knew it was Nora because the name popped up on the caller I.D.

"It's me Nora, or you done forgot me now that you got a little wifey. I don't want to talk about that right now but can you come out and play?"

"I can do whatever I want to, I am a man, remember, nobody got me under lock and key. The only reason I would be with anybody is because my one true love is gay as a smiling faggot, my girl got a girlfriend."

"Nigga, please, all these bitches be talking about you, who you think you playing with? I have known you for almost 4 years now and the only reason you want me is because I am the only woman who didn't open her legs for you."

"Think what you want to think. What you want to do? Club or O.T. (out of town)?"

"Neither, I just want to smoke some weed and pop some X and chill with the only person I can trust. That I know aint going to try anything."

"How you know that? I am the bad guy."

"Preme, please, how many times we been in the bed naked and drunk?"

"A lot!"

"How many times have you hit this pussy?"'

"None."

"How many times we been on X together?"

"More than I can count."

"How many times have we had X sex?"

"Never."

"So what do that mean, Mr. Bad Guy?"

"You are a fucking tease." I said and she started laughing.

"I'm about to hit the block to holler at A.G., where you going to b at?"

"I'll be around there in a hour."

"Cool, I'll be in my truck."

"You drive a truck now?"

"Yeah."

"What happened to the Bentley?"

"I still got it and it's not a Bentley."

"Well it look a Bentley, then it's a Bentley to me. If it walk like a duck, it's a motherfuckin' duck."

"I hear you but I'm get at you later Ma, one."

"One Preme."

I hit Mook up, got a 12 pack of "X" grabbed up some purp and Nora's favorite drink, Malibu and pineapple juice. I got 3 bottles for her and grabbed me 3 big bottles of Remy V.S.O.P.

"Stop, drop, shut 'em down, open up shop, oh, no, that's how rough riders roll." DMX killed the airways, blasting from my system as I hit the trap house. A.G. was standing in front with a couple of niggas from the hood. Hanging out his back pocket was the bet bag and Poppadoc was right by his side. I got out the truck and dapped everybody as I came up to A.G.

"What's up tender dick? I see wifey let you come outside to play with the big boys." A.G. said as we dapped up.

"All I want to hear is that money of mine being counted in my hand." I said with my hand out.

"It's not your money yet, you still got to put the work in to get paid." A.G. said. We talked in code so nobody could put salt in the game.

"That job is already done, trust me. I might even

put in a little bit of overtime."

"Bullshit, we been down this road before."

"But this time A.G., it's a new street, same road but a new turn off."

"We'll see."

"Here is my money." I said giving A.G. the cash I got from the safe at my other apartment.

"Poppadoc, you know what time it is." I said. Then we bullshitted, I told A.G. if Cinnamon call tell her I'm in the middle of something and I'll call her back later. Just then Nora, short, fine ass pulled up. Nora is mixed with black and Brazilian, but she look like Jada Pinkett with an ass like Ice T's wife, Co-Co. She was one of the baddest bitches in the city but she only fucked with girls. She messed with niggas back in the day but the fools dogged her so much that she switched teams. She was the girl in the relationship; her butch ass girlfriend name was Donna. Donna used to be down with Isis but when Isis fucked one of Donna's girls they fell out. They still did business together but the friendship was over. Nora and I have been cool for a long time, I am talking before she was gay. We got drunk one night at my spot, she had a clown ass nigga at the time. We were about to get down and dirty but her loyalty to her man turned her hot body stone cold.

"I can't do this Preme. I'm sorry but I don't cheat on my men like that." She said buttoning up her shirt, I wanted to say bitch, why you come to my crib and let me play all in it if you wasn't going to let me fuck it. But instead, I let go and let her know it was cool.

"Look Ma, it's cool, we just got a little drunk, nothing happened. I know you're more than a one night stand." Truth is, I did respect her loyalty, if she wasn't gay and Cinnamon didn't come into the picture, she would have been my number one, maybe even my only one.

"What's good A.G., Pop, and everybody." Nora said as she was walking up to me.

"Everything, baby girl." A.G. said, winking at me.

"You ready? The truck right over there, or are you taking your car?" I asked her as we hugged and I winked at A.G. letting him know it was on and popping.

"I can leave my car, where should I park it A.G.?" Nora asked A.G. as she still was in my arms.

"Just give me the keys and I'll take care of it." A.G. said. She gave him the keys and I dapped him and were out.

"I can read your mind baby, I know what you're thinking, and it's alright." Avant played as we rode down the highway 287. We pulled into the Embassy Suites. I got us a nice room with a Jacuzzi. I filled the Jacuzzi up, put on India Arie CD as I stripped down to my boxers and lit a blunt. I popped 2 X pills, opened my bottle of Remy by the time she came out in just her sliver silk bra and panties. That ass is so phat. She asked you for a million dollars just to touch it and I bet you would get the money but I've seen her like this so many times before that I learn to enjoy the view without touching.

"Brown skin, you know I love your brown skin" India Arie sang her hypnotic melody. Nora popped 2 pills and fixed herself a drink, the way she like it.

"You want to jump in the water?" I asked her pointing at the bubbling Jacuzzi.

"Naw, I just want to talk." She said as she sat on the huge king size bed.

"Talk about what?" I asked then changed the CD to a mix of love songs, it was called Body and Soul, and I got it off B.E.T. The X had me feeling like Mr. Understanding.

"Cheating" she said, plainly.

"Cheating?" I asked looking at her like I know you aint talking about me.

"Yeah, I stop fuckin' with no good ass niggas because all they did was break my heart and cheat, and now this no good ass bitch cheating on me. I can't win for shit." She said, sounding hopeless.

"Your body's calling, your body's calling me." R. Kelly, Body Calling took over the sounds in the room as I got next to her.

"How you know she cheating? The way that girl acts about you, I can't see it."

"Well, you better open your eyes because I heard her with another bitch last night. She thought she hung up her cell after she told me that I love you bullshit but she didn't hang up. Her and the other bitch was going at it. When I started hearing moaning for an hour, that pretty much was the writing on the wall that she was fucking on me." She started to tear and sadness was in the words as they left her mouth.

"Fuck her. That's her lost. Look at me, don't be hurting yourself because she fucked up, that's her lost, not yours." I said. She looked in my eyes, she had beautiful green eyes that seemed to mirror my reflection as she looked at me.

"Preme, that's why I like hanging out with you, you always make me feel better, if you were a girl this pussy would be all yours. Now, tell me about your new girlfriend. I hear you about to be a daddy. I know you like that."

"You know I do, I'm having a little boy. I love her but to be real with you, I love you too. If you did fuck with men you would be the one having my baby not her." I said because the X was on full blast now and I couldn't help but tell her what I really felt.

"You always say that."

"Then you know I'm telling you the truth." I said then we kissed as Mint Condition set the mood for my cheating heart. "What kind of man would I be, if I lived unfaithfully and what kind of girl would you be if you did the same," the song What Kind of Man Would I Be. We kissed long and hard our drinks hit the floor, as we sipped each other. This was the first time we ever even locked lips. We kissed but in the cheek, never like this. We were crossing a road with no return. Our kissing continued. I was so comfortable with her in my arms, her tongue moved in my mouth aggressively. It was like she had the same longing for me as I had for her.

I stopped her and said, "Wait, this ain't right you might just b still hurt from your girl and that X telling you this is your chance for get back. I don't want you doing something to us that you might regret in the morning because there is no turning back in the morning." I love our friendship so much that even if we did have sex I wouldn't have told A.G. shit. I would have let him keep the money and let him think he won too. I could tell her body wanted me because she got me up by sucking on my bottom lip. I knew that pussy was calling my name. She looked me in my eyes.

"I want you, Preme, I'm ready to come on your team," she said as we was locked in each other arms. She moved back on the bed, I stood and watched her as she teased me. She opened her pussy lips and showed her creamy heaven. "You can look but don't touch because I don't give niggas none of this pussy," she said so sexy.

My dick was popping through the slit in my boxers. I climbed on top of her because the games were over. I ripped the thong from her body and slid deep in where her fingers had opened. I kissed her with the force of a beast popping her bra straps, peeling it from her as well. Her nipples filled my mouth and her ass filled my hands.

"Oh, that's it!" she moaned as I pounded in and out of her. Then next thing I knew she rolled on top of me, as we kissed.

I popped out of her tight wetness and she turned around putting that dripping, hot, sweet pussy in my face. She lowered it onto my watering mouth. She had her soft lips wrapped around my dick that was covered in her own cum. The way she sucked her juices off my dick I almost lost it, as I dove my tongue deeper into her hot sweetness. She moaned loudly, I knew she couldn't take much more of the tongue lashing I was giving her, as her body quivered yet she still sucked the life out of my dick, with her mouth. I grabbed her hips and put my tongue in her asshole.

"Oh shit Preme." She screamed out. I had to do something. I was about to cum just looking at her ass bouncing in my face. I let my tongue play in her ass as she climaxed then I let her off me because it was time to put that work in. I kissed her passionately, turned her around and eased into her from behind. "Yeah, that's it Preme, take this pussy." She cried out in the heat of her lust. She tried to run as I pushed deep, pulling her back hard and began pounding into her with all the force of mankind. I was going in and out of her. She was so wet that it seemed as if the sound coming from her pussy was going along with Keith Sweats Nobody that was now playing.

"Oh God Preme, I'm cumming again." As she called out I started pounding her harder. I wanted to bring her back and keep her on the home team. She grabbed the pillow as I pushed in and out of her hard and fast with deep strokes. "Preme, it's cuming, can you feel meee?" She screamed. I couldn't hold out any longer myself and I exploded like an atomic bomb in that pussy. Our bodies were dripping in sweat.

The room smelled of our raw sex. That was the start of our beautiful love affair. I never told anybody, not even A.G. I let him keep the money. She was more than a bet to me. Everything was great. I was having my cake and eating it too. Nora broke up with Donna. She didn't fuck with nobody but me. She played the number 2 position out of respect for the baby but if she knew that child wasn't mine then I knew it would have been a problem. I gave her a job at Supreme Wash because of her education. She was my manager. Cinnamon didn't care because Fugee and everybody told her that Nora was gay. But, Cinnamon fifth month is when all hell came raining down. I was at Supreme Wash, in my office, doing some paperwork. I was there all day when Nora came in my office. It was in the back of the business.

"You had lunch baby?" she asked.

"No, not yet," I said as I got up to put some money in the safe. She stood by my desk then slid her panties down from under her skirt. "I got all you need to eat right here Daddy." She said as we now were eye to eye. Without losing eye contact with me, she walked over to my big leather chair backwards and sat down. She opened her legs and placed one of them on my desk, showing me her exposed hairless pussy. "Come and get it while it's hot, I've been keeping it hot all day for you." She said as she began rubbing her clitoris that was sticking out like a little pinky. I don't know what the fuck I was thinking. I didn't lock the office door or nothing. I just walked over there like a fool and dropped to my knees and just went to having my lunch. She sat at my desk, in my chair, with her legs spread wide opened. She had both her hands on my head in my dreads, guiding me as I pleased her.

"That's it, eat up my sweetness." She moaned

as she slowly moved her mid-section in circles and grinded her pussy against my face. She was dripping wet and creamy like hot chocolate. She threw her head back in pure pleasure as her eyes rolled in the back of her head. "Taste my cum, it's good to you Daddy?" she moaned, just as she looked down at me she moved. I know now why. She = Cinnamon. Cinnamon had walked through the door with my lunch in her hand. I should've known something was up because she pushed my face deeper between her legs and grinded harder. She was eye to eye with Cinnamon, I think that's what gave her the powerful orgasm that rained in my mouth.

"Preme, what the fuck you doing?" Her voice cut through my heart like a switch blade.

"Oh, shit!" I screamed as I turned to face her with Nora's cum dripping off my lips. Nora closed her legs and just sat there and watched the show that was about to take place...

CHAPTER 8

"How the fuck could you? I am holding your damn child and this is what you do to me, to us?" Cinnamon voice was full of pain and rage but not at the chick that looked her in the eye and busted a nut in her man's mouth just out of spite, she wasn't mad at her one bit, all her anger was at me. I broke the two things nobody had but me, her heart and her trust.

"Look, let me explain what's happening." I said like a real dumb ass.

"How that fuck you going to explain Preme, I brought you some fucking lunch but I guess you're full now because I see you already ate out. Look you still got something on your face." SMACK. She smacked me in the face with food in her hand and everything then threw the drink in my face. "That's to help wash down your fish sandwich nigga, fuck!" She turned to walk out, I grabbed her.

"What the fuck I tell you about hitting me?" I said with light hearted anger.

SMACK. "Get the fuck off me, go to your bitch." She yelled after smacking me again trying to break my grip. I tried to turn it all around on her but she wasn't going for it. I was too wrong to hit her back.

"Just wait, let me"… SMACK.

"Let me go Preme!" She yelled as her hand rang across my face with so much force I saw stars and let her go. She stormed out without letting one tear drop, even though I seen them in her eyes. I guess she didn't want Nora to know how hurt she was.

"Nora, I got to go after her."

"You better let her cool off first because she might kill you right now, I know I would."

"Shit, I fucked up, I really fucked up." I was hurt because I hurt her and for the first time I felt I was going to lose her.

"She'll come around, don't worry, trust me. I'm a woman, I know." Nora said, half-heartedly.

"Nora, I'm not going to lie to you, I love you and you know that but I am also deep in love with her. She's having my baby." I said looking her in her eyes, letting her know my love for Cinnamon was real.

"Well, fuck it then. Go be with her, fuck you. I'm out!" She said then she stormed out the office. I called Cinnamon over a million times that day, she wasn't at home, she was at her mother's. They wouldn't let me talk to her, so I went to the one woman that loved me no matter what I do or did, right or wrong, she was still there, my Grandmother. Philly was out front doing what he always did, making a way for him to get high. Don't get me wrong, Philly wasn't a stank broke down crack head, he had his Lexus and he dressed fair, he was more like what you would call a smoker. He hit me up for some bread, I didn't even play with him, I gave him 3 times what he asked for thinking if I looked out for him things would look up for me. I went up to my Grammy Gam room and sat in the chair.

"Hey, Grammy." I said sadder than a kid who lost his best friend.

"What's wrong with you Preme, that baby alright?"

"Yeah but I might have messed up."

"What did you do?"

"I got busted cheating." I got choked up my Grandmother is the only one I still felt like a kid around. I'm not going to lie, I cried when I thought my Cinnamon was gone forever,

"Boy, stop crying, you did nothing that no other man don't do."

"But I made a big mistake and I know she is gone." The tears still coming down my face, as I talked.

"Boy, you didn't make no mistake. You wanted that other woman and she wanted you. That's not a mistake that is a hard lesson because now you see what it's like to live without Cinnamon and it hurt don't it?"

"Yes."

"Boy, you have to realize that a bird in the hand is better than ten in a bush."

"What does that mean Gram? Is she coming back?"

"If she really loves you she'll be back. I think she do. I never seen you act this was over anybody before. Those tears you a mess my grandson the ladies' man. I'll call her so clean your face up before Philly come in and see you. You know he won't let you live this down and it's going to cost you a pretty penny for him to let it go. But remember what I said about the bird in the hand."

"Always and thank you Grammy, you always there when I need you." I gave her a kiss as I went out the door feeling ten times better. The one thing about Grammy Gram, if she say it's going to be alright I

know things are going to work out. The only thing
was to do everything I could to make it up to Cinnamon. She didn't talk to me for a couple weeks, keep
in mind me and this girl only been together 5 months
and I bought her a four karat engagement ring and
matching bracelet. I knocked on the door of her mother's house leaving a huge life size stuffed lion, 13
hundred roses and a 5 foot I'm sorry card plus a boom
box that played Ruben Studder "This is my sorry for
2004". I left everything there before the door opened
and I went back home to my own house. My stress
was on full blast. I was in our king size bed listening
to Lenny Williams.

"Girl you know I, I, I love you, no matter what
you do, I love you baby with all my heart and soul."
The song I Love You played when she came in. I had
her night gown. I held it to my face just to smell her. I
spent over 2 thousand dollars in the last 2 weeks trying to get her to talk to me. I had the ring and bracelet
under her pillow. The princess cut diamond cost me
over thirty grand and the bracelet was sixteen grand
but it was 2 and a half karats in rose gold. She loved
the color of rose gold. My band that I got for myself
said Cinnamon Always and Forever, in her ring was

Supreme Always and Forever. The diamond tennis bracelet had both our names on it with Until the Death. I felt that this was the only way I could truly show her she was all I needed, by giving her the one thing I never gave any woman and that was my last name. "Sometimes, you get lonely, oh, oh, ooh, you get lonely." Lenny sang that song of love. I laid there in my boxers, sad as a clown that can't smile. Listening to Lenny sang my pain away. The smell of her essence in my hand was driving me deep in the pit of sadness. All I could do was think about the nights we made love in the bed and the times I spent talking to her stomach. I knew a blood test would scream like Maury 'You are not the father' but the love I had for her unborn child was more powerful than D.N.A. in a murder trial. I dialed her mother's number once again for the hundredth time that day. I haven't left the house since I was at my Grandmother's. My cell phone had over a million messages, I didn't want to talk to anybody but Cinnamon. I really ached for her. Thank God A.G. was my right hand man and never came with that left hand shit. He held things down while I was going through my personal drama.

"Hello, Mrs. Bryant, did she see the flowers today

and the card?"

"Yes, just like the day before and the day before that."

"What did she say?"

"Why don't you ask her yourself, she said she was going over there to talk to you."

"She did!" my face lit up like the fourth of July. I hung up the phone without saying bye and was about to get dressed when I saw her in the doorway. I walked over to her, looked her in her eyes and kissed her without words. She started to cry as our lips touched each other because the love was real. I held her close in my arms then I started kissing every teardrop that fell from her face.

"I'm sorry baby, I love you, my life is hell without you by my side, I don't know what happiness or heaven was until I had you. Since you've been gone, I can't think, I can't even move, I'm stuck. I'm stuck, I'm stuck because I'm in a world without you and my baby. I said as I dropped to my knees, to her stomach. "I miss you and my son. Daddy will never let no one or nothing come between us, again, in this world of sin." The sound of my voice made her belly move as we kissed, letting me know he missed me too.

"He may forgive but Preme that shit hurt me. I knew you might fuck somebody but I didn't think in a trillion years I would see you doing it. That bitch got her rocks off watching me. I was in shock when I walked in. She saw me, I was at a loss for words, as she looked me in my eyes, grabbed your head and started moving her hips and I knew she was Cumming in your mouth. That bitch aint shit. I should've killed the stank whore, you was sucking on." She said with anger and attitude.

"Look, fuck that that shit is over. I got something for you that she'll never get." I said as I walked over to the bed and went under the pillow. I pulled out two jewelry boxes, I left the box with the bracelet under the pillow. 'I love you, I need You,' Lenny Williams still echoing in the background. I dropped to one knee, looked up at her like she was the goddess of lost souls. I opened the boxes, the first one was my ring, then the other one was hers.

"This life is hard time alone, like being locked down in a cold cell on a bid. Before you my heart was full of pain that I never knew was there, sadness behind my every smile. Then, when I laid eyes on you, my heart ached no more. A man can only find happiness when his heart is at peace, so Cinnamon, I know I done started the trial and tribulations of our relationship but there in one more trial that I am going to plead guilty to and that's I love you. I want to always and forever this thing. I'm willing to testify before God, my love for you. So, I guess that will make me a snitch but I don't care as long as I get us life together." As I spoke, looking in her eyes, showing her my heart and soul, I felt one tear slide down my cheek.

"Preme, are you asking me to marry you?" She said as the tears started to rain down her face.

"I'm asking you to do life with me, to share forever with me, as wifey. Will you do life with me?"

"Yes, I bid with you baby. I love you. I'll always hold you down Preme, always." She said shaking as I stood putting the ring on her finger. We kissed and her clothes was on the floor in no time. "Tonight baby I'm giving you all I have to offer, you is going to know you got the best pussy at home. And when I'm done you will never want another woman again. I'm going to give you my heart and soul."

I have to admit, the way she was talking and acting she was a woman on a mission. She wanted to show me she was all I needed and nothing more. I laid back on the bed wearing nothing but her body as she was riding me in unison with the music. I sucked her passion filled nipples that were erect and I tasted her sweet milk of life as she was sliding up and down my dick, gyrating her beautiful thick hips in circles. Her breast popped in and out of my mouth as her body bounced up and down on top of my excitement for her. Her pussy was so wet and hot with each time her body came down and met my thrust up. I felt all of her anger, rage, tension and frustration that was build up from her seeing me with Nora. I think it was the fuel for the hot fire that was between her legs.

"Oh shit, girrrl." I moaned as she was working the pussy, making her walls grip and pull on my dick, better than a super slut. My mind was gone, lost in the desire between her thighs. I was loving the pleasure she was giving me. I gripped her phat soft ass cheeks that was slamming into my balls. I slid two fingers in her asshole and worked them in and out as she went up and down. She started to squeeze her ass cheeks together each time my fingers went deep. She was fucking my hand with her ass as she was working her pussy on my dick. She slowed down, looking me in my eyes and started kissing me then sucking on my bottom lip as she rode me.

"Who's dick is this?" She moaned as she bounced harder grinding and moving her hips from side to side when she came down. "Answer me, who's dick is this in my pussy?" She moaned louder, gripping my dick with her pussy muscles. I was gone in her hot heaven.

"Yours baby, this dick is yours." I moaned out pushing up faster.

"Fuck this pussy, it's yours, I'm your wife, I'm your wife." She screamed as I started giving her that thug love making. That pussy was all mines, forever. I started slamming up into her, pushing for that nut that was at its point. I pulled her down one last time, she started to really show off her skills as she felt the hot blast of my sperm shooting inside her. "Preme, I'm cumming too." She yelled out. We made love over and over that night, trying to make up for the two weeks apart. The love we shared was good to me and her until three weeks later.

I went to court for my charges but my lawyer had my court date pushed back. I was bringing Cinnamon from her check-up. I missed it because we had some shit going on, on the block, one of our spots got raided and me and A.G. had to bail about eight of our homeboys out of jail. That's one of our golden rules, no-body sit in jail if they work for us, if they get knocked then you best believe we were coming to get them out, no questions asked. So after that, I thought I would have had time to make her check-up, being that those things normally take a minute but the police gave the bondsman the run around. By the time I got back to the doctor appointment to be with Cinnamon she was waiting for me when I walked in. The one thing I can say about her is she understood my street life. She never got mad when I had to take care of things. I didn't have to give her a play by play of all my move-ments. The less she knew, the better and she truly understood that.

"I'm sorry baby, shit got a little crazy." I said walk-ing up to her taking her in my arms.

"It's okay, your son is doing great." She spoke as we kissed and embraced. We walked out the car hand in hand. I opened her door to let her in then went around to my seat.

"You hungry?" I asked.

"You know my fat ass is always hungry, Big Dad-dy." She said as I was backing out the parking space and made our way out the parking lot.

"I want some chicken and some French fries." She said.

"Sounds good to me. KFC or Popeye's?"

"Popeye's."

"So, what did the doctor say about my little man?"

"He said that he's doing fine and that he's real active and that I should take it easy because I got less than 12 weeks to go. That doctor is so crazy though but I guess doctor or not a man is a man."

"Why you say that?"

"Because you know how my check-up is done. They put me in a chair, legs wide open no panties or nothing."

"Yeah, and?"

"You know how the doctor have to put the gel on his hand so he could put his hand up inside to check the baby?"

"Yeah, so?" I said. I was getting pissed because I didn't know where this crazy doctor, man is a man shit was going. I was sorry I even asked the question. I was ready to turn on the radio, until she said

"He said that he hoped you know and understand that you were a very lucky man."

"How could he know my luck doing a check-up on

you?"

"He said most women the need a lot of lubrication before they can have a full check-up. He said most check-ups take a large amount of gel. Then he said but in all fifteen years of doing medicine he never seen a woman vagina get so warm and wet on his finger from light stimulation. He was like he really didn't have to use gel on me, his fingers could slide in and out easily and naturally without the use of any gel. He said that's something any man would be lucky to have."

For the first time in my life I felt something I never felt and that was jealousy that turned into pure anger and rage. I turned the car around at full speed in the middle of the street. I didn't care about no other cars on the road, they blew their horns but fuck them. I was pissed and in a mission to see my good friend the doctor.

"What the hell is wrong with you Preme? You try-ing to kill us?" She screamed, her voice edge with fear because of my driving.

"That fucking pervert doctor. I'm going to fix his ass, he's supposed to be checking on my son not finger popping you playing in your pussy!" I spoke through clichéd teeth. I was doing a hundred miles per hour going back to the doctor's office.

"Preme, calm down baby, he wasn't finger popping me, that's his job to put his hand down there." She said. Thinking that I really lost my mind.

"That's his job and he wasn't fingering you huh? Then was it like the other times when I was there and the lady did it?"

"No because the lady doctor just put gel on her hand and forced her finger up in me. This doctor took his time, he put the gel on my clit, rubbed it, and then eased his finger in and out until I was ready."

"That's what the fuck I'm talking about, the lady do her job. That other motherfucker was trying to do you."

"You might be right, I did feel a little funny how he was looking at me rubbing my clit before he put his fingers in."

"I know I'm right. Don't worry, I got something for his ass." I pulled to the doctor's office, got out my car and seen the good doctor coming out. I grabbed that white motherfucker up by his collar. "Motherfucker, today you the lucky man because the next time you try that pervert shit on my wife I'ma kill your cracker ass." Smack. "You hear me you freaky motherfucker?" Smack. Smack. I had him with one hand wrapped around his neck and the other hand smacking and back handing him across the face.

"Help me! Help me!" Smack. He cried out only to be smacked again in the mouth. Security came and pulled me off the small, white, freaky motherfucker. The good doctor started saying he didn't mean anything by it. Begging me not to kill him but before I let him go I got one more good lick in. You know the police came but I didn't go to jail this time. The good freaky doctor didn't want to press charges only because Cinnamon said if he did she would press sexual charges on him for fingering her and making sexual comments. That was enough to have his license taken and his reputation ruined. He told the police it was just a misunderstanding between old friends that worked itself out. I told Cinnamon from that point on there were to be no more male doctors between her legs. She had no problem with it. When I thought one problem was taken care of my cell phone rang.

"WHAT!" I yelled in the phone, still a little pissed about Mr. Wet Hands.

"Preme, Gram is in the hospital, you have to come quick, and it don't look good." Philly good." Philly yelled in the phone. His voice was cracking the whole time. His tone was bone chilling. I knew something was really wrong.

"What happened? What hospital? Is she going to be okay?" The questions just started shooting out. My anger was now replaced with fear, the fear of the unknown. I loved my Grandmother she was my mother and father. If I lost her it was like losing three parts of my family. My Grandmother, my Mother and Father, would all be lost if she passed.

"She's in I.C.U., I just got here. I don't know everything yet." As the words left Philly's lips I felt tears of pain building inside not a drop in my eyes but my heart was crying out.

"I'm on my way." I hung up the phone, Cinnamon knew by the look in my eyes that something was really wrong.

"What's going on Preme? Is everything okay, who was that?" She asked as we sped out the parking lot. I had my foot to the floor once again weaving in and out of traffic.

"That was Philly, my Grammy, she is in the hospital right now."

"Oh, my God, is she okay, what happened?"

"I don't know but them fucking doctor's better make whatever is wrong with her alright and I mean that shit."

"Baby, it will be alright, we'll do this together." She said with a voice full of sadness. We pulled in the hospital parking lot. I didn't even park the car, Cinnamon did. I just jumped out the car, the only thing on my mind was my Grammy. I rushed through the doors of pain marked I.C.U. Philly was standing there with tears in his eyes. I knew by the look in his eyes this was going to be the saddest day of our lives.

"What happened Philly? You were supposed to take care of her?" I said with anger and bitterness, blaming him.

"She had a stroke, the doctors said they doing all they can but it don't look good." Philly eyes had tears running with his pain as he spoke.

"A stroke? Where was she? I asked trying to hold back my own tears, trying to keep the old saying that men don't cry but every real man I know done shed a tear or two, even me.

"She was at the church. The whole church is out in the waiting room, only family can come back here. They was cooking food for the homeless or something like that, some shit like Gram like to do, just Gram being Gram." Philly said sitting with his head in his hands.

"Damn, they better make sure she make it!" I yelled. Cinnamon came in by now. She could see that me and Philly were riddled with stress and worry. I sat there thinking what I was going to do without my Grammy Gram, who was I going to talk to. I was praying to God but nobody knows but me and him, I needed him to make her better just until my first real child was born. I wanted my child to know the love of my Grammy Gram. But God didn't hear me that day because out of nowhere in the middle of my prayer the cold voice of death came.

"Mr. Divine?" The white man came in a white coat calling my name.

"Yes." Me and Philly answered and stood.

"Are you the sons of Angela Divine?" He asked, looking at his clipboard.

"Yes sir," we said almost simultaneously. We both stood anxious, while hoping and praying he would tell us everything was alright.

To our dismay, he looked at us with a solemn face and shook his head as he spoke, "Well, I'm sorry to tell you this, but your mother, Ms. Divine, has passed on," he said as in a voice as peaceful as a summer breeze.

"What did you say?" I asked as I was walking up on him.

"I'm sorry, your mother is no longer with us"… Bop. Bop. I swung a two piece and knocked the doctor on his ass. I blacked out and the next thing I knew I woke up in the same hospital strapped down to the bed. Cinnamon was crying by my side and Philly was in the window of the room eyes blood shot red. He turned to me just when my eyes opened.

"What happened?" I asked a little dizzy, what I didn't know at the time when I blacked out, they shot me up with some shit to calm my crazy ass down. I broke the doctor jaw but once again no charges. The doctor knew I wasn't in my right state of mind when I hit him anyway.

"You blacked out Preme." Cinnamon said with sadness in her voice that could have broken the hardest heart. I knew what had happened I just wanted to make sure it wasn't just a bad dream.

"Why I blacked out? What happened?"

"Gram passed Preme, she gone." Philly said still

looking out the window now.

"DAMN!" I yelled out my pain.

"It's just me and you left Preme, I'm not going to be getting high no more it's over, I mean it. I'm getting the fuck out of here, I'm going down south. That's what she always wanted me to do, go down there to start over." Philly heart was in every word that left his lips and I know he wasn't telling a lie.

"Philly, if that's what you want to do and you mean it I got your back, whatever you need. I know Gram would have wanted it that way." I said as the tears fell like rain in a storm because this man started to cry.

"Thanks Preme." Philly said….

We had the funeral, everybody and their mother came to pay their respects, and even people that never met my Grandmother came just out of respect to the game. A.G. tried to hold up as her casket was being lowered in the ground, so did I. A part of my soul went six feet under. My Grandmother was my only understanding in this world of misunderstanding and now she was gone, all I had to hold on to was the streets. I snapped, all good that I had in me was being slowly lowered into the Earth as a strong sun shower came down. My homie sang Sam Cooke, A Change is

Gonna Come, "I was born by the river, in a little tent, oh and like that river, I've been running ever since, it's been too hard living but I'm afraid to die 'cause I don't know what's up there beyond that sky, it's been a long time coming but I know a change gon' come." He sang and the rain came down as the thunder cracked, the tears fell from my eyes, with each drop of the rain but that was to be my last cry of pain. My life was as gray as the day with the sun shining because there really would be no more really sunny days because she was gone, the best part of me was really gone once he hit the last note of her favorite song...

"I'm stopping right there for now Black, I'll finish tomorrow." Preme said still having the pain of that day in his voice.

"I feel you, I understand" Black said and went to sleep.

CHAPTER 9

"Fuck that, that bitch got to die. I don't care who don't like it. I just buried my fucking brother. I'm putting them bitches in the ground. Hell will freeze over and the devil will give out free ice pops before I let them bitches get away with that shit." Taz said to his crew as they sat at the table in their trap house discussing their next move. Taz was Leakey's younger brother and a certified cold blooded killer. He was no more than 17 years old and had more bodies than an average Vietnam veteran. He led a crew of young boys called J.B.F.L. (Jack Boyz For Life) They robbed, killed and stole, mostly out of town. They lived by the golden rule, never shit where you eat. But somebody broke the invisible line and now it was time for street justice to be served. Taz knew the game, his brother ended his own life but after he seen the D.V.D. he knew his brother was long dead before he even pulled the trigger. The fact that Isis played his family name on some faggot shit, turning his gangster brother into a punk, made Taz to an enraged, hungry, ghetto vampire and all he wanted was Isis sweet blood.

He wouldn't have been mad as much if she would have just shot him down in cold blood in the street, let him die like a man for the money he owed. That would have been something he could have charged to the game because of the code in the hood. If you don't pay the connect and get caught slipping, that was your ass. But Isis took the shit to another so Taz was planning on taking it a step much higher. Light, who was as dark as night but got his nickname Light because if you played with him the wrong way then he would light your ass up with that Mac 11 he kept with him at all times. Then there's Brick, he got his nickname not from slinging bricks of coke but from beating his step-father to death with a brick for beating up his crack head mother. Next you had D.C., which stood for double crosser, he would cross your ass like Broad and Market Street if you not one of the Jack Boys. The four men team was only loyal to each other. They lived for money, power, and respect that had that tatted on their left arm and M.O.B. (money over bitches) on their right arm.

"Yo, what you want to do, I heard that bitch Toya set the whole shit up. I told my baby mother Big Liz, that work at Chuck E. Cheese and shit because Toya be up there all the time with her stank ass daughter." Brick said to Taz as he passed him a blunt.

"If that bitch set my brother up then I got a plan for her slick ass." Taz spoke while putting the blunt to his lips and took a deep pull, filling his lungs with smoke.

"How you know Toya had something to do with it?" D.C. asked as he sipped on his Hennessy.

"Because my people seen her truck and the word on the street is that one of Isis' top bitches set the shit up. Isis love that bitch, so if we take what she love then we even." Brick said.

"Fuck that even shit, that's for white people, I don't want to get even I want to get ahead." Taz said blowing smoke out from the blunt.

"How?" Light said as he lit his own blunt that he just rolled. But before Taz could answer Brick call phone rang.

"Yo, y'all hold up, this is Big Liz." Brick said looking at the caller I.D.

"Speak of the motherfuckin' devil." Taz said as he took another pull from his blunt.

"Yo, Liz, what's poppin'." Brick said into his cell phone.

"Toya is in here and she having a birthday party for

that brat of hers. Isis was up here but she left, I tried to call you but my cell phone battery was dead." Big Liz said giving Brick the run down.

"We on our way, how many of them bitches up there with her?"

"None really, they all left. It's just Toya, her brat and some other little girl."

"Thanks Ma."

"Thanks Ma my ass, you better have my money nigga!" Big Liz snapped at him in the phone.

"I got you chill, one." With that, Brick closed his phone. "Let's roll. Toya is at Chuck E. Chees." Brick spoke standing, putting his phone in his pocket.

"Good then, I'll tell y'all my plan on the way." Taz said.

"Mommy, this is the best birthday ever, now that I'm 7 years old, you can't call me a baby no more, right Tea?" Kyra said looking at her mother with her long hair in pig tails looking like one of Russell Simmons's daughters. Her and Tea-Tea who was Isis' niece was having the time of her life at Kyra's 7th birthday party. Everybody else went home but Tea and Kyra was having so much fun that when the party was over they begged for another hour because they felt like twins now that Kyra was the same age as her best friend Tea. Toya spoiled Kyra because her baby father left her and Kyra before she was even born, in fact when Toya told him she was pregnant he said 'so, what you telling me for. I aint nobody's baby father but that's your baby, good luck.' Then he dumped her on the spot without another word. The only man her child ever knew was Isis. Well, even though Isis was a woman, she stood strong like a man. Toya loved Isis with all her heart. Isis was the only woman she ever been with. They had an off and on relationship. No matter what Isis always took care of Kyra as if she was her own child. Tea was Isis' deceased sister daughter and all the family Isis had left by blood.

"You will always be a baby to me, even when you're a hundred and seven years old." Toya said smiling at her world of joy.

"How can I be a baby if I'm a hundred and seven years old? I'll be an old mommy like you." Kyra said pointing at Toya.

"No you will not be, you will just be my real old baby." Toya said as Kyra and Tea laughed at what she said. They played a little longer then made their way into the night of the parking lot, bringing an end to a perfect day. It was late, it seemed like they were the only ones left in the whole parking lot. Toya hit the button on her key to make the back door of her Navigator open. The lights of the truck lit up the darkness as her and girls put the bags and boxes in the back of the truck.

"Don't move bitch!" The masked man yelled with the big chrome 44 pointing at her. The two little girls was about to run for help but they were quickly grabbed up by two more men that came out of the night like the first man. The girls were cuffed and their mouths were taped and thrown in the black minivan parked next to Toya's truck. The men moved so fast the little girls never even got a scream.

"Please, don't hurt my babies. I have three grand in my purse, take it!" Toya pleaded thinking if they let her get to her purse she had her 380 cocked and ready, it was on and popping.

"I don't want ya money bitch, I want your life. Cuff this bitch and lets be out." The first masked gunman said pulling Toya by the hair. Toya was cuffed, gagged and thrown next to the girls in the van. The children eyes were full of fear as the tears fell. One of the mask men jumped in Toya's truck and they left one behind the other like nothing happened. Big Liz seen everything going down on the security camera being that she was the security guard, she took the tape out and replaced it with a new one.

"Cha Ching", she said mentally counting her money...

"I love you, I love you, each and every day" Faith Evans song I Love You played softly mixed with the sounds of love making. Gemini and Isis made love naked in her large super king size bed.

"oooh uhh Isis." Gemini was moaning laying in her back, leaning on her elbows with her head back and her legs open wide as Isis feasts on her sweet sensual buffet. Their bodies were moving in poetic harmony. Isis perky breasts and her long nipples, they really looked more like chocolate pacifiers. Isis was rubbing her erect nipple on Gemini's clit, then she came up, nipples glistening with Gemini's cream so that Gemini could taste her own sweetness as she sucked it off each of Isis' breasts. Isis started going back down Gemini's body kissing and sucking all the way until she reached Gemini's chocolate heaven. Isis stuck her very long tongue deep in the core of Gemini's hot pleasure. "oh God Isis oooh, uhh, I love ittt, taste meee." She moaned grinding her hips slowly making love to Isis face and Isis's fingers that was just as deep in her ass. She was flat on her back pulling her own nipples while enjoying the oral bliss Isis was giving her. Isis got up, turned Gemini around after she sucked up every drop of her last orgasm. Isis then came up behind her with one hand on Gemini hip and the other on her huge twelve and a half inch strap on. Gemini was on all fours as she reached back to spread her big beautiful ass open for Isis. She knew Isis loved fucking her this way because of the screaming orgasms she has. Her body covered in sweat, each bead of sweat sparkled like diamonds off Gemini's perfect body. Isis wished at times like this she was a man so she could really feel all the creamy love she was tasting. Isis put the large mushroom shaped head of the long thick strap on in the inviting opening of Gemini's dripping wet pussy. "Ooh Isis." Gemini moaned as Isis opened her sliding in every massive inch in one stroke, watching her ass jiggle rotating in the deep penetration.. they started out slow motion but things quickly sped up as Gemini started throwing her ass back, working and sliding back and forth off Isis' strap on like it was her full time job. "Isis, you make me cummmm." Gemini yelled, in the heat of her passion.

Ring. Ring. Isis was still pounding into Gemini making her reach the high of her climax. Ring. Ring. The phone screamed. Isis knew if somebody was calling her house phone this late it was important, only people she called her family had the number. Ring. Ring. Isis reluctantly slid out of Gemini quivering body. Isis was pissed because she missed her own climax that was starting to build.

"Hello." She yelled, horny and angry into the phone.

"We got your bitch." The voice said in the phone with a harsh tone.

"What? Who is this?" Isis asked, now more baffled than angry.

"Don't worry about who I am, you better worry about what I want, if you want to get your niece and your girl back you dike bitch." The voice in the phone said coldly.

"My niece?" Isis voice now full of fear, thinking about Tea, who was all she had left of her deceased sister.

"Here, talk bitch." Taz said as he put the phone to

Toya ear.

"Isis, they got me, Kyra, and Tea. They said if you don't give them a half mill they going to kill us." Toya talked in a tone to let Isis know she was scared to death.

"What?" Isis couldn't believe it, she knew that this was part of the game but after that video she was sure that niggas would think twice before fucking with her.

"Now bitch, do you understand what this pussy eating bitch just told you? If you don't pay the money this is what's going to happen…." BOOM. The shot from the 44 went off.

"AAAAh, Isis he shot me in my leg!' Toya screamed in agony,

Isis could hear the kids screaming in the background. Her heart was breaking, tears filled her eyes. Isis was hard core, she had the will stronger than any man but at this moment she was all female. She felt raped and powerless, the only thing she could say was "Please" in a weak voice.

"Please my ass, you stank gut bitch, you better have my money, you got an hour or the next bullet goes in one of these pretty little girls pretty little face." CLICK. The phone went dead. Isis sat in shock for a minute, tears running down her face.

"Isis, baby, what's wrong? What happened?" Gemini has been with her for two years and never seen Isis cry, never seen Isis look weak. She was the most cold blooded queen pin she ever known but right now she was broken and one thing Gemini knew it had everything to do with that phone call.

"Somebody got Toya and the girls." Isis spoke as she jumped up and stepped out of her strap on and walked over to the wall safe.

"What? Who? Why?" Gemini asked with worry in her voice.

"Money, it's about money, don't worry, I'll get them back safe and sound and whoever did this, I'll make them pay ten times more than what they asking for." She was talking to Gemini but she was really trying to convince herself that everything was going to work out. She had the money, she kept over two million in two wall safes in her house just for shit like this. She called it her bail fund whether it was for the police or the niggas in the street, she could cover it. She knew this shit was a part of the game, she was told that a long time ago, just pay the money and make them pay it back later. The number one rule was to make sure that you get your people back safe, no time for fuck ups or letting anger override your intellect. Isis filled the Gucci duffel bags with the money. She had her cash in hundred thousand dollar stacks, so it was easy to count out.

"What do we do now?" Gemini asked as she started to get dress.

"We wait!" Isis said dryly, now fully clothed.

"Look bitch see what y'all did to my brother? Y'all took his manhood, made him kill himself. Now you want to turn your head. Look, you too, you little bitches, I don't want to hear that crying shit, this is why y'all here, your mother did this to you. Look what she did to my fuckin' brother." Taz yelled at Toya and the little girls, his voice was mixed with pain and hatred.

Toya leg was bleeding and in pain where Taz had shot her. Her and the girls were tied in a chair, looking at T.V. playing the movie Isis made. The movie once turned her on. The power Isis had over a man but now it was making her sick to her stomach knowing her daughter and Tea was looking at the sick street justice, robbing them of their seven year old innocence. She didn't know if they were going to make it. They were locked in the basement of what looked to be a morgue. Not only that, none of the men were wearing mask anymore, that's what made her fear of death a grim reality. Toya knew who they were, the Jack Boyz, but she wished she knew that Leakey's brother was the leader of them. She then would have had Isis kill them and she and the girls would not be where they are now. She thought, I could kick myself for not doing my homework but it looks like I don't have to because I know they are going to kill me, I just hope he let my baby and Tea go.

"Bitch, it's time to call ya bitch and she better have our money." Taz said dialing the number in Toya cell phone. One ring and Isis voice was on the line.

"Hello." Isis said softly.

"Bitch, it's been sixty minutes but before I ask my question, I want you to hear something." Taz said walking over to Kyra. SMACK.

"No, please don't hit my baby, hit me, beat me!" Toya screamed when Taz smacked Kyra clean out the chair, with so much force she was knocked out before her body hit the floor.

"Okay." Taz said. SMACK.

"Oh God, please hit me, leave the babies alone." Toya's voice was full of agony after she seen Taz back hand Tea, knocking her little frame unconscious. Isis heard everything through the phone and couldn't help the tears that were running.

"Please! Please!" Isis begged.

"Did I tell you to talk dike bitch?" Taz yelled in rage.

WACK. Taz chopped Toya in the eye with the butt of the gun. Blood was rushing down her face, she was hit so hard that she was knocked so dizzy that she didn't even feel the pain. Brick and D.C didn't really like the little girls getting smacked around, they both had small daughters of their own and felt sorry for the kids but their loyalty was to their homie so they were like fuck them kids it's just another day on the job. Besides it wasn't like they were their children anyway. Light didn't care one way or the other, he was glad Taz plan was working out, shit, all he saw was his cut of a half mill. If Taz wanted to beat the brats, babies, or old ladies it didn't matter to him one bit hell, he'll do it himself. It was all about that paper. He smiled and sat back and watched the show Taz was putting on.

"Now bitch that I got your full attention, I don't want you to do nothing but what I tell you from this point on, nothing more, nothing less, do you understand?" Taz asked.

Silence.

"You may speak, good thing you didn't say nothing because if you had without me telling you one of these little bitches would have been getting fucked by the six inch barrel of my 44 and once I rammed all six inches between her little tender legs, I would have pulled the trigger, so you then could get out your black dress, oh my bad your black suit, I forgot you think you're a man. Now you may speak, do you understand? Nothing more nothing less!"

"Yes." Isis said. Her tone was of one that was broken and defeated. She knew that she was dealing with a real cold hearted killer. His heart was colder than hers and for the first time she found somebody on Earth she was scared of.

"Good then, this is what I want you to do, nothing more nothing less. Take my money to the big church on 7th street, put my bag of bread on the steps and go the fuck back home, I will be watching the whole time. I want you and nobody else but you to drop it off. If anybody else comes keep in mind I'm pouring gas on one of these little bitches. If I see anybody else besides you, you can call me Usher because I'm going to let her little ass burn, but if all my money is in the bag, nothing more nothing less. I'll let her and the rest of these stank bitches go, understand? Speak." Taz said.

"Yes."

"Do you have a stop watch? Speak."

"Yes."

"Good, set it now, when this line go dead you should be at the spot by the time it says twenty minutes. Speak."

"Yes." The line went dead. Isis threw the phone, rushed out the house, not telling Gemini anything, just rushed out, bags in hand. She jumped on her black C.B.R. 1100 and she weaved in and out of traffic of the city streets a 80 and 90 mile per hour, it was late 3:00 am so it really wasn't too much cars out anyway. She made it to the church, her stop watch read 18.9. She made it just in time. She took her helmet off to let whoever know it was her if he was looking then she dropped the bags off, jumped on her bike and raced back to her house hoping that this nightmare would soon be over. Brick watched as Isis pulled off. He would have killed her right there but Taz said no, he wanted her to live and see what she did to her own family by her actions. He was hoping after he did what he had planned that she would kill herself. Brick looked to make sure nobody was there, grabbed the bag, and dialed Taz.

"I got the money."

"Good." Taz said.

Isis and Gemini waited for hours looking at the phones. Isis smoked blunt after blunt and like a man she watched the free movements of Gemini's ass as it bounced up and down in her sweat pants when she walked the floor pacing, full of worry. Isis used Gemini's ass and the blunts to calm her nerves. Gemini knew Isis eyes was on her ass so she made it shake a little harder with each step just to relax her but all her actions were in vain.

Ring. Isis grabbed the phone.

"Hello!" She said in a nervous tone.

"Well, ya did good my little pussy sucking bitch, I counted my money and it's all here, even a little extra. Speak." Taz said in a smooth voice.

"Where can I pick them up at? You got your money!" Isis said ignoring what he just said about extra.

"I'll send them tomorrow, you fucked up, I told

you nothing more nothing less but you try to butter me up by putting extra money in the bag. Speak." Taz spoke smiling.

"What extra money?" Isis asked puzzled, she knew that she put a half a mill, nothing more nothing less.

"I counted the money in the very nice Gucci bag and it was five hundred thousand dollars plus there was a half a penny. That means there was more, so you didn't listen but Toya is something that you can listen to, please enjoy." Taz then held the phone to Toya's ear.

"Hello Isis."

BOOM. The sound of the 44 cut Toya off.

"Isis, he shot Tea, nooo!" BOOM. "Oh God my baby, kill me, no, I can't live without my baby, you killed Kyra. Isis his name is Taz." BOOM. After the last shot the line went dead.

"Noo! Oh God NOOO!" Isis dropped to her knee screaming. Gemini joined her because she knew without asking that Toya and the girls were dead just by the pain in Isis' voice...

The next morning the doorbell rang it was around noon. Isis' home was full of her crew, everyone was in tears waiting for the news that the police found the bodies. They now just wanted to put their friend and children to rest. Ena opened the door, there were some delivery men there with flowers. Long black roses, over a hundred of them and three large white boxes in 3 delivery men arms, there were 5 men all together. Two of them had the flowers, she let the men in to bring in the flowers and gift boxes. Ena thought somebody heard what happened being that in the hood bad news travel fast and they were trying to show love to lighten up the mood. Gemini, Ena, and Isis opened the boxes. Isis opened hers first and was in shock, she was looking into Toya's eyes. Her head was cut off and her mouth was full of her own vagina, her eyelids were cut off so she was looking Isis dead into her eyes when she opened the box. Ena and Gemini were just as horrified because even the little seven year old young girls' heads were done in the same manner as Toya, even down to having their own little private parts stuffed in their mouths. The card read 'paybacks a bitch, it even cost more when you take little hoes to eat to. Ha Ha I'm getting ahead of myself. But the good news bitch, I know these bitches won't talk with their mouth full…

Taz and his crew Light, Brick and D.C. was on

cloud 9, each of them were one hundred and twenty five thousand dollars richer.

"Damn Taz I have to give it to you, your plan to be ahead was the shit. Now it's time to step our game up. Let's all get them Hummers we talked about." Light spoke stacking his money.

"I'm with that but Taz, you a sick motherfucker, why you cut their pussy out?" Brick asked in a joking tone but he really wanted to know what would make a black man do some shit like that, only white people do sick shit like that, niggas don't spend hours cutting out little girls and grown women pussies, so he wanted to know what was really up with his homeboy.

"Yeah man, I'm with Brick. What the fuck made you do that crazy ass shit? Don't get me wrong I don't care about that bitch but the little girls, shooting them was one thing, I don't give a flying fuck about that but when It comes down to cutting out a little girls pussy, that's some other shit." D.C. said looking Taz in his eye without a smile on his face.

"Look, I know that was some crazy shit, I don't know what got into me but that bitch did some sick shit to my brother I had to do something sicker for my family name. I wanted that bitch to see what she did and kill herself, like she made my brother kill himself after that bitch turned him into a faggot." Taz said still looking D.C. in the eye.

"Man, fuck that shit, it's over, them bitches is dead and gone now, let's go get our fucking Hummer." Light said breaking the tension...

CHAPTER 10

"Now, it's lunch time count, let's get back to the story. You on your last 48 hours and I want to know how this love story is going to end. So far Cinnamon seem to me to be a real ride until she die type chick. You seem like the one that was fucking up. Even after she seen you between another bitch legs eating pussy, she stood strong by your side. What happened to Nora anyway? Did you fire her? Where was she when your Grandmother died? Did Philly really stop getting high?" Black was shooting the questions out left and right.

"Damn Black, one question at a time. First off Nora was pissed with me because she was jealous of the love I had for Cinnamon and the unborn baby but she worked through that and got over it. I didn't fire her because she was good at her job and I could trust her to run the business when I ran the streets. She played the background the whole time after my Grandmother passed. She seen me fucked up every day. I'll get to that in a minute. Philly did stop getting high that day, he got a cell phone store down south that I got a small part of. I sent him ten stacks last year to help him get it off the ground. His business is doing well from what I hear. My Grandmother left him a house down there in the south and left me the one she lived in up here. I rent it out now to some people I know. But things for me and Cinnamon went from sweet to bitter fast."

I got up in the morning to my now usual blunt, two X pills and orange juice for breakfast. My Grandmother has been dead a week now and X and weed was now my get up and go. The money was coming in like water in a hole in a roof, me and A.G. had the hood on fire. Some nigga from New York named Juice tried to set up shop in our hood. We would have let the nigga live if he got the work from us but he told one of our homies that Jersey niggas don't know anything about the game and he was going to take over. A.G. called me that morning and told me we needed to sit down. Cinnamon was still in the bed when I left. I was high and the X had me feeling like I don't have a care in the world. We made our plan on how to get that nigga Juice. The only one that was going to do this was us and Tangy. I put work in with A.G. because he was like my brother for real. I got my first body with him and he got his at the same time. We were much younger than we were small time dealers. We were hand to handing on the block and robbing niggas here and there if we saw them slipping. This day a truck driver nigga named Big Jack and his wife came for credit like always. This wasn't anything new, he drove an eighteen wheeler and made big money plus he always paid you back twice what he owed you. He even let his wife trick off with us every now and then. Nobody fucked her but she gave a leave job that would make Super Head keep her mouth closed. But anyway, back then I wasn't as big as I am now. I wasn't 6'3" 230 pounds, I was more like 5'1" and a buck looking for five. So was A.G., we were little dudes in a big game. We both had guns, 38, and we kept them with us, for the stick up kids. Big Jack was a big nigga, he smoked like a campfire but he was every bit of 300 pounds and he was known for beating ass when he got drunk. But this day, he had me and A.G at his house he said that's where the money was he owed me. A.G. came because back then we did everything together. This wasn't new for Jack to leave his money so I went with him to get my paper. He owed me $200 but when I got there he only gave me $40 in order to get some more. He said he'd pay the rest when his wife got off work. I didn't think nothing of it neither did A.G. Big Jack was cool. I mean he was cool for a crack head, he had shit. He didn't live in the streets and his house was nicer than my shit. Angie, his wife, came home and seen us in the living room watching their big screen T.V., she spoke then went in the back room with Big Jack. About a half hour later she came back in the living room in her silk robe and said, "Which one is going first?"

"First? What the fuck you mean first?" I snapped at her.

"Jack told me he owed you a little money and I was going to give you guys a lot of ass for the cash." Angie spoke as she opened her black robe and turned around. She was sexier than a motherfucker. She looks like that video bitch Angel Lola Luv, nice tits, phat thick round loose ass. I like my woman like I like my chicken, legs and thighs. Plus this bitch had a phat shaved pussy, I wanted to fuck her for a long time but Jack only let her duck dick. She didn't look like a fiend in no way, shape, or form. She had a big bubble butt. When she gave me head I always picture myself hitting her from the back. But I needed my money not a fucking nut. Tricking aint going to do nothing but keep a nigga hand to handing. Philly told me that it's always money over bitches at all times, was a number one rule, the only thing a trick nigga play in this game is the sucker.

"Hell no, I don't want no pussy. I want my fucking money. You keep that stank ass crack head pussy, I aint no fucking sucker ass trick bitch." I said. A.G. started laughing as I was putting Angie in check. Then Big Jack came in the room looking pissed. His face said he heard everything I said.

"What did you say to my wife little nigga?" Jack said, walking up in my space with anger in in his voice. I didn't give a fuck, I wasn't scared of no fucking crack head, plus if he acted up I got something for his ass.

"I said, deaf nigga, I don't want no stank ass motherfuckin' crack head pussy, I want my motherfuckin' money nigga!" SMACK. The nigga slapped me to the floor.

Pop. Pop.

"Motherfucker, you smacked me!" Pop. Pop. "Die nigga, who the fuck you think I am, ya bitch?"

Pop Pop! Click! Click!

Holding the gun in my hand I jumped up, and before I knew what was happening, I had put six shots in his chest.

"Jack, no, my God, Jack! You killed him!" Angie screamed.

Pop Pop Pop!

Angie fell dead with three shots to the back of the head. A.G. had shot her without saying a word.

"Let's be out," I said.

We bounced and never told anybody. We stayed laying niggas down, taking over, our game went into overdrive. Tangy put work in too. She shot a bitch in the middle of her head when she heard the bitch was snitching, plus she been with us and helped us get some big time niggas before we had Isis as our connect.

Tangy been acting like she was hustling buying work off Juice for three weeks now, mapping the house out. The only people he had with him were his baby mother and a newborn. She said the girl told her the baby was two months old. Tangy used to wear tight shirts and jeans all in her ass. A shirt that hugged her body, with no bra, so he would be all on her and not on his game. The first time he was all business but when he started giving her way more than she paid for, we knew he was ready. She called him and told him she needed to re-up and that she wanted to maybe chill with him later. He said he couldn't leave, his girl was at work but she could come through and chill, until his girl got off work.

This niggas was thinking maybe he could fuck Tangy before his girl came home and everything would be all good. Trick ass nigga, that was why he was about to pay with his life. Tangy called the nigga again and now he told her his baby mother was on her way but if she wanted to chill it was still cool, he was about to order a pizza for them but his girl said she would love to have Tangy for her dinner, fuck the pizza. The nigga and his girl was freaks that was good for us, we were going to play on that shit. Tangy played along and told him don't order nothing until she got there. That was so we could put a good plan in action. It was late but no too late when Tangy got dropped off at Juice crib. I dropped her off in a rental car. A.G. went to Tommy to use the car he used to rob people, it was a Domino's Pizza delivery car, so it was perfect to have that car parked in the driveway. We would have taken Tommy, he's a real rider, he get down for his but he is a grimy snake ass nigga that can never be trusted. He's been known to flip on his partners and jump them in the middle of a lick. He likes to smoke that dream boat that dust and some-times that nigga mind be all the way gone. Tommy gave A.G. the whip. Tangy called us, acting like she was ordering pizza to let us know that everything was a go. I was high on five X pills, me and A.G., the only thing about that X is whatever mood you in it's going to take you to the next level. If you on some playboy shit, you'll feel like Heff, if you on some sex shit, then let's just say you'll be freakier than Janet Jackson and if you on some gangster shit you'll do shit that Neno wished he thought of.

I pulled the car in the back of the red Range Rover. A.G. sat in the car until I knocked in the door. We called Tangy to let her know we were outside, so she could open the door.

I knocked once on the door, Tangy opened it and grabbed the pizza box with the Mac 10 in it for her. I had my Gluck 40 and A.G. had a 357. As Tangy took the box, Juice was coming down stairs, he was kind of a big nigga, he look as though he did some time, he put you in the mind of 50 Cent but that shit didn't matter I had something to take all the air out of his chest. That X had me feeling like King Kong's father.

"What do I owe you for the pie?" Juice asked me pulling out a large bank roll.

"You owe me your life if you don't act right, you bitch ass nigga. You know what time it is grab for God's hands nigga." I said pointing the gun in his face.

"Shit, nigga caught me slipping." He said.

"Damn right dumb motherfucker, your slipping ass is going to fall." I said, looking dead in his eyes letting him know that all games was played on the basketball court, this shit was real.

Tangy acted like she didn't know what was going on. She knew the Mac 10 was in the box but we were playing chess just in case somebody else was in the house we didn't know about. A.G. quickly came in and closed the door, I told Tangy to pat him down. She pulled a Gluck 9 from his belt under his shirt. Then I told her to reach for the clouds, I had both guns pointing at them. A.G. was looking around downstairs.

"Is there anybody else here?" I asked the nigga but he was a stone cold G, he didn't say shit. I could tell this wasn't the first time the nigga has a gun in his face. He stood there calm, draped in all red, come to find out the nigga was a Blood. I knew right then we were going to have to kill him and everybody in the house when I saw his flag hanging out his right back pocket. The one thing about them Blood niggas is if you kill one then they coming like roaches, you going to have to kill them all and we didn't need war. Because if there was war money stopped and people die, so this one will have to be quiet.

"Nigga, I asked you is there anybody else in the house."

Silence.

WHACK. WHACK. I chopped him with the gun then the nigga fell to his knees in pain but never cried out. I really was liking Juice, he was holding it down. Tangy acted like she was worried about him.

"It's just us and a baby plus the child's mother. She's upstairs, please don't kill us, I don't live here." She said like she was in fear for her life.

"Smart girl." I said. A.G. went up the stairs and came down with Juice's baby mother, at gunpoint. She was holding a little baby boy that was crying. We cuffed the gangster ass nigga because I knew he would try something if we fucked around and slipped up.

"Look nigga, we aint got all night, where's the safe and the bricks?" I asked standing over him.

Silence.

WHACK. I chopped his ass again.

"Fuck you nigga, I aint telling you shit. If you want it, find it." This nigga said and had the balls to spit his blood that I put in his mouth in my face.

POP. POP. I shot the nigga in both kneecaps, his face twisted up but he still didn't cry out.

"Please stop, I'll tell you, leave him alone," his girl pleaded.

WHACK. I smacked his girl with his gun for opening her mouth.

"I didn't ask you shit bitch, I want this bad ass nigga to tell me or maybe he want to see how good you can suck my dick, holding his baby in your arms." I said and for the first time I heard this nigga scream out in pain. Not from him being hit but from the sight if his baby mother being strike and her almost dropping the baby.

"No! Don't hurt them!" He yelled out in agony.

"So, that's your weakness, where's my money and

bricks nigga?" I said.

"If I tell you, I know we are as good as dead." He said. He was right but even if he didn't he was good as dead, that was the real reason we were there anyway, to kill him. The money and bricks was a plus.

Rat. Tat. Tat. Tat. Tat.

The Mac 10 went off. Tangy took it out the pizza box and was shooting somebody behind me and A.G. I don't know if it was the X that had us slipping but a nigga had walked up behind us going for his gun. If Tangy wasn't there one of us or both of us would have been dead. We were so busy trying to break Juice that we didn't even hear the nigga come in the house. Come to find out it was Juice little brother.

"Oh no bitch, you killed my brother, the little nigga was only sixteen." Juice yelled with rage and anguish in his voice, as he watched his brother twitching his last drop of life away.

I grabbed Juice baby from his baby mother arms and walked over to the stove. I put the baby in the oven and turned it on broil.

"Now, Tangy, stand by the front door, I don't need no more surprise guess." I said. A.G. cuffed Juice's baby mother who was about to lose her mind. The baby was crying as the oven started to heat up, plus I know the gun shots scared the shit out of it. I could smell it when I put it in the oven.

"Now, if you don't want to see me bake this shitty ass to a crisp, tell me, where's the fuckin' safe at. I know it's getting hot in there." I said. I was at the point where I didn't care that his brother was dead. I just wanted to break this nigga, kill him, and go.

"Alright, take him out! You fuckin' win! You win motherfucker! It's under the refrigerator in the floor just take my son out the oven before it's too late!" Juice said with his head down. I took the screaming baby out. The oven didn't burn the child, it was getting warm though. I put it on the table and me and A.G. moved the refrigerator and there was a digital safe, it was a nice size.

"The numbers?" That baby was screaming from the kitchen table, fuckin' up my high. I just wanted to get the shit, kill these motherfuckers and go.

"0-31-2-12-96-7-11-2" A broken Juice said looking down at the floor, in defeat. I felt sorry for the broken street warrior so I wasn't going to let him see his family die. In fact, I was going to play like the nigga saved his family. I did the numbers on the keyboard of the safe and it opened.

"That's what I'm talking about, since you did the right thing, you won't see your family die but you know I have to kill you." I said.

"Do what you have to do nigga. Hell's been calling me anyway, I don't mind picking up the phone as long as my son live, I'll fry but I owe you one when you get there." Those were Juice's last words, I didn't say anything more to him. I pointed the gun at his head.

POP. POP. POP.

"Juice!" His baby mother cried out as Juice lifeless body hit the kitchen floor. A.G. put the gun to her head.

"Wait, you said that I didn't have to die." She said with tears running down her face. I didn't like this bitch, she was loyal like he was. She was no longer worried about Juice or the baby, she just worried about herself so I had to make her pay.

"Wait A.G. not yet, I said he wouldn't have to see his family die because I respected him. He was a real ass nigga but you are a fake ass stank bitch so this is for you on the way to hell," I said as I walked over to the baby crying on the table.

POP! POP! POP!

"Nooo!" She screamed as the child stopped crying, bleeding on the table, lifeless like his father.

POP! POP! POP!

A.G. shot her in the head.

POP!

I shot the bitch in the face even though she was dead just because I hated her type; only by your side when you got it all but leave you high and dry when you fall.

That nigga had about sixty gees in the safe plus eleven bricks of coke. We took all the shit, then poured gas all over the house and all the way out the back door. I cut the eyes of the stove on. Tangy pulled off in the car with A.G. I lit the gas then jumped the fence and heard the explosion as I pulled away in my rental car. My cell phone rang and I answered it.

"You straight?" A.G. asked.

"Yeah." I replied.

"I'll meet you at the spot." A.G. said.

"No, I'm going home to check on Cinnamon."

"Alright, one."

"One." I replied. After I hung up the phone with A.G., I popped two more pills and lit the blunt I had already rolled and turned the radio up.

"Try me… Try me…" James Brown classic played as I rode deep in thought. This was the only way I could think, listening to old school music it seemed to soothe my aching soul. I was on my way home but I never made it. I ended up outside in Nora's driveway. "Try me, try me" James Brown still playing. I cut the car off. This was my first time seeing Nora since the day we got busted by Cinnamon. I was missing her and the X had me wanting her. I knocked on her door, the funny thing is now that I think about it, time I pulled in her driveway the night sky lit up with lightening and when I cut the car off I heard the rumble of the thunder. Time I stepped out the car the rain came showering down on me. That night was a display of how I was feeling without my Grandmother. I knocked on the door, I was soaking wet to the bone, and my dreads were hanging down dripping on my shoulders. She opened the door wearing a bra and her nipples were hard instantly once the cool air touched her body. I already knew she slept in the nude. I could tell that I just got her out her bed or either she was going to get ready for bed.

"What do you want Preme?" She said in a tone of longing not aggravation.

"I want you, can I come in?" I said. She stepped to the side and I walked in.

"Look at you, you're all wet, out in all that rain at two in the morning. What, you and your wifey had a fight?"

"No, everything going good with her but the fight is in me trying to stay away from you." I replied. I know my remark hit her deep because she tried to pass by it.

"Take them clothes off so I can put them in the dryer. You high aint you? I can see it in your face, you rolling on some good shit too." She said still trying to ignore what I said.

"Yeah, I'm on it. That's the only thing that keeps me going since you and my Grandmother left me." I spoke as I removed all the clothes I had on,

"I'm sorry about your Grandmother. I know you loved her but she is at peace and you got to let her rest with the Lord. As for me, I am always here for you I just can't deal with being second best." She was talking as she was picking up my clothes. When she bent over her back was to me, I could see she had no panties on. I knew she didn't but when I saw it I was brick hard. My dick was standing up like the sun in daylight. That motherfuckin' X was on full blast and I wanted that ass. She turned to see me standing there butt ass naked, rock hard walking up to her.

"No Preme, please, we can't do this, not again." She said dropping my clothes pulling away as I grabbed at her. I grabbed at the silk belt that was holding the robe closed, it opened freeing her nakedness showing all of her beautiful essence. Her nipples were hard, I knew she wanted me, her eyes were locked on my mighty erection wanting to be deep inside her.

"I told you when I walked through the door I wanted you and I'm going to have you tonight." I said as I was still walking up to her when I spoke. She was facing me backing up to the wall. Now we were face to face, body to body when she said,

"What about tomorrow night, who will have you then?"

Not wanting to answer the question I just dropped to my knees and threw one of her legs over my shoulder, spreading her thighs and put my mouth on her hot creaminess. I knew sucking that pussy was her weakness and the only thing that was going to be on her mind was tonight. Tomorrow was the next day and she would deal with it when it got there once I started eating that pussy.

"Don't do this to me Preme, I can't take it." She moaned as her head fell back on the wall in full pleasure. Her hands were in my dreads, her eyes were closed as my lips, tongue, and finger went to work. I was sucking on her pulsating clit as she worked her hips. She was trembling. She started to really grind her hips making love to the three fingers I had inside her and the lip on my face. "Ooh, uhh, ooh, PPPreme, ddon't doo thiss, oooh, Goddd," she moaned. "I'm starting to cccum, that youuu want, taste meeee, it for you, oooh." She was shaking, pulling me into her wetness by my dreads as I was devouring her. She screamed, "I'm Cumming hard PPPreme, I'm cumin!" I let her passion rain down in my mouth as she exploded she was trembling as her juices came down into my mouth that was now locked on her grinding opening. I didn't miss one drop of her sweet tangy nectar. I let her leg down then kissed my way up her body until I was kissing her other lips, letting her enjoy some of the sweetness she just gave me. My dick was pushing hard on her belly as we were in a lustful embrace. I picked her up and took her to her bedroom where we made love all night. I woke up, she was gone, and she left a note letting me know she went to work at Supreme Wash. My clothes were washed and folded and she put her house key on top of them so I wouldn't miss it. Her note said that she would try to deal with Cinnamon but I don't have to worry about nobody else, male or female because all she want was me, that's why she gave me the house key because she had nothing to hide. I got dressed, went to my rental car, looked at my cell, and I had over a hundred missed calls. I called A.G.

"What's good with you?" I said after he picked up on the second ring.

"Shit, you nigga, Cinnamon been calling Tangy all night looking for you. We thought you was going home. When she called and told me you never made it I got worried because you already know what went down then you didn't pick up your phone after last night. Where the fuck you at anyway?" A.G. asked questions but I could tell in his voice he was glad to hear my voice.

"Man, you wouldn't believe me if I told you."

"Try me."

"I was with Nora all night, I was on my way home but ended up at her spot."

"Still chasing that pussy, tender dick ass nigga?" A.G. asked and started laughing in the phone after his last comment.

"No nigga, I been hitting that, that's who Cinnamon busted me with at Supreme Wash." I said putting his ass in check.

"Get the fuck out of here, I thought it was some chicken head that work there, well that's what Cinnamon told Tangy."

"She is the only one I got working there, remember?"

"Damn, you right, I should've put two and two together. What you about to get into now Preme?"

"I'm about to hit my crib, check on my girl, then make that run!"

"Naw, it's my week nigga remember?"

"Oh shit, you right, I did do that shit last week so then I'm going to chill for the rest of the day with Cinnamon."

"Tender dick, when you going to pick up this money from last night?"

"I'll get it leave it with Tangy before you make the run. One."

"One." He hung up the phone. The run is when we

drop off packs and bricks to all our spots. We only trust each other to move around that much work and pick up that much money. He did it one week and I did it the next. It was a good system, we had a good team, no worries on that note. I walked through the door of my house, Cinnamon was gone so I called her on her cell phone.

"Where are you?" She asked me picking up the phone on the first ring.

"I am home, where are you?" I asked.

"At my mother's, I'll be there in a minute, we missed you last night." She said sweetly.

"I had something I had to take care of, I told you that when I left." I said defensively, thinking she was trying to be a smart ass.

"I'm not questioning you or nothing, I know you do what you do for us. I just wanted you to know that we love and missed you last night, that's why I called you so much. But before I come home my mother wanted to know if you want to go to the mall with us. They just opened a Baby's 'R' Us and we going to get some things for the baby."

"You and your mother shopping. Hell No! I'll be better off getting my teeth pulled than going shopping with you two. Shopping right now, I don't want no parts of that, you and her can keep that shit. Last time you and her was in the same store y'all was about to fight over what crib the baby was going to sleep in. me and her bump heads too much but you can come get some money and have fun." I said.

"I got my bank card, I don't need cash, plastic is a lot better than cash."

"Do what you do, I love cash money, I'll be here when you get back, I'm not going nowhere, in fact I'm cutting my cell phones off. I'm just going to spend as much time with you and my son as I can."

"I'll try to hurry then, we love you."

"I love y'all too, one."

"One Daddy." She said before I hung up with her then cut my cell phones off. The only way people could call me is if they had my house number and nobody but A.G. and family had that. I went in my stash of X, popped four of them things because I knew I wasn't going anywhere.. I went over to my bar, fixed me a glass of Remy V.S.O.P. plus rolled me some of that good purp, took a long shower and laid in the bed. That was my routine for four days, I stayed high and fucked up. I never got out of bed unless it was to take a piss or shower. All me and Cinnamon did was enjoy each other's time, I spent hours at night talking to her belly, we wasn't even fucking like that, we did about four or five times and when we did it was hot and passionate but I just really was enjoying the love and peace of my home. She wrote in her diary as I talked to the baby growing in her belly at night, everything was going good, until that rule came into play, all good things must come to an end. I woke up one morning still high and a little tired from the home sex me and Cinnamon had the night before. I couldn't finish watching my football game with Jay, she was so hot in the ass but away I popped two more X pills to get me going. Cinnamon was in the shower and she did something she never did, she left her diary out, I always wanted to know what she wrote in the damn thing. The X was telling me it was now or never as I looked at the book that laid next time on the bed, it was like she left it for me to read so like a fool I opened Pandora's Box. I wish I had never read that woman shit, even to this day the words are burned into my brain and heart because even though I loved her, my blood ran cold that morning but hot with rage and pain. I never forgot what it said I mean word for word, I opened the book, I guess it was the last couple days she been writing, then I started to read the pages of sin a million times over and over but the words wouldn't change, it said what it said. Written in black and white in her hand writing, my Cinnamon's handwriting, so I knew it was her it was really her. It started off like this: Dear Diary, am I wrong? That is a question I have to ask because at the moment it's really haunting my mind, see the other day I see Joe-Joe in the mall, it was a good thing that Preme didn't want to come, I think he would have beat Joe-Joe ass for G.P. but anyway when me and my mother was shopping for the baby I was surprised to see him in the mall with some bitch that he met down south. I'm not going to lie or hate on little Miss Thing, she was well put together, I mean the little bitch had me jealous as hell. But anyway, he told me that he came back to Jersey because his mother had passed from breast cancer. I didn't even know she was sick she was always so full of life. I really felt bad for him plus me and his mother was real cool. She was the type of woman you could tell anything to and know it was going to stay with her. So anyway he seen my big ass stomach poking out and asked me about the baby.

(This is where I started to take the wrong turn and really begin fucking up) I was supposed to tell him like I told everybody else that this was Preme baby. I was supposed to let him know that I got rid of his child but he looked so sad about his mother's death, I just couldn't bring myself to say the words so I just told him the truth and that all rights of the baby was going to Preme and he was now the father. Joe-Joe was so pissed, for a moment I saw a man in him and I think if Preme was there Joe-Joe would have wanted to fight. He had me kind of turned on, my pussy started tingling. I never seen him act like that before. I was so glad my mother was nowhere around then she would have known that Preme was not the father. The little Miss Thing that he was with started acting like she didn't want him talking to me no more but he checked her ass then sent her hot ass to the hot ass car. He cooled down just in time when my mother walked up and seen us talking. (For the record, my mother really hate Joe-Joe with a passion) she can't stand the air he breathes. So I had to let her know why I was talking to him, I let her know his mother had died and everything. Then I did something else stupid. I asked her to leave us alone for a minute. She gave me an ugly ass look but she did but not before saying she was going to look for something to buy Supreme my husband to be and baby father, loud enough to piss Joe-Joe off and make his face sour like a lemon plus I think she was really trying to check me. That was a real shock to, my mother never done anything like that shit before, I think deep down in her own way she really like Preme. But this is not about Preme and my mother, this is about me and Joe-Joe. When we talked I seen I still had love for him, I haven't really thought about him until that day. Out of sight out of mind I guess but I still feel him, I mean he is my real first child's father. Don't get me wrong, Preme is the best I'm blessed to have him, he does everything for me as if the baby was his own flesh and blood, I love him for that, he is a real good man. I don't care what the streets say about him, even Joe-Joe tried to tell me that Preme was a cold hearted killer. But I don't see it, Preme is a man, about respect, if you respect him then there's no problem but if you disrespect him then he is going to get that ass. I know he is a real hard fight I just don't see Preme killing people for no reason but love is blind. But once again this is not about Preme this is about me and Joe-Joe. Since I seen him in the mall, I really been fucking up. Me and him been talking on the phone late night when Preme is sleep, for the last four nights. The first time was the day I seen him in the mall. I called his cell that night using mine, I only really did it to see how his father was dealing with the loss of his wife but after that I should have hung up but me and Joe-Joe started talking about things in the past, when we were together, the good old days. Most of the shit was silly and stupid then our conversation took a quick erotic turn and I should've ended the call then but I wanted to talk more when he said, "remember when we got busted by my Uncle John, the preacher?" I'll never forget that night, Joe-Joe and I had just came in from the movie and we was in his mother's kitchen doing our thing when his uncle walked in the kitchen and seen me bent over with both hands on the breakfast table, pants down, thong kicked to the side, and Joe-Joe killing me from the back. He was a man that day, slamming into me so hard that my knees kept hitting the table Uncle John screamed "Oh my God Joey, this is your mother's house!" Joe-Joe quickly pulled out of me and fixed himself. I couldn't face that man, I just let Joe-Joe talk to him in the other room but ever since then his good old Uncle John was trying to fuck me making passes, he even went so far as to say, "I want to show you how a real man can bless your pussy." I never told Joe-Joe because he wouldn't believe me no way and even if he did he still wouldn't have done shit, he love his Uncle John. But back to the matter at hand, we talked and talked about the hot good sex we had. The more we talked about sex, the more I felt myself getting wetter and wetter. I was in our bed feeling the fire, wearing a bra and panty set as we was talking so dirty I started doing the unthinkable. I put my free hand between my legs and started rubbing my throbbing clit through my panties. Then Joe-Joe told me that he been playing with his dick the whole time we been talking. He was like the sound of my voice was making him so hard that if we kept talking about sex he was about to cum all over himself. I don't know if it was just hearing him say that or it was the fact that I was so horny but I told him I was doing the same thing for the last hour and if he kept it up I was going to cum all over my hand. That's how my sin started; me and him had the hottest best phone sex I ever had, well, the truth is, that's the first phone sex I ever had that night. He had the outside of my panties so wet that I said fuck it and put my finger inside them and just started teasing myself. I was moaning in the phone, fucking my fingers until I came in a big rush with so much force, pushing my juices all over my hand. I was really in to it. I can't lie, I lost my breath it felt so good, really good. I was so loud and the most fucked up thing about all of it was I was acting like a slut being lost in my own pleasure that I forgot Preme was laying right there beside me while I was letting Joe-Joe phone fuck. I was so lucky that Preme was still on those pills and when he came down he slept hard because if he would have woke up and seen me with my hand in my panties, legs open, moaning on the phone, he would have killed me for sure. After I helped Joe-Joe get his nut I told him I'll call him tomorrow and hung up the phone with my pussy on fire. Don't get me wrong Joe-Joe is not a better lover than Preme, Preme put it down in the bedroom every time, I mean he is a man, he knows how to make a woman cum and nobody can take that from him. But Joe-Joe is more like a boy in a man body when it comes down to sex. I had to show him what I liked, I think back then that was one of the turn on for me, I was his teacher but the real reason he had me hooked and I hate to say it but it's the truth, Joe-Joe got the biggest dick I had ever seen in my life, it's so long and thick, the way it hook to the left with it's over sized head, I never seen or felt anything like it. That's why I stayed with his ass so long down south, I knew once I left him I wouldn't find anything like it again. He is the only man that I ever had that I never cheated on or even thought about it, that nigga had me fighting niggas over that dick. Don't get me wrong, Preme is not small, he is above average and his even a little thinker than Joe Joe's but Joe-Joe is blessed, really blessed from God because I know he got Preme by at least two or three full inches. That the only thing I do miss. No one ever touched the spots in me that Joe-Joe had. I lied, I can't say I miss his dick because I bought one that look just like his, my black dildo is the same size, even down to the big ass mushroom shaped head. It looks like I cut the best part of him off and took it with me. So when Preme not around or on one of his runs or in a deep sleep, I go in the bathroom and Joe-Joe, I call it King Kong Joe. Sometime we go so hard I get to the point where I can't even close my legs for a few minutes. So anyway, the next night I call him, he told me he wanted me to listen and he put the phone down, I thought he was about to play an old school song from back in the day but then I heard a woman moaning "don't put it all the way in, it's too big." He was fucking his girl and had me listening. I was about to hang up but my horniness got the best of me. I just kept hearing her cry out time he pushed deep in her, I felt a jealous fire burning between my legs as lust had me in its grips. I laid on my bed for twenty minutes listening to her moaning out in plea-sure and time I was about to spread my legs and join in the phone went dead. I wanted to call back but I know I wouldn't get an answer. But I was so sexually build up I had to do something. I got of bed to get me a quickie. I didn't pull King Joe out because if Preme woke up I knew he would want some pussy and that hook on the king be having my walls sore and I didn't want to be sore for Preme because he be on that X and can go for hours. I got out of bed wearing nothing but my lust. I was so wet that I was at the point to start dripping. I had to bust a nut. I started playing with myself thinking about Joe-Joe fucking me like he was doing the girl on the phone. I did it right in front of Preme while he slept. I stood there looking at him rubbing my clit hard and fast then I stuck four of my fingers inside me, the whole time looking at Preme, I was picturing that Preme was sitting in a chair at the foot of our bed, my back to him as he watched how I ride Joe-Joe making him, disappear inside me as I go up and down on his long monster. Then, Preme come up behind me in jealous rage and stick his dick in my virgin ass so I was getting fucked by two men I loved. I was in the zone, I know it was some freaky twisted shit. I was moaning as my legs got weak, I almost started to fall when I started cumming heavy and thick on my fingers. My cum was running down my legs. I know that was nothing but wrong but that next day Joe-Joe sent me a twenty minute video text of him fucking his girl from the back and that's when shit got out of hand. I was looking at the video text on the guess phone in our guess room of our home, Joe-Joe phone fucking me, Preme was up with company and everything. He and Jay was downstairs watching football. I was getting my fuck on for an hour, I wish I would have had King Joe then it really would have been on. I made Joe-Joe cum twice but the phone thing wasn't working for me, I wanted some dick, real dick. Even though Joe-Joe was stuck in my head, I hung up with him. I knew Preme was downstairs watching those damn Cowboys with Jay but I also knew what to do to pull him away from that T.V. The only way to get Preme is to show that I'm real hot and need to be fucked, around Jay and it was bye-bye football, that's just what I did. I put my night shorts on that's way too small, they look more like thongs if anything, the way my ass cheeks be busting out the side, I had no panties on and the fabric is pink and so thin that it was like a second skin. You could see everything from the back and front with ease and the matching tank top was no better and you know I didn't wear a bra. I walked downstairs looking like I wasn't wearing nothing but pink skin. Preme was X'n so I knew when he seen me it was on. I walked in the living room, the first person to see me was Jay, I let him get a good look before I turned around and bent over to pick up something off the floor. I looked in back of me still bent over and I saw Preme looking. I started walking, swaying my hips, making my ass bounce, and I bent over one more time to pick up something else and both of them was looking at me with pure lust in their eyes. I said, "You boys should pick up after yourselves." I went back up the steps and Preme was behind me. He stood at the bedroom door without saying a word. I kept bending over in the room like I was picking up things and the next thing I knew he was on me ripping everything from my body and I was bent over the head of our bed and Preme was really fucking me, I mean really, really working my body but even with Preme punishing powerful strokes all I seen was Joe-Joe in back of me. My mind was so far gone, I couldn't come back to reality as Preme was pounding in me with all he had, faster and harder in and out of me for bouncing my ass around the house in front of Jay. I was starting to cum, I had to grab a pillow and stick my face in it as my orgasm exploded. I screamed out Joe-Joe name, loud in the pillow, Preme was so into fucking all the hot wetness he didn't hear or had any idea that I wasn't calling for him nor was I throwing my ass harder than ever as I was cumming, he really didn't have one thing to do with it, he wasn't on my mind at all. Thank God for pillows, I came so hard and so much that I was weak and in tears that was the best sex me and Jo- Joe never had. Now this morning I woke up before Preme and went to see Joe-Joe at his father house, he came to the door in his boxer shorts, his father and girl were gone. I didn't have much time because if Preme woke up I would have just told him I went to get us something for breakfast. Joe-Joe opened the door, he knew I was coming, I told him I was on my way. When he opened the door my eyes went straight to the opening of his boxers, he had his dick sticking out. It laid hooked to the left, really long but not at an erection. He stepped to the side, and I walked in and went up the step to his room. I had on my Baby Phat sweats, and no panties because I knew when I got up, I wouldn't be going anywhere. I know my ass was jumping as I went up the steps because he couldn't keep his hands off of it. He knew we didn't have much time so by the time I got to the top of the steps Joe-Joe was ready for action, his dick was sticking out the opening of his boxers, it looked so huge, it was ten times the size since I last seen it, I wanted to suck it and I never did that to him when we were together. He had me so wet the way he stopped me at the top of the steps kissing the back of my neck telling me he was about to make my pussy his again as his hands was on my hips and he was pushing his hard dick in the crack of my ass making my sweat pants stick in the middle of my ass cheeks. We got to his room, no words was said. We kissed his hardness pressing against my pregnant belly. Then he turned me around, bent me over in his bed, pulled my sweat pants down, opened my ass, I was waiting for him to fill me the only way he could but he made me scream as I felt his tongue enter my ass. He had three fingers in my pussy. I was screaming his name begging him to just fuck me and my cell phone rang, I knew it was Preme, I could tell by the ring tone, the song My First Love let me know it was him for sure. I told Joe-Joe to stop that was Preme but that seemed to make his tongue grow deeper and his finger work harder, I was cumming more than ever, I never felt like that in my life but I pulled away because I remembered that my truck was parked outside in front of Joe Joe's father house on Preme block, it was morning, I knew nobody was out but when I missed his call because I couldn't pull myself away in time because of the feeling it took everything I had to crawl in the middle of his bed, nude from the waist down, wearing nothing but my Air Max. I called Preme back, ass in the air on all fours, I thought some-body seen me, Preme picked up on the first ring. I told him I was in the store that's why I missed his call, he just wanted me to buy him a box of blunts, as I was talking to him Joe-Joe came up behind me in the bed rubbing his big mushroom head of his dick on my clit and pushing it in my opening. I wanted to pull away but I pushed back moaning his name in the phone, I didn't even hear Preme no more as Joe entered me. Preme called my name through the phone. Then I woke up, covered in sweat and in between my legs felt like I was working in a whore house and every trick in America came in me last night. I was so wet, I had a fucking wet dream and I look to my right and Preme was sound asleep. I can't believe it was all a dream the whole time and all this happened this morning. Me and Joe-Joe were supposed to have lunch before he left to go back down south next week. I gotta make my dream come true and give him one last good fuck before he go back down south. Just writing it is making me wet. I'm going to show this nigga what he's going to be missing. This will be our last fuck. Don't get me wrong, I love Preme, that's my man, I'll never fuck a nigga with his child in me or when he is my husband but we didn't say "I do" yet and this is Joe-Joe baby, so if I let Joe-Joe get one good ride for the road that can't be wrong, can it? I'll get at you again next time. I got to take a hot shower to wash my dream off, I smell like good sex…Cinnamon

She was in the shower for almost an hour, I read it over and over then read it again just those three pages. I couldn't believe this bitch was doing this freaky shit to me like that, she even planned on fucking this whack ass nigga or was I the whack ass nigga because she was talking and getting phone fucked by this nigga in my bed lying next to me. He had her playing with her pussy thinking about me watching her bounce up and down on his dick and she did all that in my face, while I'm sleeping. But the kick in the face that make me the whack nigga is I'm fucking her and she calling his name, but what gave me the whack nigga of the year award the fact the she was she was cheating on me with a fake dick. I lost my mind for a moment I was so angry I forgot about what goes around comes around, I forgot I spent a night away fucking Nora, I forgot she walked in on me with a mouth full of Nora's pussy. I forgot all that and made myself the victim. She still didn't bring her ass out the shower, so I went looking for this motherfucking King Joe, looked all around the room but I found it in the one place she knew I would never look, her night stand. She knew it was safe right there because I never went in it, shit she could have put it in mine, the only thing I had in it was a Gluck and two fully loaded clips. I pulled this thing out and it made me even more pissed, the fucking thing was as long as Shaq shoe and if that was that nigga shit then that made me super pissed and jealous. She came out the bathroom fresh out the shower, glistening, I know she oiled down in the bathroom. I was high and angry. She had her back to me when I came up on her. I was so mad my dick was brick hard, I had her long ass sword in my hand A.K.A. King Joe, she didn't see it as I was coming up on her. I was so pissed I didn't give a fuck that she was pregnant, I grabbed her by the back of her neck, slammed her body tight against the dresser, bending her over.

"So you want me and that punk ass nigga to fuck you bitch? I'll make one of your fucking dreams come true." I said through clinched teeth as I put my arm around her naked waste with dildo in my hand, kicking her legs apart and shoving it in the opening of her pussy.

"Preme, no!" She screamed as I pushed it as far as it would go. Then rammed my dick inside her ass ripping open her asshole, she never had sex anally she said she was saving that for her husband, that day I was her husband. "AAAH Wait!" She yelled out in pain as I started working that dildo in her pussy ramming in and out of her asshole. She tried to break loose so I let the dildo go and grabbed he by her hips forcing her to take all my anger and frustration. I was pounding in her ass so hard the dildo popped out of her pussy and hit the floor. Tears was raining down her face as she tried to hold her belly, screaming out, "I'm sorry! I'm sorry, please stop please stop, you're killing me, I never had sex in my ass, you're hurting the baby, Preme, please!"

"Fuck that baby bitch, this is what you wanted aint it? This is what you wanted bitch." I said coldly as I fucked her hard with each word. I was pounding in and out of her until I felt myself about to nut then I really started smacking and drilling dick in her ass. I started to cum and pulled out and released my cum in the crack of her ass. I let her go, she fell to the floor next to her friend King Joe, tears falling, crying and holding her stomach. I walked to my night stand, picked up the drink I had on it, sipped the Remy that was in the glass, looked at her pitiful looking ass and threw the rest of the drink on her. "That's your shower whore." I said and spit on her. I started to get dressed, as I walked out the room she got off the floor and grabbed my arm.

"Please Preme, don't leave us, I'm sorry…" BAP. I backed hand her so hard she hit the floor before she got all her words out and I left her there on the floor to think about who the fuck she was playing with.

"Man, that's some cold hearted shit young blood, you crazy motherfucker. Damn man I can see if she fucked but what you did to her was rape. You raped your pregnant girlfriend. What she did was fucked up, I can't fault you for being pissed, now if you just smacked her back to reality I would understand that but rape, I can't understand that." Black was shaking his head as he finished speaking in disbelief of what his ears had just heard.

"You're right I was wrong, I do regret what I did because I knew deep down she still love the nigga. I knew even if I was playing Daddy that nigga was the real father but I loved her and the child more than he did because he wasn't at any of the doctor appointments, he didn't spend seventeen grand on a baby shower. He didn't put her in a house, he wasn't the one talking to her belly late night, even when she was sleep. He was not going out late night to buy grill cheese and bacon sandwiches from across town because that's the only spot she liked them from. I didn't care what she wanted, all she did was asked and I was going to get it because she was giving me something that money couldn't get and something that I never had and that was a son, she put me in a place that every man live for and that's fatherhood."

"Count clear! Count clear!" The C.O. yelled as the doors unlocked.

"We'll finish this later. Right now I have to check on Kong Fu." Preme said standing and walking to the door.

"I'm coming with you." Black said as he started out with Preme to the door.

"Do what you want, I can take care of his ass, I got plans, watch my work." Preme said as they left the cell.

CHAPTER 11

Face met Fugee at the mall the day before he killed her brother but he had no idea that Jay was any relation to Fugee when he killed him. She was walking to get in line and he was behind her at the food court. He was stalking a nigga that he was mapping out how he was going to jam him up later on that week that was until he saw Fugee, he couldn't help but lose all concentration because of the earth quaking ass in front of him. Fugee is a master of the erotic step, she was always known for stopping a man from breathing with the sexy sway of her hips. Face went from planning a stick-up to wanting to pay for her food and when she went in her purse to pay for her things Face quickly went in his pocket.

"Please, let lunch be on me, for you making my day one to remember." Face said. Then Fugee turned to see who was asking to buy her meal. She quickly sized him up. Looked him up and down, he was nicely dressed in the latest fashion as she put him through her mental computer. He has nice jewels, the only thing she could find wrong with "Mr. Lunch man" was the three slashes across his face. But she thought the mark or scars on his face was sexy, she felt that it showed attitude and gave him character plus by the way he was standing she knew he was a hard core gangster. That means he must be the bad guy in the bed, hair pulling and ass smacking, "Who's your daddy thug life". She thought as she said,

"The only way I'll let you buy me lunch is if you plan on eating it with me."

Shit, damn, I'm going to have to let that nigga off the hook but she is really worth it, he thought to himself. "I love when a plan comes together." Face said. Then they sat and talked over lunch. He was really feeling Fugee. She was now becoming more than just a phat ass and a pretty face that wears Prada. After talking to her he found out that she did hair for a living and that she had dreams of one day opening her own salon when her money got right. Plus the fact that she didn't have five children at home didn't hurt matters either, hell she didn't have any. She told him she only had four God children. Face was feeling her as she talked because she wasn't like the chicken heads he'd been fucking with since he broke up with his baby mother. She had plans and goals not only that she was working on making her dreams happen. That's why they say you can't judge a book by its cover. He told her he was the most hated man in the world for his job. He said he was into laying niggas down and taking all their shit plus they life even when they did act right. He felt that would scare her off but he had every plan of letting her know what time it was. With her body she could hook plenty of top dogs with that bread. I'll show her how we can have a salon in record time. They talked on the phone and he made an appointment to have his hair braided.

Now as he pulled up to the salon called Ladaes with her lunch, damn tonight I'm going to beat that pussy up, Face thought as he parked his car...

Shit, who the fuck Brick think I am? One of his cheap ass stank tricks. He riding high in a Hummer and I'm sitting low in a Honda. I'm his fucking baby mother and he lied to me talking 'bout they only got fifty grand that's why they killed Toya and them poor little girls, if I wasn't fucking D.C. with his big ass mouth I wouldn't have known they got half a mill. But this sorry ass nigga going to give me a thousand dollars but if it wasn't for me they wouldn't have shit. But tricks are for kids. Isis is putting up a million dollars for any info on who killed Toya and those little girls. A million dollars sure sound good to me. I know she going to kill them but with that kind of money I can buy a new baby daddy, besides he was trying to play me, now it's my turn to start the game. Big Liz was thinking to herself as she was dialing the phone. The phone rang three times, then it was answered by a female. "Hello." The female voice said.

"Yes, can I speak to Isis, I have some information about what happened to Toya and those poor little girls." Big Liz said counting her money as she talked.

"Hold on please." The female voice replied.

"Now, that will take care of Kung-Fu, when he drink that gift I gave him then it's over for him. He like getting drunk so I'ma let what he like kill his bitch ass. The best was to kill a motherfucker is to let them kill their motherfuckin' self." Preme said to Black after giving Kung-Fu some prison homemade wine with a super extra kick of death in it.

"You right in that young brother no face no case, I taught you well. Now let's get back to your story. What happened after you raped Cinnamon?" Black said laying back on his bunk getting ready to take the ride back into Preme's past.

"Stop saying rape because it wasn't rape, it was punishment fuck. I don't believe in punching my girl in the face but I'll smack the bullshit out of her if it calls for it. I may even choke her silly ass out but if I'm really at my point where I want to kill her I'll just fuck the dog shit out of her as a punishment fuck just to get the stress off my chest. That night started a whole new thing between me and her. After I found out about that Joe-Joe shit, I knew it was much more in that book of secrets, well erotic secrets. I just didn't read no more after I read the pages I opened the book to. I was so stuck on what she was saying then that I closed the damn book up. I wasn't staying at my house with her anymore after that night. Me and Nora was doing our thing until we was fucking one night, I bust a nut and called Cinnamon name. Nora was so pissed we got into a verbal fight so I said fuck her and left there too. I was popping that X hard now plus A.G. had to do a little six month bid for a gun charge. I had a warrant because I didn't go to court for my own charges. I was on the block or at my other apartment, or I would be with Tangy. Me and her always was cool like that. I stayed on the block with the little niggas all night drinking, getting fucked up off that

X and weed, love sick like a motherfucker. I hadn't talked to Cinnamon in a month by this time. I still kept tabs on her though through Jay and Fugee, they let me know how she was doing. She used to call my phone but I never would answer her calls, she even used to come down the block but somehow she would always just miss me but one night she caught up with me and I was fucked up…

"Preme, let me talk to you for a minute." Cinnamon said with tears in her eyes and hurt in her voice. It was dark but under the street lights I seen every drop that was rolling done her face. I was sitting in my car, slipping like a clown on a banana peel, I had my 45 in my belt showing, my jewels sparkling, I was flossing like Bird Man from Cash Money. I had over ten stacks in my pockets. I had the biggest bottle of Remy V.S.O.P. that money could buy. My butterfly doors up and my system was bumping Killing Me Softly by Fugees. I had about five bitches from my hood around me and my little nigga Karter, I was trying to see which one I was going to fuck when Cinnamon pulled up. I had a hand full of Sacoria's ass, kissing on her neck. It was kind of like when we first met all over again but this time she was in the wrong.

I let Sacoria go and smacked her on that soft ass of hers as Cinnamon walked over. I'm not going to lie, I was missing her like crazy, hell every chick I fucked I was thinking about her even called her name when I nutted. I didn't care about the sluts I was fucking feelings because she wasn't Cinnamon.

"Talk," I said trying to be cool as I sipped from the half empty bottle.

"Not here, take a ride with me, Pleasee." She begged with tears still running.

"The only way I'll ride with you is if you take me to White Castle so I can get me a Surf and Turf, well maybe four or five Surf and Turfs." I said then took another sip.

"Okay, wherever you want to go, just please come with me." She said, now she had a little joy in her tone knowing I was about to leave with her but I had to rain a little on her sunny day. Before I got in the truck with her, I told Sacoria to hold my car down with Karter until I got back, then got in the truck with Cinnamon. As we rode she was playing X-Factor by Lauryn Hill, she started to talk.

"Preme, I know I hurt you, I didn't mean to, I miss you, we miss you. I am seven and a half months pregnant the baby is almost here, are you going to be there with us or not? I'm sorry baby."

"Sorry? Sorry for what? Sorry that you like to fuck fake dicks, sorry you like finger fucking yourself in my face while I'm sleeping thinking about another nigger, or you sorry that you going to fuck the nigga, or I know you sorry that I am not that punk ass nigga Joe-Joe right?" I snapped on her, as the words from her diary ran through my mind.

"Preme, I fucked up, I love you and I'll do anything to fix it, just don't leave me. I can't take life without you. We can't take life without you. Please tell me what I can do to fix this." She was now begging again.

"Anything? That's a strong word." I said just to see how far she would go. I wanted to hurt her bad like the hurt that was inside of me.

"Yes, just tell me what it would take to have you back home in our bed tonight." She said. I was so high and drunk, the eight pills of X running through my blood had me feeling so many emotions. I wanted to go home the sound of being in our bed together was all I really wanted but then that Joe-Joe shit popped back in my head. I was hurt angry and horny at the same time.

"Pull this fuckin' truck over and suck my dick like you really missed it." I said out of nowhere, I don't even know where it came from but I said it so I had to roll with it.

"What? That's what you want me to do and you come home?" She said but she knew it was the X talking not my heart but she pulled over and she found a good place to park. I didn't answer her question.

She started to undo my belt, she put my gun on the dashboard, I put my seat down and leaned back as she pulled my already hard dick out the front of my boxers and she didn't waste no time opening her mouth and began sucking my dick with force. I grabbed the back of her head as it was bobbing up and down, the truck was off so all you could hear was her slurping, sucking sounds, mixed with her gagging because she was sucking my dick so good I was pushing up as her head came down. I was fucking her mouth like I had fucked her that night in her ass. She hung in there though as I made my dick slam the back of her throat and when u busted in her mouth I pulled her head all the way down until she swallowed all of my dick. Her lips were kissing my pubic hair and my balls and my dick was down her throat emptying.

"Drink every drop. Suck it all out bitch, don't spill not one drop." I said coldly. I let her head go when my nut was done but she kept sucking, she was milking every drop of my semen out. She wouldn't lift her head until she was sure she sucked it all out of me. She swallowed all of my seeds of life. Then she looked at me tears running down her face harder than before. I began to bring my seat back up and fix my pants.

"Are you happy now? Are you coming home? I did what you said, I got every drop." She said with pain in her voice.

"Did Joe-Joe get happy and come home when you drank up all his nut?" I said dryly.

"I never sucked his dick like that, I never swallowed anybody's cum but yours. I love you Preme, you got to believe me." She started to break down.

"I love me too bitch, drive us so I can get my food, don't you know when you suck all the protein out of a man's body he gets hungry." I spoke trying to hurt her more, I wanted her to feel the pain that was cutting me inside.

"I'm not going anywhere until you give me what I

want. I did what you asked me, I didn't waste nothing, what do I get for that huh? Her voice was cracking. I went in my pocket and I put my gun back in my belt and gave her a hundred dollar bill.

"It was good, the best I ever had, worth every penny, now you got your money. You're a whore and I'm a trick, now drive bitch!"

SMACK! She smacked me dead in my mouth as I was about to take a sip from my bottle. I knew I was wrong for what I said and did. I regretted it time I did it but when she smacked me and I was tasting my own blood in my mouth, I grabbed her by her neck, emptied the rest of the Remy over her head as I was choking her.

"This will help your slut ass to cool off bitch. I told your dick sucking ass about your fucking hand didn't I? You can't breathe now bitch can you? Look at the vein in your head I should kill your dumb ass." I said then let her go because her eyes started rolling in the back of her head as I yelled at her.

SMACK. I back handed the fuck out of her as she was trying to catch her breath, she was really crying now. I got out the truck and said I'll get my own food, then slammed the butterfly door down. She started the truck, sped off like a bat out of hell. I started walking and didn't even know where the fuck I was at, plus I left my damn phone in my car.

She came up behind me as I walked in the street, I thought the bitch was going to hit me but she pulled up beside me.

"Get in, I'll take you back or wherever you want to go, I'm sorry Preme, please, I'm sorry." She said broken and still crying.

"Take me back to my shit and keep your fucking hand to yourself before I kill you." I said and got in the truck. She tried to talk but my understanding was off, I didn't want to hear shit she had to say.

Tangy went out of town doing something I can't recall, Nora still had me on knock off and Cinnamon, you already know how I was doing her. I was making a run drunk and high, I stopped at a store and was slipping like a motherfucker coming out. I had a brick in the trunk of my rental car on my way to drop it off and played a scratch off ticket with my head down. I let this punk ass nigga I shot back in the day named Smooth creep up on me coming out the store. This bitch nigga shot me in my left leg. POW. I didn't fall until he hit me in my right leg. POW. I hit the ground.

"Motherfuck." I yelled as I went in my pants and pulled out my gun. Smooth hauled ass. POOP. POP. POP. I let my Gluck cry out trying to hit that fast motherfucker. POP. POP. CLICK. CLICK. CLICK…. The gun was empty. My dumb ass was with the little niggas letting off shots the night before for nothing. Luckily for me Smooth bitch ass was long gone. Unlucky for me Bash and his brother was across the street and came over as I was getting up with my empty gun in my hand. I stopped at a store on their block out of pocket like a motherfucker.

"Well, look what we have here." Bash said walking. I swung but missed. WAP. BOOP.BOP. BING. They started beating my ass, they made my bad day into a really bad day. They was going to shoot me but the cops was coming down the street. One of them motherfuckers kicked the dizziness into me. I don't know which one it was, then they ran off, taking my chain and gun. Somehow, I got to my feet, I was fucked up, nothing was broken, the bullet went right through. Both of my legs were bleeding with holes in them. I made it to my rental car, put my key in the door then my really bad day got worst.

"Freeze!" The police was all around me, it was too

much for me, I just passed out.

I woke up cuffed to the hospital bed. I was charged with the brick of coke. Luckily for me Bash and his brother took my gun, that saved me from gun charges but I still had those bench warrants, the only person I could call was Cinnamon.

RING... RING... RING... "Hello." She finally answered.

"I'm in the hospital, I've been shot." I spoke trying to gain sympathy.

"Oh, my God. What hospital? Are you okay?" Her voice was full of worry and concern.

"Don't worry about that, that's not the problem. The real pain is I'm about to go to jail now." I dropped the bomb on her while the feeling was good.

"For murder? Who you kill? Don't worry if they shot you first that's self-defense. I'm going to call our lawyer, we're going to beat this bullshit." She said ready to fight for my freedom.

"Slow down, I didn't kill nobody. I just got busted with a little brick. I know I can beat that charge because I didn't tell them they could search the car but I have some bench warrants. Call my lawyer so I could bail out. I'm coming home I can't be out in these streets slipping like this." I sad letting her know the beef was over.

"Okay, I'm on it."

"One." I said and hung up the phone, she didn't say one, bye, or we love you or nothing. I didn't think nothing of it until now. I went to the county jail and had to sit for thirty days for the warrants. My bail was two hundred thousand dollars for the brick of cocaine. Her mother came to the jail and put the money up after my thirty days was up because the day before I was to come home Cinnamon was rushed to the hospital for labor pains. I called her mother house and she told me that Cinnamon was in the hospital but she meaning her mother was going to bail me out to make sure I see my son being born. The morning came and I was the first thing smoking out the county jail. I was at the hospital in no time. Cinnamon didn't come to the jail to see me, it's not that she didn't want to I just wouldn't let her because I was still fucked up from the niggas kicking my ass. I didn't want her to see me like that but thirty days was enough time for me to heal. She thought I had Nora coming and I was still mad at her about that Joe-Joe shit, that's in her mind why I wouldn't let her come. I let her think what she wanted to, a little jealousy is good for a relationship, as long as your woman know somebody else want you if she slip, she will always hold on with a little tighter grip.

I walked through the door of her hospital room, my face was all healed but my legs were still a little sore. Her mother took me to my house to get fresh because my clothes I had at the jail was bloody and fucked up. I just took a quick shower and threw on some sweats and Timbs.

Cinnamon face lit up when I entered the room. I saw the beauty in those eyes sparkling like the stars in the night. Her brother was there, Jay ,Fugee, her little sister and Mr. Bryant. Everybody seemed to be happy to see me come in the room. Brandy, her little sister, screamed my name time she saw me and ran to me and I picked her up looking at Cinnamon in her eyes.

"Hey, it looks like somebody is trying to have a baby without me." I said with Brandy in my arms, looking at Cinnamon.

"You better had made it, now everybody we can have the baby, Daddy's here." Cinnamon said smiling. I still had something on my mind so I needed some time with her alone.

"Can we talk, baby, I just want to clear the waters for our relationship before our baby come in this world." I said looking he in the eyes.

"Sure, whatever it takes, I told you that." She said with a tear in her eyes. Her mother must be part clock because she knew what time it was and she knew it was now or never for us to put together what we let fall apart before the baby is born.

"Come on everybody let's go home, change clothes, and eat. Preme is here now he can do some work, he'll call us if anything happens." Her mother said taking Brandy from me as everybody said good-bye. I dapped Jay, gave Fugee a hug, dapped Mr. Bryant and Chuck, her brother then all that was left was me and her.

"So I go to jail and you go behind my back and try to have the baby without me?" I said joking not knowing where I wanted to start.

"No, I told your son I wasn't going to let him out until you came home. I couldn't do this without you, I love you Preme." She said as the tear start to fall down.

"Look baby, you don't have to cry no more, you don't have to let the tears of pain rain down your face. I am here. Know and understand that I'm here. I know sometime a wrong can make a right, sometime you got to let go to understand how to hold on tight. I know what you did and I know the things I've done but did and done is gone but I know what I got and I got you and all the love is for you to have. I am feeling all this love that you are giving to me and I know that's what count, me plus you is what count. I have no idea what I'm saying but I can tell you this, we are going to fight, we going to do things that we might not like but no matter what happen we'll always do it together. Me, you, and our son, let's let the past pass us and move on." I said and before she could say anything I was kissing her with all my soul had to offer. I didn't know where the words were coming from, I don't know if it made sense but I knew it was what I was feeling and that's all that mattered to me. Our lips parted as she looked in my eyes I guess to see if I was for real. I talked with so much passion her only reply was,

"I love you, now let's have this baby." She said as we kissed again.

They had her sitting in one of those delivery beds, her legs was bust wide open with a sheet draped over them, she was ready to have the baby and I was ready to be a daddy. She was like that for four days, I never left her side but the second day up there I called Mook to get right, it was hard staying up plus I was bored out of my mind.

The only thing they let her eat was ice chips and she was pissed about that. On the third day I was riding hard on that X her mother and them had just left. It was just me and Cinnamon in the room on some happy ever after shit. I was horny as hell, I haven't had pussy in over a month and all the lady nurses that kept coming in the room putting their finger in Cinnamon pussy to see what was going on with the baby, in my mind, it was like looking at girl on girl action. I was harder than a brick or diamonds. I got up off the couch after the nurse left and walked to Cinnamon and just kissed her passionately.

"What's that for?" She asked looking at me. Those eyes had the fire of desire really burning inside of me.

"Baby, I know we about to have this baby and this aint the right time or place but I want you baby, I need you now, not now but right now." I said kissing her face and neck.

"Preme, what are you talking about, you want me, what do you want me to do?" She asked but her tone let me know she knew what I was talking about. She knew I had that X in my system and to top it all off I just got out of jail. What I wanted was showing in the lump in front of my sweat pants.

"Baby, I need your heaven right now because I'm going through hell right now. Shit maybe it will help break your water so the baby can come." I said. My mind was racing with things to say to get her to be down with my request. I wasn't really trying to break her water, I was trying to shoot some more water up in there before my gun went off by itself, if you know what I mean.

"You think it would work?" She said. Her voice let me know she was really thinking about it, all I had to do was put two and two together and make four, then I would be dividing her legs, math is so good.

"I don't see why not, it's like poking a hole in a water balloon right? All I got to do is hit the spot." The science made sense plus I was playing off the fact she want that baby out of her and I know she would try just about anything. I wanted the backed-up babies out of me so if it worked or not for me it was a win-win situation.

"Preme, what happens if somebody come in, how's

that going to look?" She said looking at me a little worried but in knew that look. I rung that bell of understanding, now it's time to walk in.

"It's going to look like two people that love each other trying to help bring a baby in this world." I spit out, I was on a roll.

"Preme, you know that's not what I'm talking about, please baby, just lock the door." After she said that I wasted no time, went over to the door, pushed the button that locked it and it was on. I timed it perfectly. The nurse just left, they came in the room every hour so I knew I had a goof forty-five minutes to bust a nut up in her.

I got up between her legs she pulled the sheet up and revealed her magnificent womanhood. Her pussy was shaved clean but it was so big and puffy, the sight of it turned me on more, it looked fake. She removed her arms from the hospital gown showing her breast that seemed to be ten times bigger than the last time I saw them. Her nipples were so pointy, they looked the nipples off a baby bottle needing me to suck them. I quickly found myself pounding deep within her thighs. She was so wet the pussy was screaming louder than her. I sucked on her breasts that were full of her sweet hot milk.

"Oh shit girl, I'm cumming, oh girl I'm cumming." I moaned, enjoying the euphoric feeling of my climax.

"I love you Preme, give it all to me." She screamed. I think she was in more pain than pleasure. I emptied all thirty days of back-up sexual tension in her. I think that was the best nut of my life, it seemed like it was lasting forever. She drained me of all my energy. After I came I sucked on her nipples a little more, drinking her milk, it really tasted sweet.

I fixed myself then unlocked the door and sat back down as she fixed her gown and put everything back in place. Once she was done, like clockwork the nurse came in the room. She did her normal check-up but when she stuck her hand in Cinnamon to see how far she had dilated, she seen all of my cum on her hand.

"Mr. Divine, can I talk to you in the hallway please." She spoke in a nice upbeat tone but I knew what was going on, I seen her when she looked at her hand, her face was like what the fuck, I know this is now what I think it is.

"Nurse, is there something wrong with the baby?" Cinnamon asked but she knew what was up but she still wanted to try to play it off like she didn't have anything to do with it.

"Everything is fine, Mrs. Divine, I just need to have a word with your husband." She said as she turned and walked to the door. I got up and went in the hall behind her, feeling like a kid that got busted with his hand in the cookie jar.

"Mr. Divine, I've been a nurse for fifteen years, I have seen everything under the sun when it comes down to childbirth, that's what I though until today. I know you love your wife but she is having a baby. This is not the time to be trying to make another one if the first child had not seen the light of day yet. There's no reason why I should find your wife full of semen." Her tone was serious but she had a smirk on her face. She was an older black lady in her forties but I could tell she was hood plus a freak because she kept her eyes down at my dick the whole time she was talking. She never once gave me eye contact.

"Look, I was trying to help out, speed things up a little." I said in a smooth tone, trying to hide my embarrassment.

"How were you going to do that, Mr. Divine?" She asked with a questionable look on her face.

"I thought if I popped the bubble the water would

break and I'll be a father right now, just like sticking a pin in a water balloon."

"Ha ha ha." This bitch laughed at me in my face. I knew it was stupid what I said but I just didn't want to come out and say I just needed to bust a nut. "Well, Mr. Divine, it doesn't work like that but if you feel the need to relieve yourself here, I don't think Mrs. Bryant would like that you're tapping her grandson on the head before his birthday." She said handing me some stuff that was like K-Y Jelly. I knew that bitch was hood, she seen right through all my bullshit.

"Well, she don't have to know and you have my word that it won't happen again." I said taking the K-Y from her.

"I hope not, this is one for the record books, I'm going to clean up semen from a woman that has been in labor for three days. Masturbation is your friend." She said as she turned and walked in the room. I didn't go in because I knew Cinnamon would have been embarrassed but that nurse was cool. I finally came in a hour later after walking around that big ass hospital.

"They said they might have to cut me because I can't have it naturally." Cinnamon told me time I walked in the room.

"Whatever it takes, I'm ready to be a daddy." I said taking my place back on the couch.

"I'm ready to be a mom." Cinnamon said. Her mother came in the room and I went to sleep. I woke up half sleep, opening my eyes and I saw Cinnamon face. She opened her mouth to take in air as the white male doctor was penetrating her with four of his fingers. I didn't see anybody else in the room but him for some reason but the shit made me jump dead for his ass. I had a flash back of that motherfucking freaky ass other doctor and thought that he was freaky cracker doctor number two. Luckily for him Mr. Bryant, her brother and a few orderlies was in the room and grabbed me just in time before I got to him. He jumped back quick. Cinnamon screamed, "It's okay Preme, that's the good doctor!"

Her mother yelled at me. "What the hell is wrong with you boy?"

Mr. Bryant said, "It's alright, calm down son."

All the chaos caused Cinnamon water to break. "My water broke" Cinnamon yelled. That stopped me and everybody else in the room. The doctor told the orderly to take her to surgery now. They rushed her out the room while they removed the baby. Her mother went in. Me, Mr. Bryant, and her brother waited in the emergency waiting room for what felt like hours. I was walking the floor, mind racing then I heard "Code blue!" on the intercom, nurses and doctors started running in the surgery part. I freaked out and went running in there too, I had it in my mind if the doctor fucked around and killed my Cinnamon that was his ass. I entered the surgery room as they were removing the baby. The code wasn't for her it was for the next room over.

"You can't come in here like that, you have to be sterile." The nurse yelled, taking me to get right. I put on that blue suit the nurse handed me and a mask. Cinnamon was in another world because all the medicine they had her on. She didn't know I was there. The baby cried as they cleaned him up. Mrs. Bryant held him first but he still didn't open his eyes he just cried until he was in my arms and I spoke, he stopped crying and locked his eyes into mine and gave me what looked like a smile. He put all the torment that was in my soul at peace, the hurt of the loss of my Grandmother was healed by the gain of my son. I was tearing and didn't even realize it, for a moment it seemed as if the world stopped and it was just me and him in the room. Nothing else mattered because I was now the greatest thing a man could be and that's a father. They took him from my arms and did what they do when a child is born. I kissed Cinnamon on her head, she was now asleep. We named him after me. The world now had two Supreme Divine's that day. I went home to get everything ready for Cinnamon and the baby. She stayed in the hospital a couple of weeks to make sure everything was in order. Tangy, Fugee, and all her girlfriends stayed at the hospital. But I forgot to tell you about the moments after the baby was born. Me, Mr. Bryant, and her brother Chuck went outside to celebrate. I had some weed I wanted to smoke Mr. Bryant handed me a cigar that cost two hundred bucks, I told him good looking, I'll smoke it later but he had undercover hood in him that shocked me and Chuck.

"I know why you want to save it, you might as well roll it up, you know a blunt, that's what you call it right?" He said as we sat with the doors open to their truck.

"What you about that old man?" I asked him.

"I know this stays between us men, right Chuck?"

He replied looking at Charles.

"I aint going to say nothing, I just want to hit it." Chuck said with excitement.

I rolled the weed. We smoked out a two hundred dollar blunt. Man, we were so high we couldn't even move, we were just sitting in the parking lot.

"So, Preme, you ready to be a father? You know things have to change a little now, everything you do you have to know that your little boy will be watching you. Your mistakes can be his hard lessons. I don't say much because you are your own man but in know you are and what you do. It don't matter to me, there is no right and wrong when it comes down to taking care of yourself and your family. Food on the table is still food on the table either was but there's safe and not so safe, understand?" He said, looking at me with blood-shot eyes.

"What do you mean?" I said looking at him through chinky eyes but the wisdom was dropping, I could see clearly. I never had a father to break life down for me this was like my first man to man. Don't get me wrong I had real niggas school me on them streets but this was a different lesson. It was a man who was a father, telling me someone who was fatherless how to be the man to a child that I myself never had.

"Well, let's start with safe. Safe is Supreme Wash, your business that I hear is doing wee. One day with time and hard work you will be handing down to your son a powerful company. Now not so safe is the game you play in those streets, you get a lot of money and power with time and hard work you will leave your son either in prison or in the grave, then he will become the one thing like you, you don't want him to ever be." He said.

"What's that?" I asked.

"Fatherless." He replied coldly.

"Freeze, put your hands up." The cop said with his flash light on us. The weed was gone, Chuck was passed out and this dumb ass pig just fucked up a good moment.

"Where's the dope I smell it?" He asked as he walked over to us.

"It's gone sir, I was the one smoking and if you are going to lock anybody up it should be me. I just had my first child and was just celebrating." I said stepping out the truck.

"Don't worry about it, I just wanted some, it's

been a long night. I'm not even a real cop. I'm a rental cop." He said. We all started laughing. Mr. Bryant respected my gangster to the next level. He seen that I was a stand-up guy and no matter what I'll hold it down. He even hooked me up with a dude that could change your ID and social security number for just ten grand. He said you never know when I might have to run and make a change….

CHAPTER 12

There was still a score I had to settle with Bash, his brother and Smooth. I was chilling at this bar called J.C.'s when I saw Bash and his Girlfriend walk in, the bitch name was Kiwi. She was a real raw uncut whore that this sucker for love ass nigga tried to turn into a housewife. I knew for a fact by the time she got him and kissed him, he would've kissed about ten dicks that Kiwi had sucked before she hit the door. She was a real jump off but she was about her money, if you had a name for yourself and your bread was long it was like a key to opening her legs. My son been in this world only two days and I wanted to clear all beef before he came home from the hospital. There was no way in hell I was going to start a real war with Dollar, his bitch ass could get it too, my goons was on standby ready for war. But the way I plan on taking those niggas out, it wasn't going to be on full blast. I was going to keep it low key, M.O.B. (money over bullshit) that's what it stood for at the moment. I wanted to get Bash and his brother so bad I could taste it, for kicking a nigga when he was already down, I could understand Smooth, he was getting me back for shooting him. I fucked up I should have killed him instead of playing with the nigga. I left the door open, so I got what I had coming to me. Just like when I get my hands in him, he's going to get all the hot slugs I got for his ass and a quick ride to the casket. But anyway, I saw that nigga cum drinking bitch Kiwi looking me all in my face when she sat at the other end of the bar, so I sent her a drink. That's all it took to give her the green light. She walked up to me and I knew it was on and popping.

"What's good with you Big Preme, looking all good up in here. Thanks for the drink big time now I owe you one." She said as she sat next to me. Kiwi is not an ugly chick, she just do ugly shit, the bitch put you in the mind of Ciara with a bigger ass and fuller hips.

"Look her little ma, let's not waste time bullshittin', after these drinks let's go somewhere and sip on each other because I know chocolate and cognac goes down smother than buttermilk. You feel what I'm saying or you want to stay her and keep playing?" I said looking in her eyes so she would think that every word that was coming out my mouth was real. I even looked her up and down stopping at her plump perky c-cup breasts, so she could see the lust in my eyes.

"Chocolate and Cognac? Mmmm you know a drink like that can cost a lot of money Big Daddy but it would be good to the last drop." She said in a sexy voice taking in air so I could get a bird's eye view of her huge cleavage.

"Girl, you know I got so much bread that money owe me, unlike that small time boyfriend of yours." I said then sipped on my Remy.

"You talk like you trying to step my game up and be my boyfriend and take over all this hot chocolate passion." She said putting her hand on my leg.

"Naw, I could never be your boyfriend but I can take you up a level and show you what it's like to be with a man by giving you a night with these ten and a half inches of thug passion." I said. She slid her hands between my legs and gripped my dick. I was a little hard from looking at her breast but when she gripped it I turned to full brick mode and she had more than a handful.

"Ten and a half inches!" She said stroking my dick through my jeans/

"Are you ready to go or do you want to sit here

and play verbal chess?" I asked tired of playing games and this bitch had my dick hard for real.

"I'm ready Big Daddy." She said excitedly.

I let her follow me back to one of my stash houses, it was still decked out with everything a playboy need to get the game started. She came in the house and started taking her clothes off getting ready to fuck but I stopped her and let her know this wasn't that type of party, I had other plans for that pussy tonight.

"Look baby girl, slow your roll, I don't want to fuck you but I want to fuck with you on some business shit." I said in a way letting her know it's time to make some money but a hot in the ass slut is going to be a hot in the ass slut.

"What do you mean Preme, I came over here to get my ten and a half inches and now you backing out on me talking about some business." She said sounding really pissed. I didn't give a fuck. The bitch was going to do what I said if she wanted to or not.

"Look ma, I know you're about that money before anything else and I know you know your fag ass boyfriend and his brother jumped me after I got shot. But that's what got me and you at this point. I need you to help me get this nigga, I know you love him and I got ten and a half stacks for your love plus a new whip of your choice for your trouble." I said lying through my teeth. Her mood changed from horny to greedy.

"What I got to do? I don't want to go to jail." She said with eyes full of dollar signs.

"You don't got to worry about jail, this is hood shit, just tell me the best time for me to get Bask and is brother and stop worrying about the fucking crackers."

"Well, if you got the money now, Bash will be at the house in an hour or two. I know how hard you was at the bar, you wasn't going to last too long so I was going to fuck you real quick and good then make it back home before he got there. I was talking to him on my cell phone on the way here, he said he had to take care of something but his brother locked down out of town, the Feds got him."

"Let's just go to your house and from there I'll take care of the rest."

"Please don't do what you did last time when you beat him up in my front door, that shit almost made me lose my section 8."

"Section 8? Bash uncle is one of the biggest weight men in the hood and you and Bas live on section 8?

What the fuck?" I said kind of shocked because Dollar was a millionaire nigga and he lived like one.

"Yeah, section 8 but Dollar own the house, he own a lot of section 8 houses, this is the best one. He gave it to us but not because he love his nephew, he did it to keep me around to suck his little dried up dick when Bash not around. That is the kinkiest fat motherfucker I know, he like me to suck his dick with two of my fingers going in and out of his fat ass until he cum. I do it because he doesn't last very long, two or three minutes and pop goes the cork, it's a dirty job but keeps me in the latest Prada, Gucci, and whatever else my heart desire. He really don't give Bash too much of nothing because he is fuck-up when it comes to money, he really thinks that the little $500 he gives me a week is holding me down. The only reason I'm with him is because Dollar is damn near paying me not to leave him." As she talked I really started hating this bitch, she was so full of shit and Bash was a stupid nigga for loving this bitch. I had a plan for both of these sorry motherfuckers before I killed them that is.

We were at her house in no time. I had my gloves and my 357 with the six inch bowl that was so there wouldn't be no prints or shells but you know I also had my Gluck just in case six bullets didn't do the trick. I grabbed a little something special from the bathroom of my stash house for this pain in the ass nigga.

I told her to strip down and get in the bed when he had called and said he was on his way. I let her give me some of that brain work and bust a nice nut in her mouth to kiss her man with when he walked through the door to see how he like a cum mint. I can't lie to you Kiwi can suck a dick better than a crack head fiending for a $20 rock. That bitch wasn't shit she swallowed every drop and said she should've saved some for Bash and this nigga was in love.

I was kind of pissed that his brother got away, the nigga slipped through my fingertips but I still felt I could hurt his ass when he called home and find out his punk ass brother is getting fucked in the ass by Satan. I was thinking to myself in my own mental bliss feeling good knowing how much anguish his brother would go through when the star of the show walked in the bedroom giving her a deep passionate kiss, enjoying his mint. Step one of the payback had already started. Step two was to get that nigga cuffed to the bed, lucky for me the nigga is a freak like his fat ass uncle. He'd like for her to cuff him to the bed and suck his dick and ride him like a bucking horse, so the cuffing was the easy part. Time he came with that kissing, she was stripping him down. They wrestled naked on the bed in an erotic display of sexual play. I wanted to jump out the closet and fuck Kiwi myself the way she dominate him and put those cuffs on him. Their backs were to me and she had that ass in the air as she cuffed him to that big ass steel headboard on the bed, then she started kissing her way down his body and began giving the nigga some of that head work. I waited until he really got , into it, I waited until he was begging her for the pussy, I even waited until she straddled him, I let her bounce once maybe twice to let him get a good feel of his last piece of pussy, and just when the getting started to get good, I bust out the closet. She was in mid-stroke but she hopped off him leaving him pointing to the sky with shock and fear in his eyes.

"Paybacks a bitch motherfucker!" I yelled with so much venom that spit flew from my lips.

"What the fuck you doing in my shit, you aint like your movie?" Bash mood changed from fear to pissed as he found the nerve to question me. I still didn't know what he meant by movie.

"Fuck a movie, this is payback motherfucker. You like to kick a man when he's down and from the looks of things it's going down silly motherfucker." I said pointing my 357 at his shrinking dick. Kiwi just laid in there next to him looking shocked like she didn't know what was going on.

"Fuck you nigga, you lucky those cops came or your ass would have got more than kicked." Bash said. I guess the bitch was putting air in his balls, that's why he was talking so slick. A bitch with some good pussy can get a dumb nigga killed.

"You talking a lot of shit before this night over with you going to eat the same shit you talking before I kill you if you keep running your mouth." I said with an evil smile on my face.

"Fuck you nigga, I aint eating shit, but I know Cinnamon can eat a dick and your bitch ass aint going to do shit because of my uncle." POW. I shot off his right big toe.

"Shit!" Kiwi yelled.

"AAAAAH!" Bash screamed.

"Say one more stupid thing and I'll take another toe, you got nine left, don't open your fucking mouth unless I tell you, understand?" I said letting him know I had enough of his shit, this was my show now.

"Please Supreme, I'm sorry, please, I don't want no more problems. She wanted…" POW. I popped his ass again as he pleaded, this time I shot off his left big toe.

"Oh my God, please Preme!" He yelled in agony. Kiwi's mother sat in silence with fear all over her face.

"Shut the fuck up nigga, I didn't ask you to beg me for shit, I asked you did you motherfuckin' understand. Yes or no? Nigga!" I yelled.

"Yes, oh God, yes, whatever you say." Bash said with a voice full of pain.

"Good then, you talked a lot of shit about me and my wife. Kiwi, come here. Bitch I said bring your dick sucking ass over here bitch!" I yelled at Kiwi who's eyes were locked on Bash's bleeding feet that was squirting out blood in the air. She jumped at the sound of my angry voice and came over to me. I had both guns pointing but I was only using the 357 to do all my shooting. I had a bottle of liquid Exlax in my pocket which I told Kiwi to take out and when she did I told the bitch to drink it.

"Why?" She asked like she had a choice.

WHACK. I chopped her dumb ass for asking me questions plus I wanted her to be on the same page as Bash. She fell back on the bed with a little blood on her forehead. She didn't yell out in pain but the look of shock was on her face. She knew she was in just as much shit as Bash was in.

"Drink bitch or I'll shoot your nipple off!" I demanded. She started drinking, tears running down her face. I didn't give a fuck cry bitch.

"Leave her alone, she aint got nothing to do with this, I fucked up." Bash said with anguish in his voice. This nigga really loved this stank ass bitch. This had to, well he had to be the most tender dick nigga in the world.

"So you love her?" I asked him with a smirk on my face.

"Yeah, let her go, she don't got shit to do with this." The sorry ass nigga tried to sound honorable.

"Kiwi, tell Bash, the man that's the love of your life, what you did for me before he walked through the door into your arms." I said. I knew after he heard what she had to say it would hurt him more than his missing toes because there is nothing more painful to a man in love than an unfaithful woman.

"I sucked your dick." She said plainly.

"Then what you did girl with the big nut mint I was so nice enough to give you for all your hard work?" I said enjoying Bash face as it balled up like a two day old newspaper.

"I swallowed it." She confessed.

"Now, let's tell your loving husband how did I get into this nice section 8 home, that his uncle was so kind enough to let y'all broke ass stay in?" I said toying with Bash emotions, with this game of 21 questions.

"I brought you here to get him." She said, putting one last knife in Bash's broken back.

"Bitch! Bitch! You stinking, no good, dirty, cum drinking bitch, after all I do for you, you sorry ass trick bitch. I'm going to kill your ass as soon as you reach hell bitch." Bash yelled with tears in his eyes. I know he was not even feeling the shots anymore. His heart was broken and he was feeling the pain of betrayal, so I understood the tears and I was eating the whole thing up.

"Bash, Bash, that's no way to talk to the woman you love. Didn't anybody ever tell you in real love man you got to take the good with the bad, you talking all type of shit, when she was the woman and confessed to you now you want to kill her. I just don't understand." I said smiling like I just won a million dollars.

"Please Preme, can I go to the bathroom?" Kiwi asked, holding her stomach that was bubbling. Keep in mind I'm the only one with clothes on. I was the ring master of this butt naked chaos.

"So you ready to take a shit, huh?" I asked like I didn't know.

"Yesss!" She answered jumping up and down. I walked over to Bash who's still running his mouth until he felt the cold steel of the 357 barrow on his naked nut, the feel of cold steel full of that hot led shut his mouth but his eyes were open wide.

"Open your motherfuckin' mouth, don't close it now, you like to talk shit, now you going to eat what you talk, or we going to play nut cracker." CLICK. I clicked the hummer back of the gun and pushed hard on his balls. He opened his mouth good and wide.

"Kiwi, go take your shit, feed your man all that chocolate love of yours." I ordered.

"Please Preme, don't make me do this." She

begged. I pointed the 45 at her.

"Chicken head bitch, didn't I just tell you to go lay a fucking egg in his mouth or do my gun need to get some of that good brain of yours?" I said with the fires of hell in my eyes. She knew what time it was and got on the bed and put her ass over his opened mouth. She pissed first and it showered on his neck and then a large big ball of hot shit dropped in his mouth. He gagged, the she farted really loud and a ton of wet brown baby looking shit came out of her ass, it was so much it filled his mouth and covered his face. He was vomiting and choking. That bitch shit was stinking like an old dead motherfucker. She had the whole room lit up. But I knew when they find these motherfuckers it was going to make headlines.

"Open up your shitty ass cheeks and rub your nasty asshole clean over his face." I ordered. She opened her ass and rubbed her shitty ass all over his nose and face like Rakeashy from W.W.F. that nigga face was smothered in shit like chicken and gravy.

"That's enough bitch, your job is almost done, get the fuck down." I said. She did tearing. Bash was trying to spit the shit out his mouth. I put the 45 in my belt and opened the 357 to take out three bullets and I left one. I pulled my 45 out after I backed the 357 then pointed the 45 at Kiwi.

"Now, Kiwi, I know you think you the shit now and everything but you have a choice to make and those bullshit tears don't mean shit to me. You can live or did it's up to you. If you want to live take this 357 and put a bullet in that shit eating motherfucker's head but if you want to die with that shit all on your ass all you got to do is tell me no. Remember, we still can have that deal we talked about if you still want to live plus I'll even give you twice what I said before for being a good sport." I said as I handed her the 357. She was crying, she didn't say a word, she knew it was him or her and she wanted to live, it was written on her face plain as day, as she took the gun out of my hand. I put my 45 at her head just in case the bitch tried to think too much. "Put it to his temple and look into his shitty ass eyes." I said, sounding like the devil himself.

"Please Kiwi, don't do it baby, I still love you." Bash begged, still spitting shit out his mouth.

"Kill him!" I yelled pushing my 45 in the back of her skull, her hands were shaking but then. POW. Bash brain was on the pillow next to him, mixed with

Kiwi's shit. Kiwi fell to her knees crying, dropping the gun. I picked the 357 up and put the three bullets back in. I said in a cold tone, "Open your mouth bitch". I was looking down at her on her knees. She closed her eyes and opened her mouth. I think the dumb bitch thought I wanted some head because the way I was standing in front of her but when she felt those six inches of hard steel enter her mouth her eyes opened wide for the last time. POW. Before she could say anything I pulled the trigger and dropped the gun next to her. Then, I left feeling satisfied. It was one down and two to go….

"Man little brother that's some crazy sick gangster shit, what the hell was you thinking? I have never heard no shit like that before in my life and I have come across all types of cold blooded killers but you my young gangster brother, you take the motherfuckin' cake and a piece of the good damn pie." Black spoke looking at Preme, once again shaking his head in disbelief with a shocked tone. Black knew that Preme got down for his but he never thought that Preme would make a nigga girl shit in his mouth then make the woman the nigga love look the nigga in the eye and kill him. That type of shit was unheard of,

Black was thinking to himself.

"I can't tell you for the life of me what was on my mind at the time. At first, when I took the ex-lax I was going to make him drink it and hold the gun to his head, punch him in the stomach and tell him if he shit on his self I was going to kill him but he started talking shit so I thought his bitch aint shit and you are what you eat so I let his bitch shit in his mouth. The newspaper called it the sickest murder suicide that they ever heard of, that was the good part, it played out my way without the war. Money kept flowing. Life was so sweet for me once again. Me and my son was on cloud nine together. I was being a real father doing the family thing hard but I still couldn't keep my dick out of Nora. She was my erotic addiction. She loved the thug in me. She even knew I had something to do with Bash and Kiwi death but I never admitted it. She said that shit sounded like some crazy shit I would have done to that nigga for what he did to me. Nora, made a joke out of it but she was dead on the money."

I had a good run. Me and A.G. took over Bash and his brother's blocks and I started having my cake and eating it to but it all came to a crashing end a year after my son was born. The shit hit the fan my last day of trial for the brick charge, well shit popped off the night before, that's when things started going down-hill straight to the open gates of hell. Cinnamon was at our home, chilling with the family, Jay, Fugee, and my son. I called her and told her I had some things I had to take care of and I was going to be late. She told me Jay and Fugee was over there but they was about to leave. I talked to my son then hung up my cell phone as I rode down the streets of Plainfield...

CHAPTER 13

"My days are cold without you but I'm hurting while I'm with you, see my heart can't take no more but I keep running back to you." Ashanti's Foolish boomed form my speakers as I rode down the street on my way to Nora's crib. I had put her up in a town house across town and even bought her an Escalade, it was money green. I loved her so if she didn't live with me I made sure she lived like me. She knew I was really stressed because of the way my trial was going. I was looking at ten years for possession with intent to distribute. I pulled in her driveway wondering what she had to tell me, I was hoping whatever she had to say was good news, I put my key in the door, made my way to the bedroom, I walked in and she had little candles everywhere as she stood there in a very see through short night gown that rested on her full hips. She looked like a beautiful exotic African goddess as she walked over to me with a remote in her hand. She started kissing me with so much passion, love, and desire. It felt like it was our first time being together all over again. She must have pressed play before the remote hit the floor because as we were locked in loves embrace our bodies was in tune with the voice of Musiq: "Love….so many people use your name in vain love….for those who have faith in you sometimes go astray yeah love…through all the ups and downs of joy and hurt yeah love….for better or worst I still chose you first…." The song Love was the theme music for the feeling in the room. She started crying and trembling in my arms.

"What's wrong baby girl?" I said in a voice full of concern, looking deep into her eyes trying to find her trouble.

"I'm pregnant." She said, with tears now running down the sides of her face as she looked up at me. I was taken aback by what she said but I knew it was going to happen sooner than later. I've been trying to get her knocked up since day one so without missing a beat I said,

"So, what's the problem baby momma?"

"You not mad at me?" She said, now she was getting excited.

"Why should I be mad, I love you and if we going to have a baby that's good news, not bad, in fact, that's the best news I've heard in a long time. I was starting to think something was wrong with you. I've been trying to get you pregnant. Why do you think I never pull out?" I said, still looking in her eyes, holding her in my arms.

"But what about Cinnamon and your son?" She asked, trying to read my thoughts as she looked in my eyes.

"What about them? Cinnamon is going to have to accept you just like you did her and my son will love his sister or little brother." I said, reassuring her.

"You mean it Preme, you not going to leave me high and dry with a baby?"

"Nora, I am a man. I take care of mine, name one thing Cinnamon have that you don't."

"She got you lying next to her every night that I am here alone." She said, with tears starting to build again.

"That's bullshit and you know it, it's night now and where am I?"

"Here but…"

"But nothing, I am always here for you because I love you." I kissed her before she could say anything and the next thing you know we were by the bed where we stripped down. My clothes were making love to her nightgown on the floor. We were kissing and caressing as the music played the theme of our love scene. I laid back as we kissed. She made her way down my neck then to my chest. She sucked my nipples setting my body on fire, as she sucked my chest she had one handful of my hard dick sliding it up and down. I closed my eyes, enjoying her foreplay; next thing I felt was her warm mouth on my dick. She used both her hands to work them up and down my shaft, unison with her mouth. Her mouth was so wet that I could hear slurping sounds mixed with the music but it was still in perfect harmony as the candle light was flickering. I was on cloud eighty nine watching her work her lips, and tongue on my passion like it was the sweetest thing on Earth. Her head was bobbing up and down in slow steady motion. Once she felt my dick was harder than cocaine when it met baking soda she made her way back up my body, kissing and licking until she reached my lips.

"I love you Preme." She moaned, looking me in my eyes as my dick entered her wetness. We kissed as she was rotating her hips in circular motion taking the deepest penetration I could give her. Our lips parted as she cried out, I guess I hit a spot because I was working deep inside of her. She started to suck my neck riding me at a slow pace, just bringing her ass up half way off my dick then she would slam it down meeting my thrust.

SMACK. SMACK. I was smacking and gripping her soft ass, she moaned but never broke her lock on my neck. I can't lie, the shit was feeling good, she had me in a pure sexual bliss. SMACK. She started bouncing that ass up and down hard on my dick faster as my hands were crashing into the flesh of her tender ass cheeks. She was working her inner muscles, gripping and pulling on my stronger muscle. She was dripping wet, that pussy was as good as it could get. I lost it before the song went off. When she felt me unloading my sexual tension in her wetness she took all of me as she slid way down on her hips and stomach was touching, I could feel the bottom of her ass cheeks on my balls, as she started to gyrate her hips it felt like her pussy was pulling every drop of my climax out of me. My toes curled for the first time in my life, I was at a loss for words. After my climax we laid there a while. I told her how much I loved her, we took a shower together and I punished her this time from the back. I made sure she got hers three more times before

I left.

When I was driving down the street I was in deep thought on how I was going to tell Cinnamon about the baby. I knew one thing, I wasn't going to wait, I planned on telling her as soon as I hit the door. The way I looked at it, like this, I'm there for her child and her plus I've been nothing but a father to the baby, I love him as if he was my own flesh and blood, in my heart he was my son, my first born. He had my name and all, so she should have no choice but to look at mine the same way. Fair is fair, she did me wrong so this could be a way to make us even. The only thing I didn't think about was the big ass hickey Nora put on my neck. If I would have paid attention, I wouldn't have walked in the house and told her that I had another woman pregnant that I just got finished fucking all night before I came home to her. No, I wasn't thinking about none of that as I pulled in my complex and Tank played what was on my mind through my speakers. "It aint worth telling a lie, it aint worth seeing you cry, it aint worth it, that's why I'm right here begging you, please don't go, please don't go." Tank had me sick as I parked in my driveway and cut the car off. I entered my house, went upstairs, stopping by my son's room, he was sleeping peacefully. I went to the room, kissed him on his little head, then went to face the music in my own bedroom, with the weight of the world on my shoulders. I was in a true love triangle. I loved Nora but I also loved my Cinnamon deeply. I really loved Cinnamon more I guess. I didn't want to lose her, she gave me the best thing a man could have in life and that's a Jr. Nobody outside my Grandmother ever really gave me anything and she gave me a life when I didn't think life was worth living. This was all going through my mind as I watched her sleep. I stood over our bed playing with my engagement ring and she woke up.

"What's wrong with you?" She asked, with sleepiness in her voice. She looked so sexy laying there on her side, our silk sheets resting on her sensual frame.

"We need to talk." I spoke looking her in the eyes then hit the lights like a God damn fool.

"It can't wait until the morning?" She asked covering her eyes so she could focus to the light.

"No, I have to tell you now, in the morning I might not have the nerve." I said. She said nothing just looking at me. "You know I love you and I want to marry you. That's why you are the only woman I ever gave a ring to. I don't love no one more than I love you, you are my world but I have been sleeping with someone." I stopped to see her reaction, she still said nothing. Her face was blank but her eyes were on fire. "I do care about Nora, yes, it's the same woman you walked in on me with in my office but remember after I tell you this I love you more than anything but the reason why I'm telling you this now is because she told me tonight that she's pregnant and I know four hundred percent the baby is mine. I'm sorry if I…"

SMACK….she leaped from the bed and smacked the living shit out of me. I grabbed her before she could smack me again. "How could you Preme? Did you fuck her tonight too Preme, after she told you? Did you have fun fucking her while I was in here playing with myself, instead of being home handling your business you was out there fucking her making babies. That's it Preme huh?" She yelled with tears running down her face. She was deeply hurt I didn't want to tell her anymore truth tonight, so I lied.

"No, I didn't touch her, I came home to you." I said. Then she spit in my face only because she couldn't smack me because I had a tight grip on her.

"Fuck you nigga, you is a fuckin' cheating liar, let

me go. Get the fuck off of me!" She yelled trying to break free.

"How the fuck you going to call me a liar after what I told you? Was you with me tonight? Did you see me with her tonight? Haven't I been a man and came in here, woke you up, to tell you the truth and you going to disrespect me by calling me a liar and spit in my motherfuckin' face like I'm some punk ass bitch." I was yelling shaking her, trying to put fear in her and make her think about her next move but Cinnamon didn't give a flying fuck about what I was doing or saying.

"Look at your fucking neck bitch and you trying to play me like I'm some dumb crazy little bitch, let me go Preme. I can't take this I need air." She said sadly. I let her go, she didn't swing, she jumped out of bed and started grabbing her clothes. I looked in the mirror.

"Shit!" I said when I saw the big ass hickey on my neck. I said it so loud she heard me.

"That's right nigga, shit, that's all your love is for me, shit. Here, take your ring." She spoke throwing the ring I gave her at me. I didn't say anything, I knew it was useless at the moment. I just got cold busted in a lie. I just felt if I let her take a ride and clear her head we could work it out later. I knew she love me too much to let me go like this.

"You not taking my son nowhere this late, let him sleep," was all I could say.

"Did I say I was going to take him? I need air. I'm really not feeling you right now." She said, still crying but now fully dressed in a pair of sweat pants and T-shirt then left the room without another word. I let her go because I knew she was coming back because she didn't take the baby that let me know it wasn't over. After she left I went in my son room and picked him up so he could sleep with me. I set my alarm clock for 8:30 a.m. because I had to be in court by 9:00 a.m. but it never started until after ten. I went to sleep and woke up to my screaming alarm. My son wasn't next to me, so I got up, went in the guest room and Cinnamon was on the bed breastfeeding him, looking beautiful as ever.

"Are you coming to court with me today?" I asked. She said nothing. I stood there for a minute then turned my back, went in my bedroom, took a quick shower and got dressed in my Sean John black pinstriped suit. I didn't have time to kiss her ass and fix what happened, I felt I could put everything back together later, after court. Even if she didn't come and show her support, I still had Nora, she was going to be there for sure and A.G., Tangy, Fugee, Jay, my aunt and mad homies from my hood was coming to hold me down. So if Cinnamon needed to cool off today I was like fuck it, I'll let her get this one if it helped matters. I had all this on my mind when I walked back in the guest room. I kissed my son on his head as he sucked her breast then I did her the same way. Then without a word I turned around and headed out the door.

"Good luck and fuck you nigga." She said.

"I love you too," was my only reply.

I dashed through traffic to get to the court house, thinking the whole time how I was going to make things right with Cinnamon. I also was thinking about how it didn't look good yesterday when the rental car lady got on the stand and said she told the police they could search the car and that I signed a paper that said nothing was in or wrong with the car when I rented it. To me that shit looked totally fucked up but Vince, my lawyer, told me not to worry about it, the jury would clearly see the rental car place didn't own the car at that time, I did, the car was mine until my time was up. So during that time, I had all rights to the car and only I could have given the police permission to search the car.

That bullshit sounded good to me at the time because I didn't know any better plus the fact I paid this slick talking motherfucking lawyer over a hundred grand to get me off, made me believe every word of his bullshit until the verdict came back.

"Guilty! Guilty! We the jury find Mr. Supreme Divine guilty on the one count of possession with intent."

"What the fuck is this Vince!?" I yelled. The whole court room was in an up roar. Nora, Tangy, Fugee and my aunt was crying. My homies were cursing and yelling. The judge was banging the gavel.

"Order! Order in the court!" The judge yelled. "One more outburst like that Mr. Divine and I'll hold you in contempt," the judge said looking at me. "Vince, do you have anything you want to say on behalf of your client before I pass sentencing." The judge said to my lawyer.

"Yes, your honor, Mr. Divine lost his mother and father at a young age and not too long ago lost his

Grandmother, who was his caretaker. He beat all odds and graduated high school and now he owns several businesses in the community and not only that he just had his first child. Besides this one mistake, Mr. Divine, has been a hardworking and upstanding citizen, making jobs for the people in his community. I ask that your honor give him a month or two to put his affairs in order. Thank you, your honor."

"Anything from the prosecution?" The judge asked.

"Yes, your honor. Mr. Divine is a violent menace to society. He attacked a man at the gentleman's home, broke his jaw, then there was a report of a shooting that Mr. Divine's name was once again. He is an up and coming drug lord and leader of the Clinton Ave. street gang. I think he is a real flight risk with the time he's facing. The state recommend the maximum sentence of ten years and that we put this gangster away from our children today…" the prosecutor said.

"Mr. Divine, please stand. The state of New Jersey has found you guilty of possession with the intent to sell drugs and I'm going to deny your postponement of sentencing and I'm going to sentence you today. I give you the maximum ten years in the Department of Corrections." After the judge said ten years all I heard was blah blah blah.

"Vince, do something, motherfucker." I yelled in rage but you know what this punk ass cracked told me, give him ten more grand and we'll get started on a good appeal.

I blacked out, the next thing I knew I had his tie around his neck, choking the life out of him, he was turning purple. The judge was screaming order. I must have gotten hit with a Taser because I was knocked out from the shock....

CHAPTER 14

I woke up in the hospital, cuffed and shackled to the bed that day I knew my life was over. The first visit when I hit the county jail was Nora. Cinnamon wouldn't come, I would call my house and she would always accept the calls but she would put the phone to my son ear. I told Fugee and Jay to stay with her for a little while. Jay stayed in the guest room, he lived there for a minute. He started staying there with Fugee almost the same day I lost trial. I needed him staying there to keep an eye on her and I wanted Fugee to help bring her back to me. So sometime I would call, Jay would answer the phone and give me the run down and Fugee told me that she was still hurt about my time, Cinnamon that is, and Cinnamon still loved me but she was pissed about Nora. I sent A.G. to get my son for him to bring him to visit when Jay or Fugee couldn't. Being A.G. was his God Father she had no problem with it. She finally came my third week and dropped a bomb shell on me. I was laying in my bunk waiting on A.G. or Tangy to come visit.

"Mr. Divine, visit." The C.O. said popping my

cell door and I went to the visiting room, with the three inch thick bulletproof glass and phone. When I walked in there, it was Cinnamon to my surprise. She was looking so good, the little tank top she wore clung to her breasts, she wasn't wearing a bra and the chill of the county jail A.C. had her nipples on plump and hard. It was mid-Summer and the shorts she had on fit her like a second skin. I wanted her and she was right there in front of me, so close yet at the same time the three inch bulletproof glass made her a million miles away. I was wishing I'd tap that ass one more good time before I left. Looking at her, I was thinking I should have told her about Nora after a good round of hard core sex. I picked up the phone on the wall so did she.

"What's up sexy, how are you feeling? Long time no see but good things come to those who wait and looking at you now I can see everything in life worth waiting for." I said in my smoothest tone. The tears start to build in her eyes as I spoke.

"I'm good and I miss you. A.G. got little Preme. I'm still fucking pissed at you but I came up here to let you know I'm one month pregnant. You managed to leave something behind before you left." She spoke with sadness in her voice as the tears started to fall. I'm not going to sit here and play hard when she said she was pregnant my eyes started to water, knowing I was three weeks in on a ten year sentence, with two women I love out there in the world pregnant with my children. The only thing I could fix my lips to say was,

"I am sorry I hurt you, I love you. I am not sorry for getting the money to take care of you and our family. I play the game to win but sometime you got to take a lost to respect the win. This lost time I can respect because you and my son is in a house paid for and money still coming in. That's the win I respect. But I'm truly sorry I cheated on you and that I'm not there with you right now. But know this, no matter what my love has always been real." I said looking her in the eyes, talking from my heart.

"I love you too Preme. I understand this is a part of the game and I'm still willing to play. I still got my ring on, I put it back on the day you lost trial. I wish I would have been there for you, I'm sorry for that but I'm here for you now, ride until we die. I told you I'll bid with you for better or worst. This thing with Nora I can work through it, it's going to take some time but

I'm here. I just wish you would have not got that bitch pregnant."

"I feel you on that but let's not talk about wishes unless we wishing me home. Are you going to have this baby knowing Nora having hers?"

"Yes. You know I wouldn't do that to you. I was going to leave your sneaky ass but the baby showed me that I need to be with you and little Preme still needs you so I'm not going nowhere so tell your little bitch nice try."

"Let's not go there but you know you will be taken care of just like I was home, I have plenty of money out there. I'll be in a halfway house in no time. I might have to do two or three years behind the wall but after that I'll be in the halfway house. Jay and Fugee will be there until the end of the Summer. You can do you, I mean just keep it real, nigga behind the wall, I know you might get lonely and just…" She cut me off.

"Preme, don't even think it or say it, I'm pregnant and I don't want nobody but you. I can wait, the babies will keep my hands full but I don't know about your hot in the ass other soon to be baby mother."

"Don't worry about her, just take care of my son

and my other child that you carrying and stay away from those freak doctors."

"I might." She said jokingly about the doctor. We talked a little longer. She flashed me her breast then she made me show her what I working with. She played with herself, I did the same like we were at a peep show that we were the stars of. All and all it was a nice but perverted visit. From that point on we had an understanding. She knew Nora was a part of our life. They split the visiting days when I went to Northern State Prison.

I was the man when it came down to the day of the players ball, you know we call that the visiting hall. I had Nora coming with her girlfriend well she was more like our girlfriend, her name was Shay. She had a small frame with a handful of everything, as far as her face she would put you in the mind of Monica when she first came out, I'm talking about the singer A.K.A. Miss Thang. Shay was a sexy smart little momma plus she was 100% gangster with a splash of class. Shay accepted and respected me and Nora's relationship, even the baby that was growing inside of her. After every visit I'd take pictures with them, kissing both of them, then I would have them kiss each other. The next week Cinnamon would come, she was my show stopper. She put on, I mean she always came draped in Prada, diamonds for Tiffany, Dolce and Cabana, Dooney and Burke, she was the Queen 'B' and she let everybody know that her man had all things on smash. I always love how she had my little man iced out, looking like he was in a Cash Money video. She was a good mother and she had this beautiful glow. I think it was that same glow that made me fall in love with her. Tangy used to come visit with A.G. and sometime by herself. We talked about nothing but hood shit.

Nora had my little girl first, we named her Tasha Divine. She was so breath taking, she looked like the perfect mix of me and Nora. She had my nose and eyes and Nora's silky black hair and lips. A month and a half later Cinnamon had Jada Divine. We named her Jada after Jada Pinkett Smith because I am a big fan of hers since Set It Off plus my little girl had the same color eyes as Jada Pinkett Smith. Now, once again I was having my cake and eating it too, so you know clear as day something was about to happen.

I was about a year and a half in on my bid, one late night listening to my walkman zoning out, you know

I had Hot 97 bumping when Nora called in and dedicated a song to me. I listened to the words.

"My whole life has changed, since you came in, I knew back then you were that special one, I'm so in love, so deep in love, you made my life complete, you are so sweet, now I'm complete, glad you came into my life, you blinded me with your love, with you I have no sight." Ginuwine, Differences, put a smile on my face and everybody that was listening banged on the door calling my name and state number plus the cell I was in, so it wouldn't be no mistakes. But that short little happy bliss cost me the next day. I called Cinnamon and asked what she was going to wear to visit and she flipped.

"Tell your bitch to come see you, I got something to do!" CLICK....

The line went dead, I was pissed because this was the day I had her by herself, no kids and I made a move so we could creep off in the bathroom and do what lovers do. I had already paid the C.O. and everything now this chick was acting stupid over something she knew I could not control. I called back, this time my emotions were on pissed and I didn't feel like playing any games.

"Hello." She answered like she didn't just hang up on me.

"Hello my motherfuckin' ass, what the fuck is your problem?" I said in rage.

"Nothing, it's just everybody and their momma keep calling me, telling me that your little bitch was on the radio telling the world that she was your wife and her and your baby girl miss you plus some other ghetto chicken head shit." She spoke with a voice full of jealousy. I think she was mad because she didn't think of it first.

"So, what the fuck that got to do with my visit?"

"Why you can't keep your little ghetto drama in check on who is your woman."

"How can I check her if I didn't know it happened?"

"Yeah right, nigga please, I know you heard every word, smiling like a pig in shit but I can't make it today, I got something to do, I have plans."

"If you got plans on missing this visit I don't want to see your ass no more unless you have my children with you, you hear me?" I yelled in the phone tired of her bullshit.

"Fuck you Preme!" She snapped back.

"Fuck me, bitch who you think you talking to, you want to lose your job talking to the boss like that, you must want a brand new pink slip that says 'hey bitch you fired'!" I didn't mean one word that came out my stupid ass mouth but I wasn't going to show any weakness I had to stay the H.N.I.C. (head nigga in charge) Supreme Divine because when a bitch think she got you she'll always use whatever she got you with to break you down.

"Fuck you nigga, you can't fire a bitch like me because I quit!" CLICK. The line once again went dead. This time I don't feel like playing phone tag with her, I wanted some pussy that day. I called Nora and told her to bring her ass up to the prison to see me, her and Shay.

"We'll be there time it start." Nora said. Now why did I do that, that's what started it all.

"Divine, visit." The C.O. yelled, I was already dressed in the state best tan smelling good. I had my dreads going to the back to show off my super sharp Steve Harvey hair line. I dapped all my homeboys as I made my way to the players ball also known as the visiting hall.

When I entered it was like a whole new world, it

always feel like that no matter how many times you go. I guess it's because all the women. It was like a little fashion show, some of the women looked like real super models others looked like super whores. I didn't care they were women and they all looked damn good to me, even the big girl was turning me on, even to this day, being behind these walls, looking at niggas all day and night, changed the way a man look at a woman. The lonely nights on that hard ass bunk they call a bed made of steel and a piece of cotton they call a mattress sure makes a man turn for the tender warmth and feel of a woman. Just to smell her essence as you hold her in a tight embrace is the one reason out of many why visiting day is so important, for that's the one day out of seven that you can really see what's out in the world waiting for you. The misery behind these walls are not that hard when you know what's on the other side waiting just for you.

I walked in the visiting hall and seen my two video vixens, Nora and Shay, dresses in Baby Phat dresses, rose gold, and diamonds X and O chains around their neck with name plates with none other than yours truly name on them plus matching bracelets. The dresses hugged their every curve when they stood to greet me, they had my pants on point, I couldn't hide my erection if I wanted to. The dresses made their breast look like they were jumping out at me like the snake in my pants were trying to jump out and strike at them. I hugged Nora first, pushing up on her so she could feel the point of my excited situation.

"Mmm. I see that somebody is very excited to see me." Nora whispered in my ear easing her hand down to brush up against my excitement, then Shay was in my arms.

"Do you want me to go under the table and fix it until you bust in my mouth?" Shay whispered but she gripped my dick. The one thing I really like about Shay, she wasn't all talk, she really was a raw uncut freak. If I would have given her the green light, she would have took her ass under the table and gave me a red light special, she say what she mean and mean what she say. I thought about telling her 'go ahead, do your thing little Ma' but it was too many little bad ass kids running around.

We talked for about an hour. Nora sat across from me and Shay was sitting next to me. We ate, talked and we were having a fairly good time. At that moment in time I wasn't feeling locked down, it felt like old times with Nora but as we were in the middle of planning our little freak off in the bathroom, I knew everything was all good I paid the C.O. so it was a go, it just was timing was everything but before we were about to make that power move, who do you think came walking in the visiting room. Motherfucking Cinnamon, looking like a super star, dressed in a Gucci mini skirt, Gucci top and shoes plus the white gold Gucci shades. Her hair was in micro-braids. Her earrings were white gold bamboo with my name in diamonds, matching chain but she out classed Nora and Shay because not only did her jewels have my name but she had a fresh tattoo with Supreme on her neck. I didn't even know she had it plus her bubble ass was bouncing so hard that Gucci couldn't hide it and she had even the women looking at her.

She was pissed when she came in and saw Nora and Shay at the table with me. She tried to play it off but I knew her all too well and I knew she was hot it was written all over her face like graffiti on a project wall. I was enjoying the moment for two reasons, one to show her if she didn't come I knew not only one but two bitches that was more than willing to take her place and two if she quit me she quit herself, there's always somebody that want to work for Big Preme.

"Preme, baby can I have a little word with you alone but not to disrespect your little friends, it's just I need a word with my husband." She said in the sweetest tone but I could tell by the word play she felt like saying 'what the fuck are you doing motherfucker' but I got to give it to her, she kept her cool and played the role of a lady.

"Excuse me ladies." I said as I stood but Shay had to be a smartass and get her back for the 'little friends' comment.

"Don't be too long daddy, with your old wife, you know how much we miss you," Shay said, then Nora followed her up with,

"Yeah because we still have to take a little trip to the bathroom because you know two heads are better than one when it comes down to taking care of that hard problem you had sticking up in front of your pants." I didn't respond, I stepped off with Cinnamon by the vending machines.

"So this is what you do to me because of a little fight that I only started just to get this tattoo for you. I was coming but I knew I was going to be late, I didn't want to tell you why I wanted to surprise you but I'm the one that got the big surprise huh?" she said. She sounded more hurt than angry.

"Don't do that shit ma, you know Nora comes to see me, she is my baby mother and me and you been pass that part of the game. Her girlfriend comes with her from time to time. I'm in here 24/7 I need to see a woman, you can't hold that shit against me. I don't know what dick running up in you at night when you're home. I don't ask because you in the free world not my world. I thought when you said you quit, that nigga, whoever he is was fucking you right. I know how this shit go. Love is as good as the dick in your face." I spoke like I was Goldy from the Mack. I was putting my pimp game down.

"Preme, that's bullshit and you know it. Why if I got a nigga? Would he let me tattoo your name on my neck? Every night I'm on the phone with you until they go off and you know everybody in the hood! Tell me one time somebody ever said something about me fucking a nigga. The only men that come in our home is Jay and A.G. Jay damn near live there and A.G. always popping up, him and Tangy. Now you know if they see a nigga, they will tell you, plus you know Fugee is always in and out."

"Well, all that shit may be true but the bottom line is you said you wasn't coming, and I am not going to miss a visit. It's the only time that I am not stressed out. The visiting hall is my escape from all those slime ball niggas, like it or not Nora is a part of our family."

"No, nigga she is a part of your family, the child I love and accept with all my heart, but not her, not now, and not ever.'

"So what you want me to do? Tell them to leave after they drove all the way down here to see me? You're the one that said you wasn't coming, so I asked them to come in your place. But this is what I'm going to do, it's three hours left for visit, I'm going to let them stay for one more hour and then when they leave, me and you can go in the bathroom and do our thing."

"I thought you planned on going in the bathroom with them. That's what that bitch said. Don't lie to me Preme! If I wouldn't have walked in here would you have fucked those bitches?" she said.

Looking at me in the eye like I was stupid enough to give her a silly ass answer to a question she need not to ask because she knew what time it was.

"But you did walk in do there is no 'if' and no need to talk about it now, let's go back to the table and I'll put Nora on point."

"You think you so smart…" I grabbed her and kissed her sweet soft lips and palmed her ass. She was smiling now because I showed love in front of Nora and Shay. They kept their cool, everybody was acting like ladies. I told Nora I needed to talk to her for a minute and time Nora got up from her seat that was across from me Cinnamon took her seat but she held it all in and walked off with me.

"Nora, you know I love you and I asked you to come up here today but it is her visiting day. I thought she couldn't make it, that's what she told me but she did that to surprise me with that tattoo she got on her neck this morning." I said with Nora in my arms.

"So now what, Preme, that mean you kicking me and Shay out because of her?" Nora asked with tears in her eyes plus the tone of her voice let me know she was hurt.

"No, no, I'm not kicking nobody out, what I'm going to do is make her split her visit with you and Shay. Y'all still have a whole hour but the last two hours I have to give to her. I love you but you also know I love her too and if it was your day I would do the same thing." The words came out my mouth but I was lying through my teeth, if Cinnamon wanted to have every visit she could have had it, I just never let her know that. I loved Nora but my heart belonged to Cinnamon.

"I know but…" I kissed her but not with as much passion I gave Cinnamon when I cut her off.

"Now look baby, no more buts when we get back to the table tell Shay what the deal is."

"What about the bathroom? I wanted you to fuck me before I go."

"I will but it'll be next week."

"Are you going to fuck her?" She asked a stupid question with a stupid look on her face because she knew if I wasn't fucking her or Shay then a blind man could see Cinnamon was about to get what I had coming.

"Stop asking me shit that you really don't want me to answer." After I told her that we went back to our seats, Nora and Shay walked off to talk. Cinnamon told Nora how she was telling Shay bout her engagement ring and how I was going to marry her once I hit the halfway house. She was rubbing it in that no matter what she was number one and that she called the shots.

When Nora and Shay came back to the table Cinnamon grabbed my hands then started talking about my son Little Preme. Nora sat next to Cinnamon but she didn't like her new seat yet I got to give it to her out of the respect she had for me she let it go and went with it. Now Shay say next to me and her hand went under the table. Cinnamon was so busy being a bitch she didn't notice that Shay was under the table in my pants pulling my dick, looking in her face smiling the whole time. Nora had a smile on her face because she knew what was going on. I tried my best to keep a straight face but when I started to cum I jerked because when she felt my dick throbbing she was moving her hand up and down faster as I exploded under the table. Cinnamon still didn't notice the euphoric look on my face or she must have thought the feeling of her soft hands holding mine had me on fire. But I couldn't help but squeeze her hands as I was releasing, it felt so good I had to put my head down. Nora was enjoying every minute because Cinnamon was in La Land and didn't have a clue what was going on. Nora even covered for me asking Cinnamon where she got her outfit from, Cinnamon couldn't help but to run her mouth about where she shop at in New York on my dime. I was glad she did because if she would have asked me what was wrong I wouldn't have known what to say. But anyway after Shay got me off she had my cum all over her fingers then she removed her hand from my pants and sucked my nut off her fingers. Then as Cinnamon was telling her shopping story Nora and Shay started kissing. Nora was sucking on Shay lips and tongue trying to taste every drop of my cum. Cinnamon stopped talking mid-sentence and started looking at the living erotic art that was lip locking so poetically right in front of her. She didn't know why they were kissing but I had full understanding and I wanted to fuck.

"Baby that was so sweet, I wish I could have some more, I really miss that taste." Nora spoke looking at me with lust in her eyes.

Cinnamon was looking at me and Nora confused to what was happening. After Nora and Shay show we all had some small talk about the kids. Shay would every now and then put her hand under the table just to get my dick hard then she would stop. The hour was up and Cinnamon wasted no time letting them know it was time for them to go. Shay and Nora wanted to take a picture with but Cinnamon said they had time to do that an hour ago when they were kissing and running their mouth. I let her have her way because of the tattoo and I wanted to fuck in the bathroom. Nora was mad as the fires of hell so was Shay but not at me, their anger was pointed solely at Cinnamon for being a bitch. I hugged Nora and gave her a light kiss on the lips and told her to give it to my little girl. I tried to do the same thing with Shay but Shay wasn't having it, she kissed me like she wanted me to fuck her right there. Then, Nora, not wanting to be outdone by Shay came back and kissed me with all that made her a woman. I felt all her love in her lips. I didn't want to let her go, until Cinnamon called my name.

"Preme! You can let your little gay friend go home to play with her toys so you can come fuck me, your wife, with the ring and work on our third baby we talked about last night." She said, shining her ring. Keep in mind we never talked about no fucking other baby. She was just saying what she could to hurt Nora and Shay. Our lips broke and I could see the hurt and fire in Nora's eyes but she said nothing and they left. I know once I called her later I could fix it, Nora was in deep love with me and our history was strong. Her and Shay wasn't going anywhere, I had them under lock and key. We sat back down, me and Cinnamon, when Nora and Shay was gone.

"Why you do that little kid shit?" I asked her. She knew by the way I was looking at her and the tone of my voice I didn't like that shit.

"Fuck them, do you want to talk about that or do you want some of this pussy that's wetting my panties right now?" As she spoke she slid her hand under the table in between her legs, then put her fingers in my mouth and kissed me. The taste of her ebony had me hard as steel.

I gave the C.O. the look to let him know I was ready. I got up first, went in the bathroom then the C.O. put an out of order sign on the door. Three minutes later she came in. I only had ten minutes before the C.O. went on his lunch break, so when Cinnamon came in I wasted no time. I started kissing her lips and my hands were kissing and caressing her booty. I was kissing down her neck on her new tattoo. I wanted to suck her hard nipples that were poking through her shirt but time was of the essence. I turned her around, lifted up her short mini skirt and seen not even the borders of her expensive Gucci panties could stop all her soft tender flesh from busting free from its boundary. I ripped the fabric from her body letting her ass escape to freedom then I put the torn panties in my mouth, the taste of womanhood was ready to explode. I pulled my throbbing excitement out my pants and entered her easily from behind. Her pussy was so wet and hot, I tried to pound her like it wasn't my first piece in over a year.

"Oooh Preme!" She moaned as she was bringing back her jiggling ass on my, as I smacked her cheeks and gripped her hips. She was rotating them and moving them from side to side as I entered her. I lost it, on my fourth stroke, I slammed into her and came so hard. Cinnamon was holding on to the sink bent over. I came so much that when I pulled out of her it started to slide down her legs when she stood. She turned to face me and we kissed but the tap on the door let me know there was not going to be a round two. I put my dick up in my pants and stepped out the bathroom and took my seat at the table. The C.O. took the out of order sign off the door. I knew people knew what was going on but they didn't care. I guess they were trying to do the same thing. Cinnamon came out a few minutes later and sat across from me.

"I can't believe how much you came inside me. I was in there trying to clean myself up and why you ripped my panties off, now I'm walking around with nothing under this short as Gucci skirt. What if I have to bend over and some crazy horny nigga see me and take what's yours, then what?" She said jokingly, holding my hands at the table.

"I hope he last longer than me." I said and we laughed. We talked more for the rest of the time and before the visit was over we took some pictures. I even lifted her skirt when we were kissing in one of them. I was giving the old school cameraman that I was cool with a little shout out when I flashed him Cinnamon's ass. Plus I was going to put up that picture for them hard and lonely nights, to put it down when it came up, if you know what I mean.

That was the best sex at the time, I ever had. I guess it was because it's been so long since I had it. I went back to the wing and everybody was talking about how I held it down in the visit with three bad show stoppers, kissing all of them in each other faces plus going in the bathroom with one. I was player of the year on that day at the player's ball, I even showed the niggas I fucked with the flick of Cinnamon skirt up. I was the man and my name said it all 'Supreme' it don't get any better than that. Just when I thought my day couldn't get any better, my home boy Lil' Dee scored some cell phones so you know I was on it. I had some bread in the cut all he wanted was $200.00 from me for a camera phone but the rest of them niggas he was killing them for five bills, with no camera, knocking them silly niggas in their fucking head. I didn't give a fuck, I had mine. I called Cinnamon that night but got no answer so then I called Nora, got no answer, then I hit Shay up, the same thing. I couldn't understand it, I even called Cinnamon's mother house and still nobody. So I called A.G. to see what the fuck was going on.

Ring. Ring. "Yo, who is this?" A.G. said.

"It's your right hand nigga."

"Preme, what's good?"

"I don't know, I need you to check my house and see what's up with Cinnamon, I called but she aint answering her cell or the house phone…"

"Tangy just left from over there, she called me and said Cinnamon was not there nor were the kids at the house, she couldn't get no answer from her either."

"Fuck it, I aint going to worry about that shit. I just got this cell phone so this is my number, if you hear something call me. Right now the pig is callin' a count so I'll hit you back later. One my nigga." I said and hung up the cell. You know how you get that feeling somebody looking at you, I did and when I looked up I saw the fucking C.O. standing at the door and I had the fucking phone in my hand, it was like getting busted with a smoking gun and a dead body. the fag ass pig popped my cell door then asked me for the phone. I gave him the shit because I knew he wasn't going to charge me, all he was going to do was give it to another inmate that he was cool with to sell it for him, then I was going to buy it back. It cost when you get caught slipping but I had the bread to pay like I =. Three days had passed before I even got in contact with Cinnamon. I haven't talked to her or my kids. The only thing that was playing over and over in my mind was that bitch was out there fucking and sucking some nigga. I know now after this time in that time I was stupid because the bitch was fucking before me and the bitch will be fucking after me. Sex don't have shit to do with being in love.

I know now that as long as she hold you down with

that mental and keep your spirits up the best way she can with mail, phone, and money, she doing her part as wifey she can only be there for you like you can be there for her. A nigga can't give her no dick when she need it so that's what the next man is for and he don't have anything to do with me because if she was locked up I would've damn sure had me a bitch. But anyway she answered the phone. I cut deep into her like a knife into butter after she answered the call. I didn't give her time to say hello.

"Bitch, I'm glad to see you took the nigga dick out your mouth to talk to me!" I yelled in a way to make her feel she was nothing but a two dollar whore.

"What are you talking about I been…" I cut her odd before she could finish what she was saying.

"Don't try to play dumb with me bitch, I know everything that goes on in the street and your dick sucking sour cum drinking ass think I don't know that you out there with your mouth open sucking every dick that cum on your face. Did you brush your fucking teeth before you came to see me last time bitch?" I was talking like I was King Kong but to be real I was hurt and worried about her and the kids. I was talking shit but I didn't mean one word of what I was saying.

I just didn't want her to know how fucked up she had me. It's only been three days and I'm already talking like a mad man. I didn't even talk to Nora or Shay but I really didn't even care about them like that. If Nora would have answered I wouldn't have come at her like that, I just would have said something like long time no hear from or some shit like that. But Cinnamon had me on fire, the girl had my head and heart all fucked up. I was blacking out in the phone giving her that pimp verbal abuse. She knew I wasn't going to let her get one word in until I got that shit off my chest.

"So you don't got nothing to say bitch? What your mouth hurt, asshole hurt, or is that pussy sore? Let me know. I'm a man, I can take it. What's the fucking problem whore, talk, did you get paid?" I asked those things trying to break her down but if she would have said yes to any of the questions I would have sent somebody over there to beat her ass.

"Are you done Preme?" She said dryly.

"Yeah, but tell that nigga to wait, you can put it back in your mouth when you hang up, I can't understand you with your mouth full."

"I don't believe you nigga. I put up with that bitch Nora on my visiting day and you know what 'Mr.

Know It All' you want to know where I been? I been in the motherfuckin' hospital because of your sorry ass. You called those stank dike bitches to see you and your little whores jumped me in the parking lot, stumped me and bruised my ribs. I cut one of those bitches, she tried to cut my face but slashed my arm and I bit her. She dropped the blade and I cut her in her face. The police came and locked them up because when they pulled up I was on the ground getting the shit beat out of me, all because of your black mop head ass. I didn't blame them, I blamed you nigga, you shouldn't have bitches if you can't keep them in check, now what are you going to do about this shit? Preme, you're the reason this shit happened to me, now what? What the fuck are you going to do about the shit?" She was yelling and I knew she was crying. I also knew I was wrong but I didn't want to eat all that shit. I was talking before she told me what happened. So, like a jackass I let my pride talked me into trying to turn the shit around on her and play the victim.

"You're trying to put all this bullshit on me, you better check yourself. You were the one acting funny on the visit, you were the one that wouldn't let my baby mother take a picture for my little girl. What? Do you think you can take a shit and don't smell it? Life don't work like that, this is the real world like it or not shit stink. What can I do about this? She is my baby mother just like you. I can't have her killed. Shit, I'm locked up doing time, why am I doing time, trying to take care of you and my family, our children but do I blame you for my shit? No. I did what I did for you but do your blind ass see that? No. You just sitting here blaming me but I'm not blaming you for my bid, so don't blame me for the foot you put in your own ass." I stated coldly.

"Fuck you Preme, I mean it. I never felt so much hate for you like I feel right now. Fuck you nigga and those bitches." The way she said it I really felt she meant what she was saying. I mean I heard in her voice she hated me for real and that hurt me it cut deep.

"You hate me bitch, after all I done for you, bitch you fired!"

CLICK. I hung up the phone mad at the world. I knew I never should've talked to her like that after she told me what happened. I was going to make it up to her but when she said that hate shit I knew I was going to have to let her cool off.

Fugee was off to school at Job Corps out of town, learning how to do hair at the time. I wished she was home because she would have helped me fix things. Jay was over my house but him and her had some type of falling out and he told me she was crazy. At the time the one person I really needed was dead and gone that made me stress even more. It hurts when you are doing time and it feel like there is no one you can turn to emotionally.

I let a week go by without calling anybody, not even A.G. I just was doing my time. Cinnamon really did cut me deep when she told me she hated me that cut me down to the bone. The saddest day of my life happened when I came from my work detail on the wing. I planned on calling Cinnamon and try to make things right, she was on my mind and I wanted to talk to my kids. Nora sent me a letter after letter and over a hundred cards that week but I had to put her in check for the shit she pulled on Cinnamon. I knew if I didn't talk to her that would hurt her and teach her to play her position.

I came in and went to call my baby Cinnamon and put our relationship back together. I still didn't have a cell phone yet but anyway I picked up the phone.

"Mr. Divine, I need to see you in my office A.S.A.P." The sergeant said to me. Sargent Jones was cool as a fan. She used to let me cop feels every now and then when I find twenty dollars for her lunch. She told me she would have gave me some pussy if she hadn't seen my in action on visit. She said my hands were full and she didn't like to share but I could always feel what I'm missing when I buy her lunch. But this time her face and tone told me that it wasn't going to be about lunch or ass grabbing when I got in her office.

"What's up Lady J?" I asked once I came in her office and closed the door. She started to tear up as she spoke.

"Supreme, have a seat, there's something I have to tell you and I think it would be easier if you have a seat." I didn't say a word, I sat down, the room had a chill out of nowhere. I kept my eyes on her face the whole time, this was the first time I really looked her in the face, I always had my eyes on her assets but now I could see she was a very pretty woman but the sadness in her face told me that I wasn't going to like what she had to say.

"Supreme, do you know some people by the name of Cinnamon Bryant, Supreme Divine Jr, Jada Divine?" She asked her voice cracking.

"Yeah, that's my kid's mother and my children I have with her, why?" My heart started beating fast in my chest the blood started to rush through my veins, I felt pain before the words left her lips.

"I'm so sorry to be the one to tell you this but I felt it was best that you heard it from me. There's been an accident and they have all been killed in a very bad car accident this morning. The accident was all over the news this morning, fifteen people died this morning, while you were on your work detail the call came in…"

"Fuck that bullshit you talking about, aint no motherfuckin' way something happened to my wife and kids like that. I know God don't play the game like that." I stood with tears in my eyes, pain in my heart because I knew Lady J wouldn't play with me like that but I just couldn't believe she was telling me this after what I told Cinnamon and what Cinnamon told me. I grabbed her phone on her desk and began to dial Cinnamon number no answers, her mother no answer, Nora, she answered.

"Hello." She said.

"Nora, tell me everything is alright out there in the free world, tell me Cinnamon and my children are okay." I was demanding not asking her.

"Preme, I wish I could but there was a car crash…" CLICK. I hung up and flipped her desk over in pure rage, I couldn't take it. I didn't want to hear it come out Nora mouth, I knew it was over. Sargent Jones was scared, she had to call a code on me, my mind was gone when they came in. I banged with the officers until I passed out. My soul died with grief as the murder weapon.

To be Continue …

www.ingramcontent.com/pod-product-compliance
Lightning Source LLC
Chambersburg PA
CBHW061922170626
46813CB00006B/2268